# Belfast:
## Out of the Shallows

BRIAN FEARON

AuthorHouse™ UK
1663 Liberty Drive
Bloomington, IN 47403 USA
www.authorhouse.co.uk
Phone: UK TFN: 0800 0148641 (Toll Free inside the UK)
        UK Local: (02) 0369 56322 (+44 20 3695 6322 from outside the UK)

Published by AuthorHouse  04/12/2022

ISBN: 978-1-6655-9791-3 (sc)
ISBN: 978-1-6655-9789-0 (e)

Print information available on the last page.

# Contents

To Helen, Roisin, and Declan .......................................vii

Chapter 1   Just wee boys ...............................................1
Chapter 2   Newcastle .................................................. 16
Chapter 3   The Football Match....................................38
Chapter 4   Decisions and changes ............................49
Chapter 5   The Betting Shop and the Setup.............68
Chapter 6   The Aftermath.........................................98
Chapter 7   Consequences ........................................ 116
Chapter 8   Home and a Job.................................... 145
Chapter 9   Learning the Ropes and being
                Hung by some of Them ...................... 173
Chapter 10   Scotland and a Change of Career.......... 197
Chapter 11   Resurrection ..........................................220
Chapter 12   Scotland Pastures New .........................249
Chapter 13   So, the End is the End ..........................274

# To Helen, Roisin, and Declan

During Lockdown in May 2020, I sat down and wrote part of a story which had been running around in my head for several years. Lockdown created both the space and incentive to begin the work. Although parts reflected a few personal experiences, these amounted to only a few hundred words. As I wrote, other characters and situations emerged, as did a plot, and this is the result.

I want to thank all those who helped me write this work. It is á piece of fiction and none of the characters are real, although the story I have weaved around real events in the late 1960s and 1970s in Northern Ireland.

My thanks to my wife Katy and my friends for their encouragement, especially Malky McEwan, who tried to bring editorial discipline to the book despite my resistance, Douglas Walker, and Stephen Murray, who encouraged me and my late cousin Paula Evans, who did the early proofread and was a considerable source of encouragement.

Books are only stories, and stories are just dreams that are remembered.

This is a story of loss and striving for redemption. Belfast seems a long time ago and a different place. The first half of my life and yet it feels as if it happened to someone else.

Those happy days of football, and later girls, were followed by a dark period of violence, imprisonment and the search for salvation, forgiveness, an escape. The past never let me go. It returns in various guises, some more malevolent than others. There was something terribly wrong at the heart of Northern Ireland society, the government and media brushed them under the carpet for 50 years. They did not stay hidden. A range of influences and events brought them into the open. Blaming religion is nonsense. Anyone who lived there will tell you religion was a small part of it. The least violent people were those who practised whatever faith they adhered to. The violent ones used religion as a tribal identity, a source of ritual to bind in those less committed, but it was a war fought by secularists.

All I am doing is putting thoughts in my head into your head. What you do with them is up to you. Between 1968 and 1998, 4000 people died in The Troubles.

Was the Good Friday Peace Agreement what it said on the tin? It wasn't a Peace Agreement, more an 'Agreed Truce,' people were tired. The paramilitaries finally understood that, so a cessation of hostilities was manoeuvred. It could never be a lasting peace. Taking up arms would be left to another generation. You cannot partition Ireland, any more than you could partition

Scotland or England, without leaving a running sore to spark conflict and violence.

When I grew up, so much was happening in Belfast and broadcast throughout the world. My interest focussed on what went on closer to home, what happened in our street or to people we knew. Ongoing disturbances took place throughout West and North Belfast between 1969 and 1970. Something would happen on either side that dragged people back onto the streets. Many horrible murders took place.

In August 1971, Brian Faulkner, the Unionist Prime Minister, persuaded Edward Heath the solution to the ongoing problems was to bring back Internment Without Trial, not used since the 1950s. In effect they decided to imprison known Republican agitators without bringing them before the Courts. On the 9th and 10th of August 1971, 350 of 450 IRA targets were seized by the army. The odd thing is a 100 people on the list, key members of the Republican movement, got wind of the exercise and moved to Dublin a few days earlier.

My mates and I went out on the streets firing stones at the Army while the older one threw petrol bombs. Streets became blocked with burning barricades all over the Falls. Parts of West Belfast and Derry became forbidden territory for the army and police. An added tragedy took place when the Parachute Regiment shot ten civilians, including a woman and a priest in Ballymurphy. They repeated this killing of non-combatants in Derry in January 1972.

I don't want this to be a weary angst-ridden account of atrocities. It is an experience, a journey, my journey. It may not end up where you want it to. My two most important relationships did not end well, and I kept others at arm's length. I found a route out. The vehicles for that part of my journey were employment and education, but whenever I thought I was free, deep roots drew me back.

**"I pressed the accelerator gently, the engine burst into life. I heard the clicks as the others checked their guns. The adrenalin was seeping through me. I wanted to pee, but I wanted it to start even more. Tonight, I was going to be a fucking player, at last.**

# Chapter 1

# JUST WEE BOYS

I don't want to dwell on it, or I would have to face the fact it was my fault. Belfast was a dangerous place, but I was the one who took the decisions, people died. I did not linger on either decision, the second one.... it was pure self-preservation; I am sure of it. They took place a short distance from where I was brought up, where I felt safest.

Sevastopol Street lay on the fringe of the City Centre, in the lower Falls Road, "the Road" to us, an unremarkable place to grow up in 1960s Belfast. Two rows of terraced kitchen houses sitting alongside so many similar streets. My parents got married in 1954. My father's family owned a wee off licence on the Springfield Road and my dad, Gabriel, and his brothers, worked there. Dad worked in the GPO as a postman. He and my mother rented the house on Sevastopol Street.

Bridie, my mother, came from the country where my maternal grandparents owned a small farm in the Glens of Antrim. My mother's brother took over the farm. She was sent to work for a catholic doctor in the city. Bridie helped his wife keep the house and look after their expanding brood. My parents met at a dance in a Parish Hall further up the Falls and, or so he claimed, she pursued him relentlessly until he proposed. I was born in

1

1955, my sister Maeve in 1956. My mother miscarried, and then my brother Eugene and wee sister, Fionnuala, were born. Our local church played an important part in our lives when we were young.

Our world as seven- and eight-year 'olds' was dominated by adults, especially the omnipotent rule of "the mammy". A youth culture or a vibrant young generation was only stirring on the fringes. We were brought down by a grazed knee, the admonition of older people or the fear generated when bigger boys chased us.

I didn't meet Raymond (Ramie) Mulgrew for a first time, well I must have, but the way my mother tells it, she and Greta, Ramie's mother, just parked our prams facing each other outside one or others front door when we were a few months old. We took to each other, gurgling, making nonsense sounds and eventually words. He was a few months younger than me. Mammy said I spoke earlier than him and Mrs Mulgrew {Greta} always said 'Joe McFaul did more for Ramie's speech than anyone,' so there. In those days, mothers did not wear sports clothes or makeup, just old dresses with smocks over them, and slippers, even in the street.

The Mulgrew's lived opposite, but our side of the street got more sun around late morning, early afternoon, so our prams were parked at our door.

The mums looked after the succession of children, shared care for its day. Ramie's dad, Paddy, did not have a job. He helped a mate in his milk run and pottered around fixing cars with another pal, the odd time making a little cash if a car was repaired or sold. Of course, he was on the "Buru," National Assistance and later Supplementary Benefit, How can I describe Ramie, easy-going guy, no temper, a wee relaxed, funny mate, smaller than me, curly hair, freckles, unremarkable? I didn't know any Protestants; I held plenty of opinions about them, though I never spoke to a one until I was 17. That was Belfast, one city, two tribes.

I was older, just a little older, but as kids, it gave me bragging rights in decision making. A theme which continued as we got older. I was mouthier and our parents assumed I was the leader. Me and Ramie never saw it like that. True partners in crime.

I was tallish, thin brown hair and with one blue and one brown eye which, when I was teased by others, my mother assured me meant I was destined for success in life. It calmed my tears a bit. As wee boys, we roamed the streets around the lower Falls, winning battles against impossible odds; Red Indians, Outlaws, Nazis, all the goodies and baddies portrayed on Saturdays at the Broadway cinema, long life to the Roy Rogers Club, I say.

I liked Ramie's dad, so much like him. Yet Ramie's mother, Greta, never hid from anyone in the street, how little time she had for that 'waster.' I never understood why she married Paddy or why they had Ramie or Geraldine. I can guess why they didn't have a few more. Paddy could drink, according to my dad, "shush" my mother replied, "he" (meaning me) "will repeat it outside."

"Greta broadcasts it far and wide; we are hardly revealing a family secret."

3

Ramie adored his dad. They were more like pals than father and son. Geraldine, I got to know better, but more about that later, took her mother's side. They both doted on Ramie. What was not to like?

The other guy who hung around with us was Pat Kane. Pat lived at the bottom of the street. His parents moved up from Lurgan to the city and he joined our class in Primary 3. Taller than Ramie, smaller than me, always well built, hefty but not fat. You didn't use the 'fat' word around Pat, he could be stroppy. Pat passed the 'Qualy' and went to Grammar school.

Ramie and I got along well, but one incident is always brought up when the family reminisces. Even Nuala, who was a baby and couldn't have remembered it, claimed she did. We were five or six and sitting in the same row at Mass, bored out of our heads. I looked at Ramie, only our Maeve sat between us, and I made a face at him. As required, under the code of boys, he made one back. This continued, and Ramie made a rude gesture with his fingers. I didn't understand what it meant, but it upped the ante; he went too far. I went for him. I swear I passed Maeve in a flash, aiming a flurry of blows at his head. He responded in like manner with a couple of swift hits back until our mums sorted it.

My mother was inclined to give me a slap for defiling the holy sacrament of the mass, or more for embarrassing her in front of fellow parishioners. However, to police violence with greater violence wouldn't send out the right message. Walking home, we made up, though neither of us was allowed out to play. A few days later I met an older boy from our Church who said Ramie's and my scrap was the best entertainment ever at mass, praise from a fourteen-year-old was praise indeed.

I recall the "Qualy", the qualifying examination, called the 11 plus "across the water" (that's where you live). This marked the rite of passage from primary to secondary education. Ramie failed and so did I. My mum thought I might pass, a mother's pride obstructing a rational view, but the Head Brother said I should have passed, thank God I didn't.

There was no soccer team attached to St Finian's PS, a shame. The 'Brothers' schools didn't play 'foreign games' like soccer or rugby, just Gaelic football, and hurling. Me and Ramie and Eugene, when he got older, played in the streets with our friends, 15-aside soccer games with a few of the younger Dads joining in, sometimes, or just watching. Ramie was the pick of the boys in our street. He was a talented but greedy wee player. He argued with coaches over the years because he wanted to score. If we lost 4-2 in a match and Ramie scored our two goals, he was happy. The buzz of scoring was an addiction to Ramie. He didn't get off on the congratulations or admiration of others. It was something inside him.

For me the Troubles started, in 1964, we sat in class one afternoon when the Deputy Head came in. He said, "Boys, there is trouble at the Irish Republican Election office in Divis Street."

Divis Street ran from the City Centre to the start of the Falls, a continuation of it.

"Mr Ian Paisley and his followers are threatening to demonstrate there, and I don't want any of you near the place. It could be dangerous."

All responsible advice but, to a man, after the last bell rang, the entire school decamped up Divis Street to join a large crowd swearing and jeering at the Police.

We saw TV cameras, a Tricolour flying over the office, a Republican was standing in the election. Paisley demanded the flag's removal. That's what created the fuss. Paisley making a speech through a megaphone at the City Hall less than a mile away, threatening to march up Divis Street. A crowd of Paisley supporters waving the Butcher's apron (Union Jack) stood outside the City Hall. The Police broke into the Election office and removed the flag. They were attacked by the republican crowd and a Belfast Corporation bus was set alight and riots continued into the night. I saw all of us on the TV news later, one of rare viewings of the news. There were other incidents relating to housing. Social issues were bubbling away beneath the surface.

Ramie and I were never political. Pat was always going on about rights, injustices, battles and "broken treaties". We raised our eyes to the heavens; it was as boring to us as football was to him. As wee lads, we wanted to kick a ball and mess around with our mates, that's the top and bottom of it. We 'mitched' school when we were 11. We ended up with a severe talking to, no slaps. We then, settled down, a little. Pat told us that the Grammar School teachers got more vicious as exams approached, perhaps they got extra pay for kids passing exams, anyway it didn't affect us. We became independent and went out onto the Falls Road, the 'Road.'

Northern Ireland was 'simmering' for several years. Now, it was different and exciting due to events on the streets. It started following a big march in Derry, not only Catholics, my Dad said, but other people who knew the government policy allocating jobs and houses and votes was unfair. Students marched in Linenhall Street in Belfast to support what happened in Derry, the RUC overreacted and cracked a few heads.

Neither Ramie nor I got excited when the Peace Line was built between our street and the streets on the Shankill Road, forbidden territory. Ramshackle initially, then it improved, if that is the right word regarding barriers built to stop people from killing their neighbours! It would have been odd in any other city in the United Kingdom to have a wall built to stop neighbours from intimidating each other out of their homes or, as with Bombay Street, burning their houses. We never discussed it, except in wee boy terms of, "if they come here, we will sort them,"

A lot has been written about moving from boyhood to the end of your teens. It should be an exciting time, music, and girls, especially girls. In fashion and music, from what was on TV or magazines, Belfast was different with its 'Ulster Sunday.' No sense of freedom, not as much fun as there should be. The poverty, the tension, and the violence were all engulfing. Coping with one or two was possible, we could not, as a society, cope with all three.

We went to dances in the Parish Hall, discos and sometimes we went into town to the King George VI Youth Centre, risky, not a lot of Catholics, or the Astor, on a Sunday night. The older ones went to Romano's and the ancient, last chance saloon girls, Maxims! As the troubles took their grip, we stayed on our own turf. In the evenings we wandered around 'the Road.' Later, a few girls joined us, and the more mature guys paired off with girls. The rest of us just moved in a gang, slagging the girls off, seeking to provoke a response.

I remember one night up at the Falls Park, most of us paired off. Ramie was ill and wasn't there. I walked holding hands with his sister Geraldine, seriously. We snogged. It was the first time I kissed a girl, and I was 16. Who would believe it today? Me and Geraldine were lying on grass at the side of a hill. Others were dotted around the park, but we kept a safe distance. I don't know why, but I put my hand up Geraldine's jumper.

Well, I know why I did, why I thought she would go along with it was a different matter. Anyway, she slapped my face and called me a "dirty little pervert," which was harsh. I only tried to be a dirty little pervert. She headed off home.

She told her mates who told my mates, and my status rose at least ten points because of the attempted grope, what immature teenage guys admire!

A couple of Sundays later, I was prevailed on to go to mass. When Mammy issued a three-line whip, you just fell in line. As we walked to the church, we caught up with the Mulgrew's.

8

Paddy wasn't there, and Ramie was walking ahead, so when my mother and Greta started chatting. Geraldine dropped behind and whispered to me: "You dirty little pervert, God will know what you done!"

I panicked in case the Mothers' heard. More imminently alarming and likely to bring retribution than the Almighty, so I shot off to catch up with Ramie. I was certain he didn't know. None of the guys mentioned it when he was with us. There are rules concerning what you say about a mate's sister. For months after she hissed 'pervert' at me. I used to grin and poke my tongue out, waggling it to provoke her.

On the streets, it was me and Ramie and Pat but only on a part-time basis, as if he was living a double life. When we arranged something, he would cancel or not appear or leave early with a mumbled excuse. Ramie and I laughed at him behind his back. He didn't have much of a sense of humour.

"Ramie, could Pat have a woman?"

"Aye, an older woman, 22 or 23." More to do with our fantasises than likely to be true.

As, of course, he didn't, but the humour entertained us, part of our response to his constant disappearing.

As demonstrations, riots, and other events grew, even playing football in the street became hazardous. A decent teacher, Fred McKay, set up and ran a football team in the Parish, aided and abetted by a cast of characters, including some Dads and other adult football fans who came and went. Ramie always played; I was in and out of the team and played most positions.

I look back on the team, what became of them? I was raised alongside them. We attended primary school together, and on to our secondary school, others attended the Brothers' Grammar. We met at mass on a Sunday 'til we stopped going regularly, from the age of 15. We lied to our parents, "oh we will go tonight," or "we are going up the Falls Park to play football so we will go to a church near there."

To keep the peace, the parents never argued, although Maeve, Eugene and Nuala still attended. I suppose my parents accepted three out of four wasn't bad. Eugene used to chat to me, trying to encourage me to attend mass. He and I weren't close, but I was a big brother and sallied forth to do battle on his behalf a few times when he was wee. Despite the shock of red hair, Eugene was even-tempered, like my Dad and, although three years younger than me, Mammy claimed he was the more mature and the brighter of the two of us. Nuala was an annoying wee sister, she, and Eugene, looking back, were quite close. Maeve and I got on better. Not close growing up, more so when we were older. She always radiated calm, my mother's First Lieutenant.

People talked about the IRA, 'I ran away' as they were called back in the late 60s in Nationalist West Belfast. The struggle between the Stickies (Officials) and the Pinheads (Provisionals), then between the Officials and INLA, contained a lot of anger with comrade turning on comrade and it left most of us baffled. The violence between them was extreme, with killings on both sides. They were sides of the same coin for goodness's sake. Why aren't they fighting the Brits? But that's always the Irish way. The split is the first item on an agenda for any Republican meeting, always will be.

In 1969 and 1970; I was 14/15 and still controlled by my parents, so when I went out to watch what was happening on the streets, I could be hauled back in by parental hands.

Our parents were not political, but we could rely on Pat for accounts of what was happening. There was nothing on our street.

It all happened on the Falls Road and after 1972 it was more like disturbances, not an insurrection. Belfast from 1970 on became a more tense, and violent place, very politicised.

It came home to us, as it was bound to, in July 1970 during the "Falls Curfew", when 3,000 soldiers locked the Lower Falls down for 36 hours in a search for weapons. It started in Balkan Street, and they found a few weapons there, but the bulk of weapons dumps were further up the Falls. I heard later the army was working on an Informer's tip off.

Given the few weapons they got for a 36-hour operation involving 3,000 soldiers, which antagonised many Catholics they hadn't already antagonised, the Informer was hardly up to the mark. These days he would be registered and inspected by a body setting acceptable standards for Informers!

The Army came into each house in our street, often in an aggressive manner sometimes less so. We left the door ajar to prevent them having the excuse to break it down. They came in and my Mammy stood in front of them with her three older children behind and Nuala in her arms. She told them there were no weapons in our house. All the soldiers saw was this wee woman and her family, the Corporal in charge said, "we have to search," and they did. They went upstairs and Mammy and Eugene followed. She stood there tutting at the mess and Eugene played with a soldier! They left a bit of a mess but no violence. I never forgot that experience. It felt traumatic.

Pat's house was wrecked, his Father arrested, and his Mother knocked semi-unconscious. No doubt they gave the soldiers an Irish history lesson when they entered the house. Greta rushed down and grabbed Pat while other women in the street tended to his Mother.

I don't want to dwell on the violence much. It was always there and always, in greater or lesser definition, part of my younger self. Ramie and me, and every other teenager we knew, replaced street football with street rioting. It required a similar level of coordinated teamwork, plus skills propelling implements. It was less fun after the tear gas and rubber bullets, but it was real community involvement and empowered us in trying to take control of our own lives. Lives in the control of outsiders, 'strangers' as the Irish historically used to describe the Brits. Pat played his usual game, hanging around us for a while and then disappearing. When a violent attack on us took place, he was absent, as if he was warned. We got annoyed, and we tackled him. I remember the conversation:

"Aye, and where were you when the peelers and the SAS ran amok, cracking everybody's heads?"

"Don't you worry about me."

"We're not, Pat."

He announced; "Only fight fights you can win." Sixteen years of age, I mean, where did that come from?

Pat met us one Friday morning. IRA bombs went off in various parts of the city, including the City Centre. We intended going down town, but Pat said not to. That afternoon a massive bomb exploded in Oxford Street, near the main Bus Station, (Black Friday). I said to him, not being serious, "It's as if you knew."

He said, "I'm in the IRA,"

Oh, how we laughed. He waited until we stopped laughing and shooting our fingers at each other. He told us in 1969 his cousin, Ciaran Duddy, was on the fringes of the republican movement. The IRA was a fiction in the early days, more in the minds of old men who drank in pubs, sang songs from the Easter Rising, Wolfe Tones and Henry Joy from the 18th century. Younger guys, however, got involved. Remember, an organised IRA structure was not yet in place. Despite all the subsequent talk about the IRA, the Civil Rights marches and Burntollet ambush claimed the headlines.

The Republicans tried to elbow their way in, but they needed to provoke a reaction to garner wider support among working class Catholics. It was to come from an unlikely source, the Unionist government, which supplied it through re-introducing internment in August 1971.

Back to Pat, in the autumn of 1969, following a period of rioting three handguns became available. One night, to appear as defenders, it was arranged three lads on mopeds, or Honda 50s, brought the three guns to designated IRA guys throughout the Falls and 'Andystown' (Andersonstown was a massive Catholic Housing scheme at the top of the Falls Road).

The guys fired three shots towards Police or Police Barracks, and the riders took the gun to the next designated guy. Three guns, firing three shots in each location. The following day newspapers proclaimed, 'Civil War in Belfast,' 'police under fire by dozens of gunmen,' 'over a hundred separate incidents,' in truth there were 15 at most.

"My cousin was one of the three riders," Pat proclaimed proudly.

"Fine Pat, if that's your scene, it isn't ours,".

## Reflection Gabriel

Our Joe was a bright enough boy, but when he was young, he possessed a temper. It came from his mother's side. Some of her brothers possessed with fierce tempers. As a boy, football and his pal Ramie, the way wee boys are, were everything to them. But as he grew older, he always sought the easy way out of situations. He could have passed his Qualifying examination, but Ramie wouldn't, and he was aware he would be pushed at the Grammar school. I tried to get him to see he needed to prepare for a future, not just drift along. I regret not spending more time with him. I was a better Dad with Eugene and the girls. Joe had to be with Ramie, from day one, those boys were close. Joe, as a wee boy, was a law unto himself.

## Reflection Ramie

Me and Joe were always best mates. Before we started school, as soon as I got up, I went over the road to his house. We played every day. As we got older, the football bug got to us. Joe would accept he wasn't a skilled player, but he was a reliable teammate and never jealous of me. I was better, a lot better. We hated school, no fun. What was the point of it? Joe had my back. Joe possessed a fierce temper, when he was a kid, he did not seem to feel pain fighting until it finished. Pat didn't come between us. He was detached somewhat. Pat went through a horrible experience during the Falls Curfew. My heart went out to him that night. He came and stayed with us for a couple of nights. My Mum and Dad didn't get on, neither did me and my Sister Geraldine until we got older. I loved my Mum, and my Dad was terrific fun. We used to have brilliant laughs.

# Chapter 2

# NEWCASTLE

My Mother's two Sisters also lived at the bottom of our street. My Auntie Mary and a younger Sister, Yvonne, but whom we all called Big Yvonne. Mary's Husband, Sean McGrillen, followed Auntie Mary to the City as she followed my Mum. My Dad helped him get a job in the Post Office as a mail van driver. Auntie Yvonne had a learning disability. She was well built, could run fast, and possessed a mighty slap. These kids we didn't know came up the end of our street. We greeted them in traditional Belfast fashion, with a volley of stones. We didn't hit any, most of us were only eight. Seven years later, our aim and accuracy improved as the RUC could testify. A stone hit Yvonne. She charged the kids, and we ran behind her. When we reached their street, a woman told us to go back to where we belonged. We were on the Shankill!

She got odder, approaching strangers trying to hug them, or swearing at younger children if they wouldn't let her join in the games. Auntie Mary was less and less happy about her going outside. She was admitted to a big Hospital near Antrim and Mammy and Aunty Mary went to visit her regularly. Nobody talked to us kids about it. Yvonne was gone. We heard something here and there. She was in Antrim and then she was in a big Hospital.

Sensitive family news was always whispered in our house and the younger you were, the less you were told.

I can't be certain when Yvonne died, of the flu. It was the first family loss I experienced, though I had not seen Yvonne for two years. In Hospital, she would get looked after, even made well. Then I heard she was dead. I tried to talk to Mammy about it; she became upset and said I was too young to understand, but I was sad. Too young to know life was about changes, some better than others.

In the early Sixties my Dad was upset when a lifelong pal of his, Tommy Brennan, who worked alongside him, moved to Scotland. He and his wife Laura were disillusioned by Northern Ireland and its sectarianism. Tommy was adamant his two young children would not be brought up in this 'sick place.' Tommy came back to visit his parents, who lived in the Short Strand area, until they died.

Ramie and I left school. We signed on because there were no jobs for the likes of us. In our part of Belfast, we would be a third generation to depend on state benefits because there were no employment opportunities for us, no Mackie's Foundry, no Harland and Wolfe, no Short Brothers. Jobs in heavy industry were reserved for Protestants.

The Troubles came closer to us. We wandered across Leeson Street, a street we were to revisit, and headed towards the Grosvenor Road, which was close to the 'Badlands' for us. We were searching for the site of Celtic Park, the former home ground of Belfast Celtic FC, a famous club that closed after a riot in a match between Celtic and Linfield in the late 1940s. Rows between Green and Orange were not new to Belfast. For the next forty years, it was used as a greyhound stadium, although a perfect playing pitch was maintained in the middle of the ground.

Ramie's Dad, Paddy, swore he saw Wolverhampton Wanderers play there during the big snow of the 1960s. Schools were closed for three weeks. It was worse in Britain, Ireland thawed first, so some big football clubs came over to play friendlies. In 1986 the stadium was demolished.

We weren't comfortable in a strange area, so we headed back towards the Falls. It was getting late and darker. As we went around an entry, a lane that runs between rows of houses in Belfast, I stumbled over a guy lying on the ground.

"Is he dead? "Ramie asked.

I approached him and kicked the guy, not too hard, in case he got up. He groaned.

We bent down, and the guy mumbled. "Who is it?" Then Ramie went. "It's me, Ramie?" I mean who the…....

He was on his side now, his head was covered in blood, he was on the receiving end of a severe beating. We did not know what to do. Then, these three guys dressed in raincoats arrived. We were panicky. If they had done this and believed we were helping him, we would get a doing too.

They were friends, or comrades of his. They pushed us out of the way and two of them drew guns. It was the only time we were ever close to a group of armed IRA men. We, of course, scarpered. Paddy told us later, he was a Provisional who had been abducted by the Officials in their interminable feud. His mates got word and arrived in force to free him and exact retribution on his assailants. From what Paddy said, a quick ceasefire was put in place between the two warring Republican factions. Just as well, the guys we saw wanted revenge.

The ongoing violence, especially bombings, continued in the city with the Officials and the Provisionals vying with each other to be the protectors of the Nationalist community and there hung a blanket of tension over the city. We just got used to it. You heard older people talking about murders and bombings about 'our ones' and 'their ones,' the army, the RUC, the loyalists as if it was normal, and over time it became just normal. I bet teenagers in Newcastle, Edinburgh, and Bristol had different influences and topics.

Following Yvonne's admission to the Hospital, the two families together bought a car to take her runs out. It enabled her sisters to visit her when she could not leave the Hospital grounds. Dad contributed although he couldn't drive, but enjoyed the co-pilot role, sitting in all his glory beside Uncle Sean with various elements of the tribe in the back seat. He wasn't keen on leaving home when he wasn't at work. Sean and Mary had three children, wee Sean, Alice, and Ann: all a lot younger than me. In fact, in my memory, the youngest Ann was always a baby.

I loved being in the car. We operated a 'turnabout' arrangement, so everyone got a fair shot, but our Maeve wasn't interested. Eugene, after initial enthusiasm, lost interest. Auntie Mary often couldn't go when Ann was first born, as it was too much hassle. So, when someone dropped out, I was first reserve, alternate, as the yanks say. This proved to be a regular event, and we went to Bangor, or Tyrella, or Newcastle, Co Down. Uncle Sean would let me drive the car if we were parked in an empty car park or, more often, a field near the beach.

The car was a big old Vauxhall Victor, so comfortable with its large bench seat in the front, facilitating the six to seven passengers that always seemed aboard, squashed in the back, but I got to sit in the front, when I got my provisional driving licence. I was doing two Provisional licences, but more about the other one later. I passed my test when I was 17 years and four months. Uncle Sean insured me for his car. I did my test on the Shankill Road, less than a mile from where I lived, but I never ventured. It was strange how similar it was to the Falls, even the people.

I turned 17 in March. The Summer of 1972 was boring because the Parish under 18 team was playing in a Summer League. Not all the parishes on the Falls had teams, as a result we got an influx of talented players from elsewhere. I was not likely to get a game. I went along and watched Ramie.

In Northern Ireland, when July comes, the heavy sense of tension which hangs over the city all summer gets worse. It was an atmosphere you could almost reach out and touch.

Marches, bonfires, flags on lampposts, painted kerb stones and, of course, factor in a minor Civil War. Oh, to be young, eh, in the 1970's in Belfast.

A sunny Saturday in August, not long after I got my licence, we went to Newcastle County Down, "where the Mountains of Mourne sweep down to the sea." There was my Mum, Auntie Mary, Uncle Sean, and at least two of their kids. Uncle Sean wanted to teach me to drive because, after driving all week at work, he could see it far enough.

"It's like a busman's holiday," he often muttered through gritted teeth.

I was the answer to a mail driver's prayer. So, this Saturday I abandoned the family in a car park near the boating pool with strict instructions to be back by 5.00 pm from Mammy along with, "or Uncle Sean will drive us home and you can make your own way."

One look at Sean's face gave the lie to the likelihood of that possibility.

I was glad to get away from the herd and wandered down to the promenade alongside a bandstand come stage. Here the "Pieros (entertainers) did skits or sang on stage to passing holiday makers. Exhausted parents rested on a series of benches in front of the stage as their kids watched the live show. It was a mixture of acts, some sketches and singing current chart hits. All sung badly in my expert opinion, well, I was from the city and therefore an expert in everything! I remember fierce women in massively applied make up rattling collection boxes under your nose. To avoid them, and the off-key singing, not to mention the naff sketches, I sat on the concrete wall well away from the stage. I was just sitting there daydreaming in the August sunshine when a voice bellowed in my ear.

"JOE."'

"Wee" Beggs, all six foot one of him, standing right in my face, "Wee" Beggs to distinguish him from his brother "Big" Beggs, six foot four and counting, though three years older than us at St Peter's. Now, in five years in school, "Wee" Beggs never addressed me by name, though we were in adjoining classrooms. To be fair, he had no interest in football.

There was no issue between us, ships in the night. I doubt he knew my first name, and I didn't know his. I am sure it wasn't 'Wee!'

We exchanged pleasantries.

"How's your brother? (can't say "Big") .... eh?"

"Our Sean, in the Crumlin Road Jail for 15 years for car-jacking."

"Fifteen years for carjacking. That's steep even for them," said I somewhat sympathetically.

Not too sympathetically, because in the second year I was running down a corridor late for a class and collided with the aforementioned 'Sean.' One hefty punch laid me out for four minutes.

"Not so much stealing the car, I suspect. Shooting the two guys inside had more to do with the number of years he got," shrugged "Wee" Beggs in a world-weary tone.

Now this can't go on, "Wee" and 'Big". For God's sake, we have established the lunatic version is 'our Sean,' we are almost 18, we can communicate in first names in an adult fashion?

"So, what are you doing here?" I asked while I sought to work out how I would get around the name protocol. "Wee" Beggs had a story.

Gloomily he recounted his parents booked him and themselves into a boarding house in Newcastle for a week to get away from the city. "Wee" Beggs put his foot down, "I told them there's no fucking way I am going to a boarding house with 'youse' two for a week. I'd rather slit my fucking throat."

I doubted if he was as direct as that with his parents. Ramie swore he saw the Beggs' Father once on the front of the Falls Road, his elbow leaning on the top of a lamppost with the light just below his armpit. The yarn was exaggerated, but the genes were correct.

"Wee" Beggs, two older sisters, said:

"If you leave him here with us, we will stab him. He is as big an arse as that psycho, 'our Sean.'

A bit of self-awareness in the Beggs family on the female side, at least, I noted. So lucky "Wee" Beggs was ensconced in the afore mentioned boarding house. He said, "Each day I escape the boarding house and the Old Fellah,"

No mention of his mother, "and wander down here. I have been here since Thursday, (two whole days) and I said to myself, Enda…,"

(What Enda? I guess he would prefer to be called "Wee")

"You need a buddy, and here Joe, you are."

I soon put him right about the length of my stay and he resumed his gloomy persona.

We chatted a little about guys from school and what they were doing, from six months to five years in most cases, and he asked about the 'wee runt Mulgrew.' I think that's what he called Ramie.

I recalled there was no love lost there because of this long-forgotten incident involving a football and "Wee" Beggs's face, well not long forgotten by one of those involved! His face brightened as two girls approached us. Enda whispered to me, "My name's Alan, don't know what we will do about Joe though."

He introduced the girls in what he assumed was a posh voice. He sounded more like a pirate radio DJ trying to do a mid-Atlantic accent and losing his way. The girls were Vicky Newman and Jess Morton, Protestant girls! Both were still at school, Vicky at either Richmond Lodge or Sullivan Upper, and Jess at Methody, schools I never heard of. Enda, Oh God, I cannot call him 'Wee' Beggs, or I will lose my way. He looked at Vicky with pure, unadulterated lust. She was of average size, a sixteen-year-old girl with medium length brown hair, tight pink sweater over an enticing bosom, sprayed on jeans, and a dirty laugh.

"Vicky today is your lucky day; a woman like you doesn't get to spend much time with a guy like me. There are things I could teach a girl like you. Hee hee hee!"

"Such as, Alan?" more laughter, "Really Alan, what sort of girl do you think I am?"

"Wee" Beggs was bantering her, rather lewdly, for my taste. But she was far too amused and clearly encouraged him, not that he needed much encouragement. I couldn't catch the rest of the conversation. They were whispering, I believe, because of Jess. Vicky could hold her own, no doubt. He kind of enveloped himself around her in what he fondly believed was a solicitous way, excluding Jess and me.

My job was simple: entertain her pal. I turned my attention to Jess, a much more petite, slim girl with short straight black hair, dressed in a summer skirt and 'cardy' and a constant smile required of the one whose imposed role was, 'be the mate, keep quiet, don't flirt with the guy I fancy, and if he has a pal with him, divert the pal.' Girls have their own tactics in this game.

Jess smiled, what a smile and her eyes sparkled. I backtracked from making fun of her because I liked her.

"The Asters, a Belfast band, are playing here tomorrow night. Have you seen them or the Freshmen or the Mainliners?"

She shook her head. Showbands and US surfing music were not her thing.

"So, Jess, what do you do during the holidays?"

"I help around the church and the hall."

"Ah, right, you are a cleaner, or a window cleaner, "I ventured.

She laughed

"No, just sorting the church, the hall, helping the Minister."

God, the Minister, couldn't see me helping a Priest.

"Well, what do you do all summer?" she countered.

"I have left school; I am starting College." I lied. "I play football and" went for the clincher. "I have just passed my driving test." Her eyebrows furrowed; that impressed.

I was in the old Belfast banter mood so beloved of guys my age when we considered ourselves funny. It works best with an audience of other immature boys and fails miserably if even one female is in the group with a classic put down.

At one point, having discussed her school at length, though never having met a pupil from it until this afternoon and not being certain where it was, I ventured: "I hear Methody girls are… you know…, "No," she invited me to enlarge on the point. So, I did, "Fast."

I felt a sharp pain on my face. This was not, as you know, the first time I had had my face slapped by a girl. What on earth possessed me to go down that line? I was enjoying talking to this girl. She was the nicest person I ever met. She even laughed at my corniest jokes.

Why did I have to spoil it? I gazed at Jess, and this sounds cheesy, but it is the pure truth. I know I was 15 minutes into a conversation with a girl and the only physical connection was a slap in the face, but that did it for me, forever. Is it possible to connect so soon and know deep within yourself it, or part of it, will stay with you forever? Is it love at first sight? Does it exist? What surprised me was 'Wee' Beggs and Vicky were oblivious to the slap. They were holding hands and cuddling.

I worked harder than I ever worked in my life to redeem myself with this petite brunette with the slap of a prize-fighter. She took over managing the exchange, letting me grovel my way back. My mind was racing ahead. How did I ask her out?

"How long have you and he?" she nodded towards 'Wee' Beggs, "been friends." Some instinct led me to say, "I don't know Alan well. We were at school," (please don't ask which school)

She seemed reassured by this response, interesting. The 'lady killer's' magic charm wasn't impressing Jess. At one point I tried to retrieve hints from my 'Guide Manual of Ten Tips to get Laid.' This came from a book, an American book, which an older boy recommended and then leant me. He said it was the 'muckiest' book he ever read. I admit there was sexual content between its covers. The tone was a self-depreciatory style beloved by humorous American writers.

Tip one was to tell her she has the dreamiest eyes and Tip two was to say something nice about her hair. Trouble was I either didn't remember any of the others including the four "absolute certainties, Tips five to eight, or else I didn't have the courage to use them, or I couldn't remember the order they came in, which was vital.

Jess and I lived in different parts of a divided city. We did not have friends, events, or even shared spaces in common. I had never talked to anyone like her. We spoke for a couple of hours. She chatted about her family, devout Protestants, a concept of which I was not familiar. I thought Catholics monopolised devoutness, She listened as I talked about my Sisters, my Brother, my Aunts, and Ramie. I could have spoken to her for three days. I cannot describe what I felt, I was so.... excited, I was in a state.

All too soon, Vicky turned away from '" Wee' Beggs" and said, "We have to go."

They went but as they were starting to walk away Jess ran back and gave me a wee peck on the cheek and this fabulous smile as they walked off.

"Wee" Beggs, ever the romantic, was full of woe.

"I'm home and dry with that one. All I need is for you to take her pal for a walk."

Then he remembered, "Fuck it." he said, "and fuck you too."

I remained on the wall in silence, reflecting he needed to settle down and after a bit, he did. Meanwhile, I was wondering how I could see Jess again. Only 'Wee' Beggs could help.

A younger girl from the Piero's, with heavy stage make up, rattled a tin can in front of us and said to 'Wee' Beggs, "Dig deep, big boy."

He didn't, well, neither did I, but she was attractive and the other fish in the sea mantra beckoned. Now that he cheered up, he focused on me.

"You were doing all right with Vicky's wee pal.

I didn't mention the slap, and I assume he had been oblivious to it.

I drew a deep breath and said as nonchalantly as I could.

"Yeah, she was alright, wouldn't mind seeing her again."

This, of course, raised the possibility of me getting Jess away from Vicky, a prospect which appealed to both of us. I suggested, "I bet you see them tomorrow," but with far too much excitement, I added." Can you get Jess's number, or her address and kinda let her know, through Vicky, I would love to see her again?"

Far too much information. It gave "Wee" Beggs a hold on me. He peered at me as he tried to work out the significance of this torrent. He gave me a funny look and said, "Oh, we have love at first sight here, how cute," and he took the piss.

I cursed my lack of self-control. I should not have given him that information despite my eagerness to press the Jess business. A more casual approach would work better. "Wee" Beggs had had a better afternoon than he expected, and my potential involvement with Jess offered hope for a future encounter. I made him promise he would pursue my suit, emphasising how it could help him, a point he understood. He had five more days to work on it. The tactic of saying to a girl "my mate fancies your mate," was one I often saw on the Road. The girl would act as broker and if her pal fancied the lad, they would pair off. Many a marriage on the Road started in these sorts of old-fashioned bartered couplings, although, looking back, the guy often married the broker rather than the original object of his desires.

The following Monday, Ramie and I were walking up the Road to the Falls Park to join the guys for a kick about. It was a longish walk, and Ramie got the full on about Jess. He listened, gently teased, couldn't quite see how less than three hours on a seaside promenade could have such an impact on me. Look, I cannot explain why it all happened with Jess. I was ready to enter a relationship, albeit an immature one. It might have been 'forbidden fruit.' One thing I was sure of, it wasn't just me. I am certain Jess felt something too.

At the time Ramie was seeing the younger sister of one of Geraldine's pals, on and off, a girl called Carmel McCann. As a result, we were not running about with each other so much.

After about 15 minutes, a familiar figure lumbered towards us. One "Wee Beggs," not due back from Newcastle until Wednesday. I grabbed him and said, "What the F--k are you doing here?"

He explained a Priest, who was a regular at the boarding house, phoned to get a room for a few nights. The owner asked Mr and Mrs Beggs if their son would either move into their room, 'gross,' or sleep on the couch in the small upstairs sitting room. "Wee" Beggs forced his parents to give him the money for the bus back to Belfast to the waiting, but not welcoming, arms of his older Sisters. He continued, "I got a snog from Vicky on Sunday. Might have been more if you hadn't fucked off," he added, a tad wistfully.

"I didn't fuck off," I reminded him. "I wasn't there, well, except for the day."

God, how single-minded and selfish can this guy be? He glanced at Ramie, then he stroked his cheek where four years ago a well-aimed plastic football caught him.

Now 'Wee' Beggs possessed a mean streak, and I didn't want to rekindle that animosity.

"I was just telling Ramie about the cracking wee honey you were scoring with in Newcastle and her wee mate."

The right approach, very 'Cool,' pretending I can't quite remember Jess's name. Not too cool. 'Wee' Beggs grinned in triumph at me. "I wondered when you would get around to her."

Now, if anything creates an alliance between two guys who have had differences in the past, it's bantering a third one in the present. He and his new best pal, Ramie, did a pathetic double act that would have put Little and Large to shame…. not.

I deduced I was going to get information at some point, so I waited until these two wannabe stand-up comics finished their double act.

"Good news and bad news, Joe. Yes, Jess did like you. Thing is, she has been going out with this lad from her church for two years. They split for a while, but Vicky believes they will pick up again when their Church events start after the Summer."

He told me the street she and Vicky lived in, off the top of the Cregagh Road in East Belfast, but not her house or phone number. I wandered off with Ramie, who was quiet as I mulled through the information. Did I have a chance?

A few days later, I persuaded Uncle Sean to let me take the car for a spin. I went over to Jess's street and drove up and down it for a while. There was no sign of Jess. I parked outside a local convenience shop. I saw people going in and out but didn't focus until I got out of the car to stretch my legs, Vicky was the next person out. I greeted her like my oldest ever long-lost friend. She recognised me and remembered my name. I didn't tell her, and Enda/Alan wouldn't have wasted a breath on another male in such a situation. Vicky said, "Jess and I were just talking about you this morning. In fact, she seems to refer to you anytime we meet."

You can imagine how I felt.

"Can I drive you around to your house?" I asked gallantly and ushered her into the car.

"How do you know where I live?" she enquired, "and how come you bumped into me on the Cregagh Road?"

We drove around to a nice red brick, semidetached house.

"You have a nice house." I said, so polite and adult.

"It's not my house," said Vicky. "I live across the road. It's Jess's house. I'll just get her."

She disappeared round the back of Jess's house and the two came out a couple of minutes later, Jess pulling a blue jacket over her jeans. She jumped in beside me.

"I'll just leave you two lovebirds to it."

And with what seemed an unnecessarily broad smirk, she walked across the road to her house, hips swinging all the way, I tried not to stare too much. Jess made a face at her back. Now Vicky broke the boy's code. You never let your broker or mate tell a girl you fancy her. He can say "my mate thought you were all right," or "my mate fancied your mate," but nothing more definite. Girls will have a similar code, if you tell a guy, 'We have just been talking about you,' drive round to the girl's house with the guy, fetch your friend out with no preliminaries and describe you both out loud as 'lovebirds,' you up the ante. I suspect it was typical Vicky.

At Jess's suggestion, we drove down to Helen's Bay, a posh place I was at for the first time. We walked along the shore. We just talked and talked, held hands, and I was brave enough to kiss her. She responded. One topic that didn't come up was Wee Beggs. Funny, Vicky didn't mention him either.

When I got home, Uncle John asked me, in exaggerated polite tones, how Dublin was. I had been away for a while. Auntie Mary came out and scolded him," Can't you see he was trying to impress a girl?" Sean just winked.

Jess and I met again the following Saturday in the City Centre and went to the Wimpy Bar, drank cokes, I had no transport, but we walked up to Botanic Gardens and lay in the sun, kissing and canoodling, as the yanks would call it.

The next week, we went to the Pictures in the centre of Belfast and got the bus up to Jess's Street. I decided I must marry her and although it might seem a major step for a seventeen-year-old with his first girlfriend, well; we were all young and in love once, weren't we?

Jess was in two minds whether to go back to school and sit 'A' levels or leave with the five 'O' levels she hoped to get. She went away to do voluntary work in a church holiday home for older people in Sligo in the West of Ireland. I followed her there.

Vicky had a new boyfriend, John. He was a little younger than me, but not at all phased by having gained a Catholic mate. I forget who he supported, Manchester United?

He and I hatched a plan to hitch to Sligo and meet up with the girls. It was a novel experience for me being outside the city, hitching and camping.

We put our tent up in sand and the first gust of wind blew it down. A local farmer let us pitch our tent in the corner of his field. The girls only got an hour free each day during the week we were there, much to John's frustration. I learned more about the practical side of sex from John than from those daft lessons they gave us in school. On our second last day, the girls got the afternoon off. John and Vicky disappeared for a few hours across the sand dunes and Jess, and I ended up sheltering in the tent because of the wind and rain.

It was freezing as we were wet, and we snuggled down into my sleeping bag. I had ambitions, but Jess kept me under control, only 'just' mind you. She was a decent sort of girl. Shame. When Vicky and John got back, they were quite dishevelled, and John with a smug look, which he enlarged upon when Jess and Vicky returned to the Home. He asked how I got on, three out of ten, he reckoned he was 9.5.

When Jess got home, our relationship resumed. It was going well, far too well, and it ended as suddenly as it started. I made my way up to the Cregagh Road a few days after she got home, and I waited outside the grocer's. Jess got out of a car parked nearby. She was brief and to the point. "My Dad says we have to stop seeing each other."

Unless you are from Northern Ireland, especially in the 60s and 70s, you do not know what a barrier religion is to relationships. That was the sum total of the issue. I don't know whether Jess and my relationship would have survived. She was 16; I was an immature 17-year-old. Who knows, in a year or two, we would have gone our separate ways? Our relationship was cut off in its prime without a proper ending. So sad, Jess was in tears and ran back to her Dad's car and her Father sped off like a furious Dad who needed to go home and check his shotgun licence.

We met twice more, once in the City Centre, thanks to Vicky. The other time was on the Ravenhill Road because of an event there at the playing fields attached to Jess's school's feeder primary. I waited until the event ended, and we walked towards her home hand-in-hand. It was no use. Jess wasn't in the habit of lying to her parents, and I had to accept the end of our brief relationship.

In October, I walked over this time to Cregagh and wandered up and down but didn't see Jess. I saw Vicky with, I assume, her Mother, but she didn't see me, and this trip was futile. I needed to move on.

## Reflection Jess

I met Joe in the summer of 1972 in Newcastle County Down. My friend Vicky was chasing this horrible guy from Belfast whose name I cannot remember. I could not fathom why she was attracted to him, but Vicky lived a bit on the dangerous side with boys. We were staying with her folks in their holiday home. Back to Joe. He was with the guy one afternoon and he and I chatted. I liked him from the word go. He differed from the other boys in and around our church. I don't mean just the religious thing, but he was friendly, funny, cheeky even, but attractive. I am not sure why he was important to me or what the attraction was. He did not fit my life plan of marriage, children, and church, but he was special. Was I serious at the time, we only knew each other for a short while? I was at the time.

I was dating Robert on and off for two years. We started when we were quite young. When I was fifteen, I used to tell my friends I would marry Robert; At the beginning of the Summer, he had applied to go to University, and he suggested we split for a couple of months.

I was quite upset at first, but I was aware a lot would change in his life in the coming months, and I needed to let him see where that would take him.

We agreed we would talk again when church activities resumed in September. I went out with a couple of other boys, like Robert, nice but not as nice as him.

Then Joe came on the scene. It came out of nowhere. I guessed my parents would not be pleased, especially my Dad. He was not exactly anti-Catholic, well, a bit, but he was adamant the two communities should be kept apart. I liked Joe. He even followed me to the place out in Sligo, where I did voluntary work. It was intense, more passion than I was accustomed! My father found out we were seeing each other, and he put an end to it. There were terrible scenes in the house. My wee Sister and my Mum were getting upset.

I even told Robert about Joe. He suggested he and I got back together; he hadn't intended it to happen so soon, although I am sure he wanted it to happen at some stage.

I next saw Joe at a football match, playing against Robert's team. I also saw him again not long after when we were shopping in town.

# Chapter 3

# THE FOOTBALL MATCH

In the winter of 1972, it reverted to type. The Stormont government fell, but Ramie and I were oblivious to the political issues of the day.

A guy called Tommy Delaney, who was a coach assisting the guys in the Parish football teams, suggested setting up an under-19 team. Tom was a nice guy, not a well-organised person, but amiable, mad about football and well intentioned in trying to prevent us guys from being sucked into the paramilitary scene. Anyway, the under-19 team was formed, and I was back playing football. There was no way the Down and Connor League could accommodate teams of guys that age, so we played in a Belfast Saturday Morning League. The significant issue was there were Protestant teams in the League, most based on former Boys' club players who wanted to play organised football but had not 'made it' with senior clubs.

Two clubs from the Cregagh Estate in East Belfast were in the league. Cregagh Boys Club, which sprang to fame transferring George Best to Manchester United ten years ago and ruled the roost in boys' club football in Belfast for a while. Then there were Cregagh Rovers, an up-and-coming side. The other Cregagh boys discarded a few of the boys who played for Rovers. All the guys lived in the same area, played in the same flute bands, attended the same schools, and got 'tanked' into each other when they met on the football field. It wasn't always religion that brought out the worst in Belfast teenagers! Both teams used a pitch in the middle of the Cregagh estate and 'derby' games were keenly contested and then some! There could be two or three hundred spectators at their local derby, plus, so keen was the rivalry, half a dozen Cops. Tommy went over to Cregagh to watch one derby. He wanted to see Cregagh Boys club because we were due to play them the following week. His verdict, "Brutal, man," he answered.

"What was the final score?":

"Two taken to Hospital and four arrests," said Tommy.

Most teams wouldn't come to the Falls Road. Tommy registered our home pitch in Victoria Park, a public park near Sydenham, in East Belfast. This was how crazy Belfast was.

The only other Catholic team in the League, the aptly named Wolf Hill, registered their home ground in Ligoneil and most of the Protestant teams refused to go there and often forfeited the points. There was also Queens University's 4th team, not as talented as Queens University 5th team, no I don't why either, but there you go. In addition, there was City Hall, a team of Belfast Corporation employees and a team from the Ormeau area known as Ormeau North End, a rarity because it was a 'mixed' religious team linked with Rosario Youth club, an expanding youth resource on the Ormeau Road.

Our keeper, Mal Hegarty, was streets away the best player in the team. Derry City invited him to train with them, as did Shelbourne from the Republic. Mal at 19 had a serious alcohol problem. His folks owned butcher shops and he worked in them. He always had plenty of money. Generous enough, he bought booze for the rest of us, but he drank half. I heard he died when he was 32 of liver conditions. On the pitch, he was a superb keeper, but he missed quite a few games.

Dermot O' Driscoll was the Captain, a tough Centre Half. His Brother, Marty, played in goal when Mal was posted missing. Marty was more of a Gaelic football player than a soccer one but competent enough for our level.

Dermot was hard. A bit of a psycho, if I tell the truth, Ramie was terrified of him, despite being one our better players. I told Ramie to stand up to him, but he didn't fancy it. Once at training, Dermot booted Ramie unnecessarily, and I told him to "stop being a f--king p--ck." He punched me on the side of my head.

"Your boyfriend can fight his own battles."

I would have taken the punch on the head, moved towards him, the boys would step in and that would have been the end. O'Driscoll went too far with that crack, so I dived forward, catching him on the nose. He went down, spewing blood. It took three other guys and Tom to stop him from ripping me limb-from-limb, and two guys held me to stop me from being ripped limb-from-limb. We never shook hands. Tom cut the training and O' Driscoll never mentioned it. He spoke even less to me, fair enough, his choice.

Six years later, O'Driscoll was in an Active Service Unit involved in several ambushes on Army patrols in Turf Lodge and the Security Forces pronounced him dead at the scene of one but claimed none of their men had a hit. I think he might have been 'done' by his own comrades. His partner, and Centre Half, was big Kevin Kiernan, brilliant in the air and also an ex-Gaelic footballer. He came from County Tyrone, was a strong, quiet lad. He and Mal were pals. Kevin also drank a lot, but you would never know. With a striker and a creative midfielder, we could've been contenders, honest. Dermot, Kevin, and Mal travelled in Tom's car with the kit and the balls. I suppose because they were the core of the team.

The other skilful player was Ramie, but he didn't fancy being in an enclosed space with Dermot. Only two other players utilised this. One reason was Tom only had one eye and he drove looking over his shoulder, engaging the players in the back in conversation. He never shut up, I experienced it twice. It was terrifying. If the police did traffic duties in 1970 in Belfast, Tom would have been banned years ago.

We were due on this particular Saturday to play Cregagh Boys. Tom caught them in the Cregagh Derby and briefed us about the outcome of our soon to be encounter. Tom's team talk went like this: "Those goons are going to f--k--g murder you; the keeper is an Irish school boy international. They have a Centre Half who is slow but misses nothing in the air; he is on Portadown's books. The Full Backs are fast and tough, and they have a cracking striker. A guy with jet black hair who can run with a ball faster than you lot can - just run. Apart from that, a piece of cake."

Great Tom, just great, very inspirational, just the uplifting team talk we needed. We went into the heart of East Belfast. A small hostile crowd would turn up to see the 'Taigs' getting their just deserts.

We arrived in the Cregagh Estate, it was a cold; wet Saturday morning, and the local denizens chose their pits in favour of the game, we were pleased. There were half a dozen spectators AND including two lassies at the other side of the pitch from where I was playing in the first half.

I should have said earlier in his talk Tom pinpointed a slight, dark-haired midfielder whom he described as 'the number ten who made everything happen for them.'

How right he was. The boy scored a cracker from outside the box, and they got a penalty near half time. I didn't have a disaster, and they had to defend against Ramie, who was at his best. Typical Ramie, he scored a solo goal against the run of play. There was his usual big cheesy grin, which was for his own benefit, the sheer pleasure of scoring.

Dermot and Kevin must have gained a world record in the fouls they conceded. As a result, we were only one down at half-time. Tommy let us get our breath back and kept his advice to a minimum.

"Stand on the number ten," he commanded.

Our left back, Harry, commented, "Stand on him, he and Kiernan are going to have a kid together," which broke the tension, and we laughed. As we trotted out for the second-half, Harry whispered to me" The two wenches are on your side. I wouldn't mind doing it with the wee blond with the big hair. Mind you, what a mouth on her."

As I wandered over to my position, I looked first at the blond girl and at her brunette pal, and I felt sick with the tension. The other girl was Jess!

We kicked off and the midfielder who ran their show dominated. His name was Robert. Every five seconds, the blond girl was screaming; "ROBERT" and when I made to challenge him, she screamed, "Watch for that big thug, Robert." I don't think she used the word thug, but you get the drift. I winked at her and said to her pal as I went to take a throw in.

"How's it going, Jess?"

"Did he just call you Jess? "Demanded the blond, trying to work out if a player calling a spectator by their Christian name infringed Irish Football Association rules. She proceeded to give me grief.

I stated in a loud voice. "No, I won't take you out tonight. Stop pleading, that's an end to it."

Jess smothered a laugh. The blond almost turned purple, a Cregagh player came over threateningly and said, "What's your game?"

Be polite and sensitive in a situation with the love of your life nearby.

"Kicking your f--k--g teeth in Bozo," I whispered, so Jess wouldn't pick up the swearing, but I put a big friendly smile on my face. From a distance, it looked like an amiable exchange. He ignored me; God, I hate mature 18-year-olds.

"You OK Lorna," he said to Jess' mate, now I had her name. Lorna could not fathom how I knew Jess. She continued to abuse me, always brings the best out in me.

Once, after a few of my smart remarks and further insults from her, I suggested, affably enough, "Lorna, are we going to have two boys and two girls?

This time Jess couldn't restrain herself and burst out laughing.

The thing is, Robert moved from the kicking zone of Kevin and Dermot to safer waters where I inflicted less damage. Well, except poor Lorna, and he heard the exchange and also burst out laughing. The game paused for a free kick, to us for a change, given the home team supplies the referee. So, the game stopped. I was grinning, Robert and Jess were laughing and Lorna, well Lorna, was standing like one of those cartoon characters with a cloud pissing rain on her head.

Lorna wasn't just pretty, she was an absolute stunner, our guys were sure I was making progress, if only they knew. Cregagh scored again twice, and the match fizzled out, with Robert dominating the closing stages. Some of the Cregagh players exchanged handshakes with us, their keeper, called Bumper, shook hands, and embraced Mal. The goalkeeper's union transcends even sectarian divides. Their main striker was the fast, skilful guy called 'Murf' and scored a second-half goal.

Now with a name like Murphy, he should have been on our side. He was bumped all over the pitch by O'Driscoll, who possessed the physique, if not the skill, to nullify the afore mentioned "Murf." To pretend some of us were nicer than any of us were and to impress Jess since I was near him at the final whistle, I stretched out to shake Murf's hand.

He backed away, saying. "I've never even met a Catholic," or was it a taig, (an abusive name for a Catholic).

Robert was also standing nearby; he shrugged his shoulders, but he shook my hand. He was Jess's boyfriend, so they were back together.

Robert seemed nice enough, I suppose, an excellent player, but I just wanted him to die there and then. Jess would have burst into tears, and I would have rushed to comfort her.

Instead, I said meekly, "Well, played."

He headed over to the girls, and I stood there wondering what to do. Robert turned to me and teased Lorna. "My mate, Joe," (he picked that up quick, I wondered if Jess or Vicky mentioned me?) "Fancies you, Lorna. I can fix you up."

She lost the plot and chased him up the line, the big hair flouncing, quite a sight. Quite an attractive sight. I gazed at Jess, and I swear when Robert suggested I fancied Lorna, an expression crossed Jess's face, a wee flicker of jealousy. I saw it, or something like it.

We chatted, "How's Vicky?" "It was nice to see you at Newcastle," and "do you still like...?" whatever the groups we discussed.

"I bet you were surprised to see me?" I added, Jess smiled: "I noticed you just after the game began."

So, she had longer to compose herself, if seeing me was of any importance to her. Robert returned to his team, and an exhausted Lorna returned to Jess, eyeing me quizzically. I bestowed my most charming smile on her, partly in gratitude for her chasing Robert off and leaving Jess and me alone, even for such a short time.

I backed off. God, I wonder what would happen if I was brave enough to kiss her, --- I just said.

"Bye"

"It was really nice to meet you again Joe," that gave my heart a boost, I swear.

I went back to our team, who assumed my pursuit was of Lorna.

"Ah, shot down again McFaul, and we were sure you were gay!" said Harry Clarke and everybody laughed, including Tommy Delaney.

Ramie and I walked back across town.

"Was she the girl?" he asked. I nodded and chatted about her for an hour. I am certain he tuned out after ten minutes, but I couldn't stop talking about her.

About four months later, November 1973, on a busy pre-Christmas Saturday afternoon, I bumped into a couple in a crowded Royal Avenue and had the grace to apologise. The guy said:

"Joe, Joe, is that you?"

It was Robert and, of course, Jess, my Jess! He said, "HI Joe, are you still paying football?"

I tried not to stare at Jess and mumbled, "Oh, just dodging about. What about you?"

"I am up at Queens, but I play football on Wednesdays."

So, I spoke to Jess. "And Jess, what about you? Are you aiming for the University too?"

"No, I have left school and I am working in a bank around the back of Castle Place."

"Right," said Robert," need to rush, see you about." Jess flashed a smile, that smile, and they were gone.

## Reflection Robert

Yes, I remember Joe. We played against each other in a football match. Jess met him in the Summer of 1972. Jess and I were in the same church. When I got interested in girls, I remember talking to a pal and deciding who we liked the best. Vicky was fun. Even as a young teenager, Lorna was drop dead gorgeous, though volatile. From 14 onwards, we went out with the girls, in a harmless first boyfriend, first girlfriend, hand holding way. You got a kiss, a more passionate one if it was Vicky, I heard, but didn't experience.

The choir, Sunday School, waiting for the girls after Girls Brigade, youth club and the football team was my world at 15, 16, and 17. I started going out with Jess when I was 17. She was 15. We went out for a year, at weekends, and as my 'A' Levels got closer, we had less contact during the week.

I travelled to the Student's Union three or four times with a pal and his Brother. His Brother was saying how much life changes when you go to Uni, especially during Fresher's Week.

I suggested to Jess we take time out, as I wanted to enjoy the first months at university. She agreed. Jess dated a couple of guys from around our area on one-off dates.

Then she met Joe when she and Vicky went to Newcastle. Jess might have been serious about him. To be honest, she volunteered no information apart from her Dad going mental because he was a Catholic. Jess and I talked about whether we should resume seeing each other by the end of September. I intended to wait until Christmas, the end of my first term. After her Father insisted Joe and Jess broke up, I could see she was upset and. we picked up again. We met Joe in town one Saturday not long after I started Uni. Years later, I saw him on television. I wasn't going to mention it to Jess, but I did. He was a nice enough guy. Jess liked him, and she was an excellent judge of men!

# Chapter 4

# DECISIONS AND CHANGES

After Christmas 1973, Ramie and I embraced 1974. We would be 19, the last years of our teens beckoned. Ramie had broken up with Carmel and I was still pining over Jess, so we embarked on a strategy to meet more girls. I wasn't convinced Ramie and Carmel were done. She was always in his house, got on well with Greta and Geraldine, and she was set on Ramie. For now, we could team up again because of Ramie's 'single' status.

First, we went to Fruithill, a Sunday night dance at the top of the Falls Road. The girls there were older, and we got shot down a few times trying to ask girls to dance. Others were politer but scuttled off leaving me feeling embarrassed. It improved at the end of the evening, we got to walk a group of girls down the Road. We knew them over the years out and about the Road. There were six of them, four were two or three years older and the other two were only a year ahead of us at school, not I hasten to add our school, catholic schools in Belfast were strictly single sex.

Near Sevastopol Street, Ramie was with the four older girls, and I was with the other two. They asked me to walk them to their street. Ramie chatted with the other four and went home by himself. The girl I was talking to,

Eileen, took my hand and the three of us walked to her door where I got a brief snog from this older "woman," gosh. I would make a story out of it, there was more to come.

The other girl, Deidre, and I walked down the street to near her house, but as we reached it, she pulled me in beside a tree and we started kissing. I hadn't much experience. I went for it a little too frantically. When I put my hands under her sweater and down her pants. I became aroused. A light came on at her door, shit, her Mother shouted her in, and she rushed off, leaving me in a state! What was more important was laying it on thick for Ramie the next day.

"Listen Ramie, I got it from that wee minx Deidre and from Eileen last night, whoa I could tell you more, but you couldn't cope."

"No way Joe, a quick snog and that was your lot."

"She had a pink bra," I ventured.

"Aye, I bet it matched yours." he countered!

Ramie and I were the two last, almost nineteen-year-old virgins in Belfast, among our mates. I believe most of the claims were invented.

We toyed with trying to repeat our experience at Fruithill, but we bumped into a guy, Tom Duffy, who was a year ahead of Pat at the Grammar school. He had been in our Primary and he was waxing lyrical about the girls at "Queens," as he was at Uni. He got Ramie and I excited about the prospect of students, so we went over to the Students Union the following Saturday. As we walked up the steps, there were these two guys on the door, wearing black sweatshirts with ENTS on them. Whatever did ENTS stand for?

"Student IDs?" the guys asked, and Ramie and I backed off, and wandered down the steps.

We did not know about IDs, we assumed you paid in. We walked over to the edge of Eglantine Avenue next to the Students Union for a Council of War. There was a group of students milling around most about to go into the Union, others had come out and were heading off to local bars, the "Bot" and the "Egg," wherever they were.

We rushed up the steps with a group of about three guys and two girls; I became quite animated in my discussions with one guy who was drunk. Instead of recoiling at the onslaught from a stranger, no doubt because of the drink, he chatted back in a friendly manner. I remember one girl staring at us and I suspect the conversation made little sense, but as we went up the steps to the Union door, it would have looked like two fellow students having a blether.

At the door as the girls showed their student ID, I noticed the two guys on the door from earlier were gone and one ENTS T-shirt wearing doorman replaced them, so no 'I have already told you guys no ID no entry.' Excellent! I recognised him. It was Niall Coleman, who, with his brother Gerry, had been stalwarts of St Peters under 16's and under 18's teams when Ramie and I were in the under 14's. Gerry was the Club Captain of the whole setup. The Coleman's moved from our Parish over to South Belfast and Niall ended up playing for Rosario and being a pain to the club his brother captained.

I greeted him like a long-lost brother. "Niall, how goes it? How's Gerry?"

He eyed me, saying nothing, but recognition dawned. "Err Jimmy, Joe," his voice tailed away. Just as I was going to refresh his memory, he looked at Ramie. "Ramie Mulgrew, how's it going wee man? Who are you playing for these days?"

You might think I was jealous of Ramie. I wasn't, but I didn't want to be his anonymous sidekick. Ramie's skill was the key identifying factor, as he reminded me every day the next week. With a promise of catching up later in the bar and buying him a drink, Niall allowed us entry. We were turned loose on the female student population, who for reasons that escape me, were unaware of the opportunities coming their way.

We enjoyed the music and the atmosphere in the Students Union, very non-threatening. It was few degrees below places we went to in terms of aggression, didn't see any actual fights, always the highlight of even the Parish discos. The chat was important and neither of us were equipped to hold our own about university education.

We decided, given our interest in sport, we would pretend to be student PE teachers, which was fine. We could claim to be at St Joseph's, the Catholic Teacher Training college. If we got into a dialogue with Protestant girls, we were limiting our options. To me, any Protestant girl might be another Jess. Ramie came up with a clever ruse.

"When I say I am doing PE; I will wait for the girls to say St Joseph's or whatever and go with whatever."

I don't know if it happened to him, but it happened to me. I had danced and been "dumped" by several girls, including an English one (even 'faster' than Methody girls!), but I got into a better situation with a girl called Georgina (Georgie) Collins. Now Georges, male or female, had figured little in the life of a Falls Road boy but I was quite taken with the mop of curly hair and the alcohol fuelled devil may care attitude. I kept up my pretence throughout our brief time together and even tried to hide my working class Falls Road accent with something I considered sounded a bit more interesting but was odd. A touch of the 'Wee Beggs. About three times, she said to me, "You have a strange accent." Then she asked, "Did you use to live in Canada?"

I was about to say yes, made me seem more interesting but I didn't. Just as well because she said she had cousins in Canada and visited there with her parents, George (what else would her Dad be called) and…. I forget her Mother's name, on holiday.

She was an attractive girl who was studying psychology and waxed on about it, so I wasn't under any pressure to talk about my studying, thank goodness. Although she was a fun girl.

"So, you are doing PE at Stranmillis College," Where?

"Oh yes," I agreed.

I must remember the non-denominational Teacher Training College was Stranmillis. Then she asked. "What school were you at?"

Now everyone in Belfast knows how to detect someone's religion without having to ask the question, even the way 'h' is pronounced tells the sophisticates. It was a genuine question, unlike my response.

"Methody," I replied.

She went, damn it, "Me too, me too."

"Christ, how do I escape this?

"So, whose form, were you? You weren't my year?"

The hallmark of a guy trying to make it with young women must be being a talented liar, so I had to up my game.

"I left several years ago. Wee bit of bother with another lad which was all hushed up, I went to the Tech, "clever ploy.

"We must know lots of the same people."

And she worked back from "a few years ago."

I wanted to take control. "You might know a girl I used to go out with, Jess Morton." But this was not much safer territory.

"Jess Morton, she was in my Sister's class, lovely girl Jess."

"Yes, a wee smasher." I agreed, a little too enthusiastically.

"But" Georgie began, 'I thought….' got this one.

"I know, it was just when she and Robert split up, anyway I like Robert. He is a decent bloke."

That satisfied her, also she was losing interest in talking about another girl I liked and then she added, "I knew about that, but anyway, they are engaged now, getting married in about 18 months, too soon at their age."

I felt as if I was stabbed in my stomach. Jess was getting married. Deep down I felt betrayed. I hoped she still yearned for me. It doesn't make sense now, it didn't make sense then, but it was how I felt... The impact Jess made on my life was not easily swept away. She came to mind most days, but there was nothing I could do. Her

Father's attitude, the sectarianism, the violence in the city and the reality of her and Robert conspired a long time ago to keep her from me. It was a silly fantasy, I know. I suppose just hearing it from Georgie ruined a dream.

When the music and dancing finished, I asked Georgie if I could walk her to wherever she was staying. I was feeling, not aggressive, but rejected wanting to get back at Jess, silly... We chatted about music. I stayed away from education. She lived up the posh Malone Road in a block of new student flats, the Halls or the Oaks or something.

"Do you want a coffee?" she asked.

I nodded, never have had coffee, but this was only going one way. I was excited and nervous, afraid but determined to go wherever it was going to go. We went into something she called the "Common Room" with a kitchen attached and she made me a coffee, vile stuff, but I drank it anyway.

There was a couple lying on cushions on the Common room floor. The girl greeted us. Georgie led me down to her room. Streetlights outside the window made it quite bright, but Georgie pulled the blind. We lay there kissing and caressing. My hands had to go somewhere, so I caressed her shoulders and her upper arms. I persevered and to my surprise she, and I mean she, undid her bra and I took off my trousers. I caressed her buttocks and kissed her breasts; it was instinctive. I got more excited kissing her. She placed her hands down my pants. At one point, she took my penis in her hands. I became excited and made love for the first time.

What happened was, it was all over too quick. I know I betrayed my inexperience. Georgie, calmed my ardour, brought me back, she knew what she wanted. I imagined I would be the leader, in control, but it didn't turn out like that. It wasn't earth shattering, it swept over me.

I should have been more patient, but it wasn't a total disaster and she seemed content, lay there in my arms and went to sleep. A song came to mind, 'It should have been me,' I would sing it at Jess's wedding!

I woke up about 5:00 am the next morning. I decided I would head home. Georgie was dozing, albeit with the odd little stir and mumble. I kissed her on the back of her neck. I should say something, "Can we meet again?" and she mumbled.

"You Stranmillis folk are in on Wednesdays. See you in the Snack Bar."

Georgie was the first girl I had made love to; I felt an obligation towards her. We should have spoken more, not just sex and run! She was only the second Protestant girl I ever spoke to but, unlike sensitive down-to-earth Jess, she was outgoing and posh. I dressed and left the Halls of Residence. There was no one about and I headed down the Malone Road. I faced a long walk home but through safe enough areas, apart from Shaftesbury Square near Sandy Row.

The houses on the Malone Road were huge, even the semi-detached ones. Coming from a wee kitchen house, I was impressed by them. The houses on Jess' Street were semi-detached, with back and front gardens, posh by my standards, but they were not huge. They were three or four bedroomed, but these had at least six bedrooms and a couple of vast reception rooms. Our entire house could fit in them on one floor, a different world. It looked, from notices in gardens, as if the University owned several big houses on my route. I noticed a bicycle lying half in, half out of the bushes. No idea who it belonged to or why it was abandoned. It wasn't a domestic property but "part of the Department of Community Psychology." I took this as a sign to liberate the afore mentioned bicycle and dragged it over a low wall and onto the pavement. I headed off arriving home sooner than I expected.

My Dad was leaving for work, I knew he would say something, so I blurted. "I was at Paddy Flynn's house, borrowed his bike." A name I made up because if I used any of the guy's names as like as not, he would know their Dad.

"He is a guy from up the road," I added as I shot up to my room.

His words "could you not have phoned your Mum from his house" echoing in my ears.

This was in the day when houses rather than people had phones! In the weeks following, I was tempted to go back to Queens, either on a Wednesday or a Saturday, but I didn't.

Ramie and I should have better plans if one or other of us 'hit it off' with a girl and left the other to make his way home alone. At least at Queen's, there were buses at the end of the evening going to various parts of the city. If there was a lot of rioting, as there often was on the Lower Falls, the bus would only go to the City Centre. It meant a quick sprint from Anderson and McCauley's Department store up Divis Street, past Hastings Street RUC barracks, which offered a measure of protection. Still, looking back, and since later events like the Shankill Butchers, there was an element of risk. Ramie made it home safely. He hadn't 'clicked' with anyone, and I must admit, I enjoyed telling him about my success. The truth would have been enough, but you appreciate I exaggerated as guys do. We never went back. So much for my gentlemanly commitment to Georgie. I am sure she catalogued me as an experiment for her psychology course, well that's how I rationalised it.

The much bigger event in our family life involved my wee Brother. He announced he wanted to become a Priest, our Eugene. I suppose, on reflection, there were plenty of signs. He was serious about attending mass. I just assumed the old girl still terrified him! Our Mammy was delighted, 'my son the Priest,' it sounds like the beginning of a Jewish Mother's story. Eugene wanted to enter an Order called the Kiltegan Fathers with a seminary across the Border.

There was a lot of expense involved, so my Dad pursued overtime and was around the house less than usual. The day Eugene left, he hugged me. The McFaul's were not that type of family, so it was weird, but you know I missed him. We shared a room. We never fought over the years. For a time, he looked up to me as his big Brother I cannot remember when or why he stopped. I would not see him for another six years.

The experience with Georgie and Eugene's departure awakened something in me. I was about to change my life with ramifications for the next eight years. I also embarked on something fanciful, which proved more significant in the long run.

I spoke to my Dad about having no job, and no prospects. We were developing a hint of maturity. Over a few days, the need for qualifications kept rearing its head.

The Queen's 'experience' may have influenced me. I enrolled two days a week as a mature student at Belfast Tech in Millfield, close to where I lived. The advice I got was to study for 'O' levels in English and Maths as a starter. I loved the English classes, poetry, Shakespeare, and Irish literature. Most of us were adult students.

There were attractive girls, who were right out of my league. Boy, did they compete with Jess in providing more than a few fantasies? Maths was difficult, it was hard. I was OK at arithmetic at school, but this was a different level. In the same room I had a maths class, a break for an hour followed by English. The first week, I went for a hot drink, not coffee, but the other students were scary, especially the girls. They were Catholic and Protestant, bright, articulate, more mature than me and comfortable in each other's company. All were aiming for a late entrance to University.

When my English class finished the next week, I was sitting at the back and was slow at getting up to leave. This wee red head chatted to me, and I was attracted to her. Then her Lecturer arrived. Unlike my Maths teacher, she was a formidable woman who brooked no interruption. I didn't dare get up to leave, so I sat on, but I recognised a few familiar concepts and formulae being thrown out.

I walked out with the redhead; her name was Amanda, and I suggested we go for a drink.

Amanda laughed. "I don't think so,. I have a boyfriend."

We remained pally for the rest of the year. We would go for a drink at break or lunch. I was interested in how she talked about her boyfriend, what they did for fun, and tried to imagine how a normal boy girl relationship should work. A lot more helpful than "Ten Tips To Get Laid," that's for sure! She confessed later she was studying, intending to join the RUC! Her class was a duplicate of the one I attended but was taught differently. They were a week behind us, so I was listening to a version of what I sat through the previous week. At the beginning of the following week's session when my Lecturer reprised what we did, the double input helped the learning stick. To see more of her, I went to Amanda's class, though mostly it was to improve my learning. I even asked intelligent questions. What impressed me was finding the courage to speak out in class, which I later brought to the more laid-back English classes.

Years later, chatting to friends, I tried to find an explanation for what changed. Perhaps having sex for the first time. I used to be scared of the intimacy fearing rejection or ridicule. In addition, there was my newfound interest in Education. In different ways, Ramie and I were maturing.

The Troubles were in their sixth or seventh year. We all had friends, relatives or neighbours who were arrested by the Brits. Most of us knew someone killed in action or murdered by the security forces or the Loyalists. Pat sat in on more sophisticated conversations. I remember he made, well, a speech, "The Brits and the Loyalists have different agendas, and our aim should be to separate them. What the hell did that mean? He said, I remember it as if it was yesterday:

"We are going to have to sit down with the Brits and the Loyalists, but separately, not now, because you can't get one without the other. We will need to persuade the Brits to leave and the Loyalists to share. They aren't going away, so we need to talk to them."

"Get on with Protestants, Aye, big Paisley could be our Parish Priest, he has the collar for it."

I got a withering look in response. Pat's new friends, whoever they were, would just think of us as kids if we made those kinds of remarks.

In our group there were tensions because Carmel was still part of it and Ramie wasn't sure whether he wanted to rekindle their relationship. That it was intimate was clear from a few chance remarks he made to me, but Ramie never said much else, and I didn't probe. My experience with Georgie gave me more assurance. I punched in the girl stakes above my weight. Ramie took the mickey more than usual over my 'wee Protestant girls.

I amazed and amused the girls in our group, although the guys were just a little sectarian and sexist about it. No one but Ramie was aware how little occurred between Jess and me. The girls were given to comments like "Joe's a real romantic at heart." That started everybody laughing, but it did my street cred among the girls no harm at all. Could romance outscore sectarianism even in West Belfast.

Ramie's Dad had a horrible experience. Paddy was coming down the road one afternoon and was stopped by a patrol of English soldiers. Despite the time Paddy had a drink in him. I do not know who was at fault for the incident kicking off, I could accept Paddy was abusive and at least delivered an Irish history lesson. Whether he tried to attack seven uniformed and armed men, as was claimed afterwards, is doubtful. Anyway, the folklore went around the district claimed the soldiers knocked him down and started kicking him. Other men on the road who knew him rushed to his aid and, in a typical Belfast fashion, some women as well. Pretty soon, a full-scale riot ensued. In the middle of it, someone got a passing car and Paddy was rushed to hospital unconscious. Paddy recounted the details, even those bits after he was rendered unconscious, in pubs around the Road for months afterwards. A local political hack made a formal complaint and the case against the army was brought to court. Paddy accepted an apology and was paid compensation.

Ramie and I discussed the attack on his Dad many times. It brought the struggle closer to home, involved us in more. We discussed what we should do. Because it was close to us, it influenced us, in October 74, Pat approached us full on, "Do you want to join the IRA?"

We knew about his involvement, but he never raised our joining. Oh, how we laughed and marched up and down as if we were carrying rifles, saluting. To be fair, we were both drunk. Pat was deadly serious.

"You need to grow up." He growled and walked away in a huff.

A few days later, he repeated it. Ramie and I exchanged glances. There wasn't much happening in our lives.

"Yes." I responded, just to see where it would take us.

Ramie agreed with me. I have often wondered now, was it Pat who got Ramie in the IRA or me? Not something to dwell on.

As a community under siege we, at first, welcomed the British Army. Then, every so often, something happened. They were put in an impossible position, those in the middle often are.

The incidents in Ballymurphy, when the priest and the housewife were shot in 1970, Internment and Bloody Sunday, showed they had taken a side, no longer trying to pretend they were neutral. They left themselves open to Republican propaganda.

Their government's own poor judgement did it. Pat hammered this home and, to be frank, it was the same message, or a version, we heard from him since he was a kid.

I remember we were standing on the Road and Pat said. "Take a stand, you two are on the side-lines and you aren't kids anymore."

Ramie said nothing and I could hear myself saying: "Alright, we should. What do we do?"

Pat muttered, "Leave it with me."

Ramie said, "Seriously, are we going to join the Provie's?"

"May as well."

Now, by any standards, it was an important decision, but as was our way, Ramie and I just 'drifted' into it.

The next evening, Pat took us to a club further up the road. We walked into the club, dim lights, low ceiling and quite shabby in appearance, well worn. tables and chairs with groups of men sitting around them. I was aware there were no women in the building., The barman was going to put us out until he saw we were with Pat. We weren't underage, but we looked young. We didn't look like desirable customers. Pat ushered us into a back room.

"Come in," a voice commanded. "Take a seat."

We did as instructed. Sitting behind a table was a severe guy in his late 30s. We found out late his name was Sean. He stared at us, no smile, no introductions, no sense of being welcomed. Pat left us to it in his usual inimitable 'mysterious 'fashion, one minute there, the next gone. I was to be in this back room many times over the next year. It was dark, the stench of stale fags almost unbearable, lots of sweaty guys had been in this room. No one said joining the IRA meant 'spit and polish.'

This 'Sean' with short straight black hair like an overgrown crew cut sat at a table flanked by two other guys. All wore dark bomber jackets and jeans, working-class men. I must have met with him about five times over the course of the next year, always the same scenario, but with at least one of the other two being a different person.

Often a Gerry McQuillian.... McGivern, whatever, whom I knew from St Finian's, and St Peter's, was present. Gerry was just a couple of years older than Ramie and me, not part of the football fraternity, and not possessed of a sense of humour. He came from a well-known Republican family, and he was active from quite a young age. Any time he was present, he never acknowledged Ramie and me. He didn't know us well, but he was aware of us over a long period of years. He was not hostile, just serious.

On the fringes of all our activities was an older guy called Colum Delaney. Sean and Gerry both deferred to him. Column was the highest-ranking IRA officer we encountered, though I was only to speak on him on one occasion. You have all seen him interviewed on television over the years about political issues and always denying he was a member of the IRA. I claimed later, though Ramie laughed at me, that whoever was present, all the guys had holsters and guns under their bomber jackets, quite the right garb for this crew.

Sean asked us questions such as what street were we from, what schools we attended, if we ever been charged by the Police or in Court, did we have any relatives in the RUC or the British forces, even second cousins, the Irish are big on cousins, first, second, third even? It was clear he knew the answer to these questions, except the one about second cousins.

What he was interested in was not what we were saying, but how we were saying it. He asked about our political views, which came over as immature and what we thought of the British Army.

I was tempted to say, "loved having them as guests in our house during the Falls Curfew," but I decided not to. Humour wasn't high on these guys' agenda. He asked our opinions on the RUC and the IRA. Despite where we were brought up and what we had seen, we were ill prepared for this discussion.

Faced with these questions, Ramie did what he always does if someone in authority puts him under pressure. He clams up, I wasn't doing much better, but to break an uncomfortable silence, I said, "Well, we are going to have to split the Brits and the Prods. After all, we have to live with the latter."

I caught Pat's amazed look, but later he said he was chuffed at me, parroting his words as he said.

"First, I assumed you hadn't been listening to me, and second, I didn't believe you understood the point." He was right about the second part.

At the same time as this recruitment was happening, I was struggling to see my place in the grand scheme of things, and Ramie was seeing Carmel again. Caramel's Dad, who owned a small electrician's business, was talking to him about an Apprenticeship. I needed something to keep Ramie with me some of the time, I couldn't be part of that, not the way we were previously. just marking time until I got my opportunity.

There was a short ceasefire, the tension in the city eased, although there were gruesome murders but fewer bombings. The Provos were not as strong as they were in 1972 or even 73. This was because a number of their top men were lifted. We gathered they were feeling the pinch and needed to restructure.

They moved away from local battalions to two structures, local volunteers who 'policed' the areas they lived in and maintained order and a smaller group to go on operations, Active Service Units. They wanted people to obey orders, not gifted impresarios who wanted a gun to do their own thing. Ramie and I were being recruited with the local 'policing' in mind, but it took longer to set up than was intended and wasn't adhered to everywhere. South Armagh kept the original structure and Derry's was an amalgam.

Years later, Pat said to me over 20,000 people had passed through the IRA's ranks at that time. Only twelve hundred or so were active at any one time. It was understood Bloody Sunday, coupled with Internment and the Ballymurphy atrocities, had provided an accelerant to a slow-burning fuse. Many thousands of nationalists joined the IRA, passed through it but left because of being disillusioned or had families or were fed up with constant harassment by the Security Forces.


## Reflection Georgie

I do not remember Joe well. He was one of a number of guys I dated back then. I did not sleep with that many and he wasn't memorable. What I do remember is I think it was his first time and he was fixated on a girl from our school. She was in my sister's class. I would have been happy enough to see him if he turned up on the Wednesday after we met. If he had, we might have gone out for a while, but he didn't show, and I never spotted him around the Uni.

# Chapter 5

# THE BETTING SHOP
# AND THE SETUP

I still find it hard to explain why Ramie and I joined the Provisionals. We were apprehensive because of violence from various quarters in Belfast between 1972 to 1975. I got a formal letter of appointment from the IRA showing my conditions, years of service, annual leave entitlement, starting point on the salary grade.... don't be daft, there was no salary! I have spent too long in Local Government! What happened is Pat said: "You are in, provisionally,"

Wonderful, I thought, 'provisionally Provisionals!' I picked up we were in 'D' company with a long history of involvement in fighting the British before Ramie and I were born. Our recruitment process was for volunteers who would be on the fringe not yet trusted to be full operators involved. In the past they rejected those whom they sensed were unlikely to withstand interrogation, or flew solo, i.e., wouldn't follow orders, but there was a planned reorganisation in the offing, and they needed new volunteers until they restructured.

They were not sure about us. Our history was too immature, too lacking in political substance. It would have been fine if we were 15, but coming up on 20, we lacked something. It was strange how it turned out. I led

Ramie into the football team, but he was the better player, into the 'RA', but he proved the more talented volunteer. It was typical of our relationship in both situations. I started at the front but receded.

After the oath, we attended various classes, history classes, dealing with the Struggle's history. Pat's recommendation and our behaviour to-date made it unlikely either of us would become touts, informers, an issue that obsessed our senior colleagues, rightly so in view of the number of leaks. No longer 'street boys' nor Celtic IRA men, i.e.., singing the songs but being posted absent at the first sign of confrontation. We were part of a disciplined force acting under orders, freelancing would bring similar sanctions to being a tout.

There were younger guys who hung round club's meeting rooms or just outside the premises, we were on nodding terms with them. Serious looking, they ran errands or passed messages, though nothing was committed to paper. Ramie and I were more fun. We were discouraged from claiming state benefits because this helped the authorities keep track of people. When we went to the club, the organisation sometimes gave us money. It could only pay when it had money, so we hedged our bets and claimed both! There was also a Green Book, a manual of instructions on what to do and what not to do. Drinking was discouraged, yeah good luck with that.

At the time we joined the 'Cause', we expected immediate recognition as we walked the streets. The population of West Belfast seemed unaware two such fine urban guerrilla fighters were amongst them. At our initiation, if you could call the oath to the 32 county Republic and to the organisation initiation, I remember an explicit message to break our oath of allegiance would have serious, even fatal, consequences. Any fraternisation of any kind with the security forces would invite serious sanctions.

Unless you are a student of Irish political history, the array of organisations creates confusion.

I know this oversimplifies it, but in the aftermath of the Civil Rights marches in the late 1960s, the loyalist community expelled Catholics from 'mixed' areas. The IRA set itself up as defenders of the catholic nationalist community. Its leadership was old, based in Dublin, and little access to modern weapons.

Pat's cousin, Kieran Duddy, was one of several younger men who joined it. In 1970, a group of able younger republicans repudiated the old leadership and set up the Provisional IRA, the remnant of the old group was known as the Official IRA.

The Provisionals saw themselves as defenders of the Catholic community and wanted to take the fight to the army of occupation and unite Ireland.

The Officials were a mixture of socialists and Marxists who wanted a 32 County Socialist Republic. Among the Loyalists, there were different factions as well. This included the UVF, the UDA, the UFF, Red Hand Commando and Tara, but I don't know how they were different.

Disputes within the Officials about the direction of the struggle culminated in 1974 at the Official Ard Fheis (annual conference) in a series of resignations by individuals and group, it was innocuous enough at first. Then a new political party, the Irish Republican Socialist Party (IRSP), was formed. Unlike the Provisionals, it was not an abstentionist party; it intended to contest elections. The IRSP saw the Officials as representing moderate reformism and the Provisionals representing 'elite militarism.' The first item on the agenda of any meeting of Irish republicans is 'The Split'.

The IRSP set up an armed wing, the Irish National Liberation Army (INLA). It was to be involved in high-profile assassinations, including at least one English MP. The break away from the Officials had little impact on the Provisionals, but the Official's knee-capped some IRSP members. A series of tit-for-tat shootings between these two socialist Republican groups escalated. The Officials and the Provisionals were also targeting each other. It led to a lot of brutal stuff going on in Belfast, with a series of murders and reprisal killings. It was old comrade killing old comrade. They shared 70% of each other's ideology but couldn't cope with the ego clash. Once one group was violent, the other retaliated.

We lived in an 'Official' area but were 'Provisionals,' and our 'side' was growing in strength. We didn't mix with the other group, but if we passed each other on the Road, we nodded affably enough. If we had been INLA, it would have been different. We attended the same schools, same Parish, or were familiar figures about the Road. My cousin Peter Rodgers was one of them. I was never threatened by the Officials, but Pat was. Twice they picked him up and threatened and he was beaten up once. He knew them as well as we did, just knowing them wasn't a guarantee of safe passage.

Many of the Official guys were heavy, profound, talking in terms of revolution, societal change, uniting the working people, stuff of no interest. The vicious stuff lay with much older guys, old comrades who in the past shared prison time together, who were involved in disputes which escalated. Like most situations where violence occurs, it was a power struggle, and included a few ego trips. As with so much else in life, we just didn't get involved and when we were involved, we stayed within our own narrow compass. That wasn't planned. It was just the kind of guys we were.

We didn't pay much attention to it. Both the Officials and The Provisionals top brass were engaged in negotiations with the British. They did not tell anybody else, no doubt they had their reason, but it led to confusing orders when to engage and when not to engage. There were guys who just wanted to fight and to hell with the top guys.

There was another element during these years that worried us, especially Ramie. There was a spate of Loyalist murders where random Catholics were abducted and killed, guys who were not involved in anything. A guy we were at school with was walking his girlfriend home one night and he headed home back down the Falls. He was abducted by a Loyalist murder gang, tortured, and shot.

The Loyalist murder gangs were cruising around, killing random Catholics. Intimidation force feeds resistance, it never dissipates it. The intention was to provoke the Nationalist community into pressurising both wings of the IRA to stop the bombing campaign.

Protestants who were not involved in any activity were killed, as were Catholics in the wrong place at the wrong time. This alarmed us. Self-protection was the major reason for us joining the IRA.

The soldiers' beating of his Dad affected Ramie. He kept saying he wished he had been there with a gun. I told him waving a gun around in front of armed soldiers could bring its own problems. No longer was it about other people.

When Ramie was going out with Carmel, her Dad insisted if they were out late, they stayed at her family home rather than him risking walking or getting a black taxi the length of the Falls.

In fact, the night I met Georgie, Carmel's older sister saw Ramie and me. She reported back to Carmel Ramie was there. Carmel mentioned it to him when she was calling on Geraldine and Ramie was cross, though they were not going out.

I get joining the struggle was serious for lots of people. Ramie and I were just immature. The politics passed over our heads. We both hoped we might get personal protection weapons issued to us, but we never did. Pat did, though. We joined the 'Provies' because of the fear many young Catholic boys had, and I suppose because of the accumulated effect of the "Troubles."

The Belfast Assembly was set up with more nationalist input than the Stormont Parliament. It could have been a game changer. Established following elections in June 1973, it only lasted for five months from January to May 1974. The biggest change was it included nationalists in government for the first time. This early attempt at power sharing failed because of Loyalist opposition. They believed they lost too much, first the B-Specials, then Stormont and now this. In the Spring of 1974, the headlines were dominated by the Ulster Workers Strike when the Loyalists flexed their muscles and showed both governments who was calling the shots. That led to the collapse of the power-sharing executive. On the Falls, for a time, essentials became hard to get hold of, but the overall attitude was this strike was a bigger problem for the British than for us.

I was growing up, joining the struggle was a logical step. The Falls Curfew still rankled more than I admitted. The incident with Ramie's dad, the entire atmosphere of threat and ongoing violence in the city, made me want to do 'my bit.' Ramie had the same view. I was feeling happy, having been notified of my two 'O' levels passes. My life was emerging from the shadows. I could make a difference to something.

Our history and political/social classes were held at Casement Park, a Gaelic football stadium further up the Road, but a few were held just outside Dublin. Then we began drilling. Simple marching, so we could take part in honour guards at funerals or as stewards at meetings. I remember having to stop at the sounds of commands given in Irish. I knew the language from school, but it was strange outside a classroom. After a few rehearsals at funerals of volunteers and, acting with Cumann na an Ban, the women's section, we were ready to go on operations. We took little to do with the Cumann, how Irish and Catholic to keep men and women apart, no wonder Catholics of both genders have such hang ups about sex. It's bred in them. If you try to stop them dying together; you prevent them from getting up to activities even more unacceptable.

Ramie and I did not join the IRA to meet girls for sure. I found the female volunteers more intelligent, more mature, and fiercer. Girls or women who thought a week at the Gaeltacht, the summer schools for Irish language speakers, was a fun thing. I kept a low profile when they were about, and woe betide any male volunteer who did not march in time or lower their banner appropriately. They could make you feel two feet tall with their sharp comments. The Women's organisation was important. They supported the Provisionals in their split with the Officials during 1969/70 and one of their leading members was later assassinated by Loyalists in 1976, when a patient in the Mater Hospital in Belfast.

There were murders in the city and rural areas. The Loyalists tried to hit back at the IRA and in later years it was revealed they were sponsored both by British Military Intelligence and the RUC.

We heard about the plans to reduce our structure into the smaller cells because of the number of informers operating in our ranks. A special squad was set up to deal with informers and in about 2012, it came out its leader was himself a major informer!

We were pleased when Pat brought us up either Divis or Black Mountain in the Summer of 1976, to a quiet spot where we were first given weapons, M1 Garlands to shoot. I was OK with the prospect of shooting someone. It was them or us. It was brilliant at first but grew tedious.

We learnt how to maintain the guns, with constant warnings of how they were more important than the volunteers.

Sean came once and pointing his finger said if a comrade gets shot, grab his gun, and scarper don't waste time trying to save him, "we can always get more guys like you," he said. I hope he was joking.

We were taught to shoot by two ex-British servicemen. Ramie was the second best in our group of six. After two sessions, the guy who was the best shot was gone. Another guy who was a better shot than me went to School with Pat, although he lived in North Belfast rather than West. I recall a third guy who also came twice, proved useless and never came back. I could hit a target on the outside, although one ex-soldier said it's a pity we don't "use bayonets, you'd be a dab hand at that," This was not intended as a compliment. Thing is, I have a short fuse about criticism, and I wasn't amused. When I am going to go-off-on-one, Ramie senses it. "Steady Joe, stay calm," he whispered.

Advice worth listening to, these guys would have ripped me apart. Ramie, getting a shot on target, gave him a similar buzz to scoring a goal. He was not looking for praise, but within himself, he loved it.

Gerry came and spoke to us about shooting someone. What he drilled into our heads is you do not get a second chance. If you have a gun in your hand and an enemy around you, you must shoot. He shared stories of guys who hesitated and ended up getting shot. It was scary stuff. A few days later, Pat told us to go to the club. We were going on an operation! We were told we were to rob a betting shop on the Antrim Road, near Duncairn Gardens, a Loyalist area. It did not strike us as strange that we were sent to rob the betting shop for a few hundred pounds.

A car was made 'available', stolen, for us. I remember the first 'operation.' I pressed the accelerator gently. The engine burst into life. I heard the clicks as the others checked their guns. The adrenalin was seeping through me. I wanted to pee, but I wanted it to start even more. Tonight, I was going to be a fucking player at last. Despite this, I was nervous and revved the car too much.

Pat and another older guy went into the shop. They wore balaclavas like scarves and pulled them up when they were inside and took whatever money they could get. They fired two shots in the shop's ceiling, then came outside where Ramie was waiting. He pulled up his balaclava as the guys came out, and he also fired two shots from his pistol. His instruction was not to aim at anyone, 'unless there was a cop car passing', he added with a laugh. I was the driver, note, not trusted with even a handgun on this operation. It was well planned, executed like a dream.

The raid on the betting shop went according to plan and we made our getaway up the Antrim Road, turned off at the North Circular and headed towards Ardoyne to a piece of waste ground. We jumped out of the Mark 2 Cortina and a group of youths who had been standing around, not by chance, fired a few petrol bombs at the car. We scarpered, the older guy taking the guns and Pat the money. When we parked up, I remember the adrenalin rush.

It's as well the older guy took our guns because Ramie and I would have mounted a full-scale attack on the first Army or RUC patrol we came on and this book would never have been written. Our operation, it transpired, was a decoy because at the same time there was an attack on a police barracks on the Cavehill Road. It was expected security forces would be diverted to the raid on the betting shop. That was why we were told to fire shots and hang around outside.

Two Police Officers and a Soldier were injured by the bomb and shooting attack on the police barracks, so it was a success.

About ten days later, we were deployed in a roadblock in Turf Lodge, near where the Whiterock Road and the Springfield Road converge. God, I hate Balaclavas to this day, hot and it tickled. We were just there for a short time, showing we were 'policing' the area. The Army with RUC in attendance would appear, but we would be long gone.

I pulled this small white van in and was struck by how disconcerted the driver was. He looked anxious. I asked to see his driving licence, and I could see from his name he was a Protestant. Even more interesting was the fact his home address was Jess's street.

'Do you know the Morton's at number 44?' I could have asked.

When he was home safe, he could have reported to the Police a guy in the IRA roadblock knew the Morton's, at least it would give Jess's Father a bad day. The thought pleased me until I realised it would lead back to me and my comrades.

"You are far from home," I ventured. Look, I had nothing against the guy. Religion was not an issue for us. If one of the other boys who was burnt out of Bombay Street or intimidated from Rathcoole, when that glorious experiment in intercommunal relations went up in smoke, arrived he might want revenge.

"I was doing a job out at Fort William (in North Belfast) and heading for Finaghy (South Belfast)." he replied in an earnest manner. "I took this shortcut."

Shortcuts could get you killed in Belfast in the 1970s/80s. He was keen not to antagonise me. I was certain he was telling me the whole truth and nothing but the truth.

"Get out of your van and open the rear door." I ordered.

I could see he was quite frightened now. I needed him not to draw attention to himself or someone less affable might get involved. "Just take it easy," I whispered.

In the back of the van were old dungarees and workman's tools.

"That's fine," I pronounced. "You can drive on," and I paused, "see next time."

He looked up at me, wide eyed.

"Next time, take the long way round, eh!"

He nodded, said 'thanks', and was gone. Seamus Gilligan, who was in charge, ordered us to leave as the helicopter flew over again, a sure portent soldiers were on their way.

The next day, Pat cornered me outside our house. "See the roadblock you were on yesterday?" 'Oh, Christ, here we go.'

"Yeah, what of it?"

"Seamus said you stopped a van. He sensed there was something odd. Did you know the guy?"

"Not exactly, look he was a Protestant… he lives a few doors from a girl I used to see, that's all."

"You didn't…"

"No, of course not. I have never met him. He wouldn't recognise me under the Balaclava, but he didn't know me, and I didn't mention I knew where he lived. He was in the wrong place at the wrong time and once I was satisfied, he wasn't bringing a bomb in or wasn't taking photos, I chased him."

Pat considered this. "He could have been gathering intelligence."

I was becoming exasperated.

"Look Pat, he was terrified. He made a mistake and scarpered. I think their intelligence people might have a bit more about them. They pay enough of our guys to give them intelligence, anyway."

Ouch, a bit of a low blow for someone like Pat.

Our next 'operation' was a lot less acceptable. A guy, known as Driller Paddy Doyle, was the target.

Many of us had heard of him. In the early troubles he was given a gun and was involved in a famous gun battle at St Peter's Church when a loyalist mob attacked Catholic streets nearby and intended burning down the church. He did not lack courage and with other IRA members, including Sean, drove the mob away. Back then, he had a series of psychotic episodes.

He moved to a squad involved in disciplining local anti-social youths and Paddy became 'Driller,' because of his penchant for applying a Black and Decker drill to the kneecaps of recalcitrant youths. These were youths who stepped out of line or were involved in criminal activities. The IRA got cross at anti-social behaviour, well some anti-social behaviour! Driller had a serious drink problem and psychotic episodes. He was ordered to stand down. His life got worse, and he was thrown out of the house by his Wife because of the drink and violence accompanying his outbursts and he ended up sleeping rough. On a couple of occasions, he was picked up by the Security Forces who tried to extract information from him. Whether they were successful was unknown, but Doyle was a liability. He was tried and sentenced to death. He was not present at the "trial" when this decision was taken, but Pat was present.

Doyle was being cared for by a community charity who maintained a hostel for homeless people. They had premises on the Antrim Road and accommodated him in a room in a large, terraced house used as a hostel.

Seven other people with a range of problems were living there. One Thursday evening Pat said Ramie, he and I were to go over to the community hostel and carry out the due sentence. Ramie and I were not pleased. I would drive the car, thank God, and either Ramie or Pat would do the shooting. It was clear, at least to us, the operation was fraught with problems and that Pat would order Ramie to do the shooting.

As Ramie said, "So, do I knock on all the doors until I find Doyle's saying to everyone who answers their door? We are authorised to execute Driller Paddy Doyle; can you tell us which room is his?"

With little enthusiasm, we headed over to the Antrim Road. There were two handguns in the car. I know Ramie was determined to make sure Pat did the shooting. He did not fancy gunning down an unarmed man. Can't say I blame him.

We checked it out by driving past the hostel which was on the front of the Antrim Road. It was nearly10.00 p.m. and we hoped to strike when there were few people on the street. As we approached the hostel, we noticed a large crowd standing in the middle of the road and Pat told me to drive past them. As we did, something hit the roof of the car and made an almighty noise. I watched as it bounced onto the bonnet and then onto the road.

"What the fuck was that? "yelled Ramie.

"It was a fucking chair," I replied.

Pat told me to stop, park up and go back down and find out what was happening.

"Me," I said, "but I am the driver." He just ignored me.

We should have aborted the mission. Pat did not want to report, 'there was a crowd in the street, so we left.'

I wouldn't have worried, but I did not know who Pat reported to on these sorts of missions. Sean, I assume, and I never got the impression he was an easy-going guy who would have accepted the explanation. I wandered back down the road from where I parked. The crowd in the street was enjoying this little drama. There were only about 30 of them. It appeared more as we drove past them. They were staring up at the top floor of the hostel.

"What's going on?" I asked a spectator, turned out he was a resident.

"That idiot Doyle has lost it again, tried first to set a fire alight in his room. He then attacked two of the staff, and we were told to go outside and await the Police."

I had gleaned enough, but a car arrived, and two well-dressed gents got out.

Another chair came out of the top storey window. There was a lot of loud swearing, and we ran or ducked for cover as the chair crashed onto the road. A guy, pointed out as a staff member by my new pal, spoke to one of the new arrivals and I said to a colleague.

"The suits, that's Doyle's GP, and he has a mental welfare officer with him. They are going to section him."

I wasn't sure what he meant, but I had enough information for us to head.

Then two Land Rovers full of Police arrived and surrounded the small crowd.

"Nobody moves," barked the officer in charge.

He ordered two cops to block the main road so vehicles could not go past, which would mean, for us, a trip through loyalist 'Tigers Bay.' Pat and Ramie were trapped, especially as their only driver had been sent on foot, as I pointed out to Pat later when we drove home, 'not clever.'

The police sergeant in charge said to the doctor, "OK, you guys go see Doyle; do your bit and we will then arrest him."

The Doctor and the Social Worker conferred for a couple of minutes and said, given the potential violence, concluded they weren't going in unless the Police went first.

Now the crowd was growing restless. The entertainment factor was declining, and they wanted the incident resolved so those who were residents could return to their rooms and the rest could return to their homes. The RUC sergeant said.

"We are not going in there without the Army."

'God, it gets worse;' I said to myself. Not long after, there was a roar of diesel engines and two army pigs arrived. They disgorged about 12 or 14 bored looking soldiers who took up positions with rifle pointing at the house. I don't think they were at all interested in a minor incident like this.

So, there I was trapped with eight RUC men, 14 soldiers, a GP and a Social Worker and a crowd of 30 civilians, neighbours, passers-by, staff, and residents. Lucky old me. There was nothing I could do except watch. An ambulance arrived, but the medics stayed in their vehicle.

The RUC men charged into the house, six of them, the other two were on traffic duty. The Doctor and the Social Worker were in the middle of the scrum. Most of the soldiers fanned out around the door of the house and the tiny garden in front of the house clutching their rifles. Two or three were deployed to guard the army and RUC vehicles. The soldiers were not impressed with the seriousness of the incident and the crowd pressed inch by inch closer to the wide-open front door. One of the staff members, half-in and half-out of the door, kept up a running commentary for the benefit of the crowd and the soldiers.

"That's the Doctor and the Social Worker going up the attic stairs to Doyle's room. They are telling him who they are." he observed.

Introduction had not gone well. We knew that because of the cursing, yelling and the sound of furniture being thrown.

The lookout shouted, "Looks like they've got him."

We craned our necks to peer in but could only see the large, tiled floor and the bottom of the stairs. The soldiers stood or crouched, disinterested in the drama. They saw many worse dramas during tours of duty on Belfast streets. This one was unlikely to involve shooting at them. Matters looked to be resolved.

Four of the cops came down the hall, the other four followed, carrying Doyle on their shoulders. They made it to the foot of the stairs, with four RUC men holding different parts of Doyle's anatomy as he threshed about. There was a moment of total silence, as if a Hollywood director choreographed it. Then one cop shouted.

"OH, FUCK HE'S GOT MY REVOLVER!"

The silence was broken by a sound as if a well-trained typing pool hit their first keys of the morning together. It was the soldiers releasing the safety catches on their rifles. We scattered. I thought shooting at trained British soldiers might not be as easy as we thought.

Then there was the sound of crashing and cursing as the cops and Doyle falling down the stairs wrestling as they tried to secure the gun. By then we, the crowd began to disperse.

I used the opportunity to re-join my comrades while the bold Doyle was transferred to Purdysburn Hospital, the city's large Psychiatric hospital. This was in a Land Rover, not an ambulance. The RUC men would have been able to sedate him, not medically, of course.

When I got back to the car, Pat and Ramie were up to high doe. I told them all the events, but genuine apprehension meant they didn't enjoy the story. Given the detail I passed to Pat, he believed he could defend our position in failing to murder a drunk with a psychiatric illness.

We drove back to the club where Ramie and I ordered a few drinks and we complained to each other about how unhappy we were about our part in this operation.

Potential informing was the trigger, pardon the pun, which led to the operation. There was a lot of anxiety about informing within the organisation.

The car was removed, and Pat went into speak to Sean, Gerry McQuillan, and Colum Delaney. I was called in and gave my account of what happened outside the homeless hostel. Gerry was impassive throughout as ever.

Delaney gave me a bad time for leaving the car as the only driver. The others did not comment on this, and I suspect they knew Pat gave the orders on our team.

Later, Colum Delaney stopped me in the club. He was a big man with a shaved head. We had never spoken. He was in and out of the club fleetingly and disappeared for weeks on end. What surprised me was his accent, Belfast, but educated, almost posh, for Belfast. I hadn't noticed that when I got the row over leaving the car. He changed his accent, sometimes pretending to be rougher than he was. Another would be working-class hero! Delaney made me go through the events again, asked what each of us did, including Pat. He seemed very interested in how Pat handled it. As I finished, he took hold of the lapel on my old jacket. "Could you kill a man, McFaul?" he snarled, putting his face up close to mine, his eyes flashing. I could feel his hot breath.

"Yes, "I replied firmly, then ruined it by adding, "If I had to, I would."

He let go of me and said to no one in particular, not even me, "Does 'had to' cover being given an order, or does it just mean to save yourself?"

Very odd, never spoke to me again. Years later Doyle was in a house in the Markets on his own and played Russian roulette with his revolver and blew his own head off.

I kept going to the Tech throughout 1976 planning to do history and social sciences and Ramie was seeing Carmel again. He talked all the time about Carmel. He may not have realised but he was preparing me for a change in us. The 'lads' would have to go their separate ways. Carmel and I got on well enough. She made a point of being pleasant to me. She never tried to fix me up with any of her mates, who might have created a foursome.

Over the next few months, we were involved in several operations and twice I gave covering fire as we attacked two RUC Land Rovers and an RUC station. I don't recall any casualties on either side.

Pat called us into another briefing in the club for an operation in late October. Sean levelled with us and made it clear the following day we were on a decoy operation near Leeson Street.

The major attack was to be on Hastings Street Police Barracks, not far away from us. We would have M1 Carbines and we were to open fire on a British army patrol. This patrol blocked the escape up the Falls Road for the attackers on the Police barracks. There were two of our units since Sean was uncertain which of two streets the patrol would be. They varied their routes. We had a fifty-fifty chance of being involved.

The plan was Ramie, and I would take up position in a 'sympathetic house.' We would both fire two shots but not to worry whether we hit a target. Pat would support us. After firing the shots, we would leave the house by the back door, run to a nearby entry, (the English might call it a back passage, well they would), go down it to a red door, go in the door, bolt it behind us.

We would go into the house, speak to no one. A girl in the house would take the guns and we would go home. The three of us, as were the other unit a couple of streets away, were wearing long coats concealing the guns.

As we walked into the street, people stared at us, women standing at the doors of their houses. They recognised who we were and began to 'shoo' little kids, not yet at school, into their homes. The neighbourhood went quiet. Once the army arrived, they would notice this and be on their guard. The organisation used 'extras', unarmed civilians who would walk about the street. They included a woman with a pram. It might have a doll rather than a baby in it.

The intention was first to create an air of normality and to restrict the soldier's freedom to lay down fire. They would do that where they did not want civilian casualties. It didn't always apply as Bloody Sunday and the Ballymurphy massacre lay testimony to.

We entered the house; the inhabitants made themselves scarce. We smashed the back door to ensure the residents were not accused of helping us. The street emptied and went quiet. The army patrol might detect the tension. I wanted to pee. This was quite a notch up from the betting shop. These guys could shoot back, and they were armed and trained.

We knelt at an open widow looking onto a street which had seen a few battles of various kinds over the years. It was a tiny kitchen house like the one I lived in. This street looked even poorer, rubbish lying on the pavement and road, half a bicycle outside one door.

I felt quite sick, longing to stand up, hand my gun to Pat and run away, but I was even more afraid to do that. I looked down at Ramie and got a cheeky big grin back. He always cheered me up.

Pat's contact on the street signalled to him. He whispered. "They are here,"

I saw the first soldier on the opposite pavement coming around the corner, then the second on the nearer pavement also coming around into view. They were on the alert, moving slowly, partly crouching. Pat gave the signal and Ramie and I fired at our targets, one on each side of the street. We were under strict instructions to fire low; 'they' did not want a stray shot hitting houses. Pat signalled again, but only I fired. The soldiers threw themselves onto the ground or behind the garden walls and prepared to return fire. They wanted to direct their fire towards us but were uncertain from where the two shots came.

"First floor, house with black and white door," an authoritative voice bellowed.

They held back because the Corporal in charge sought orders from an officer to fire on a house and, in case residents who might be non-combatants were killed, a PR disaster.

Ramie said, just after I fired my second shot. "Wait, I have got a bead on one," two shots rang out simultaneously.

We should have been away. I saw a soldier roll over and a couple of his mates throw themselves at him. We were supposed to be out of the house and down the entry by now. Ramie let out a moan and turned over. I stared at him. I saw a hole in his forehead, the back of his head was a mess, blood and the inside of his head was all over the floor. I dropped my carbine and got to my feet. Pat grabbed me and my gun. We headed down the stairs. He threw me onto the floor at the bottom. "We need to go," he shouted.

"Ramie...," I moaned, "Ramie,"

"Christ," said Pat, "his gun."

Pat dived back into the room. No lack of courage, as the soldiers, at first thinking we had gone, stopped firing but resumed at the sight of Pat. It took only a second to grab Ramie's gun. He grabbed me by the jacket and yelled. "Move."

"We've got to bring Ramie," I wept, but as I moved towards the back door, but a soldier came into the house by it. He pointed his gun at me. I dropped my weapon and put up my hands. Christ knows where Pat was. We were not expecting a soldier round there.

None of the locals gave a warning. It could be they resented their street being used by us. The soldier looked at me, but Pat emerged from the pantry and shot him in the chest. The guy collapsed in a heap. I lifted my gun,

Pat grabbed his SLR, Ramie's carbine and me by the shoulders and dragged me out the back door. He hauled me down the entry, across the street and down the other entry to the red door. I was running and crying don't say a man can't multi-task.

As we crossed the street and went down the entry, Pat stopped, held me by the collar, and spoke. "Get a grip. Ramie is dead."

I wanted to throw up, but Pat forced me down the alley. The soldiers were shouting, but they were not risking coming forward in case our lack of activity was part of an ambush.

We made it to the red door and pushed through. Pat stopped to close the impressive new bolt paid for from Betting Shop funds no doubt. We went through the wee kitchen where a couple of adults and two kids were watching TV, I could barely see through my tears and just as we came into the kitchen, I caught sight of a girl coming down the stairs which went straight into the living room. She paused at the bottom step, held out her hands and Pat handed her the guns. The family never turned to look at us. We went out the front door.

"Can you make it home?" Pat asked. I nodded and we split. I went down the street over the Road and down Sevastopol Street.

I must have looked a state, staggering, full of tears, moaning to myself, or that was my impression of that brief journey. I went into our house. Mammy was in the kitchen; my Dad was watching TV.

"Tea in half an hour." She shouted. I may have replied but staggered upstairs to my room and threw myself on the bed.

I dozed on-and-off, cried myself to sleep in a way I hadn't done since I was six and had misbehaved and got a skelp from my Mammy and sent to bed without supper. My Dad always came up later and passed me bread and butter with sugar on it, a bit of a treat back then. I heard someone come into the house and my Mother scream and my Dad was talking in an animated, angry tone. The bad news, the worst news, arrived at our house.

The front door banged again, and my parents speaking, the sound of someone coming up the stairs. My Dad came into my room, sat on Eugene's vacant bed, and was talking.

"Son, I have terrible news," he began.

I turned round, but he was looking at the floor, he did not see my face. "Poor Ramie's dead. He has been killed in a gun battle with the army down Leeson Street."

As he spoke, he looked into my face, then recoiling. "Jesus, Mary and Joseph... you were there too."

I don't know why they would not have known I was there too, the last to know factor, I suppose.

He and I talked for over an hour. I told him everything, the betting shop, the incident with Doyle, even the training on Divis. To be fair to him, he listened without interrupting. I just needed to unload and he, poor man, was in an even greater state of shock than when he came upstairs to deliver the bad news. He went down to tell my Mother, and she burst into tears again, not something I associate with my Mother. Later, my Dad called up asking me to come down, time to face the music. My Mother looked at me in the oddest way, as if she wondered who this stranger was inhabiting their home. She said only a couple of nights previously how proud she was of Eugene. She understood he would never be home again, and she missed him already. Now she faced losing a second son. It was bound to happen but when it did; she was more than a little relieved.

She began: "Do you want something to eat?" I shook my head. "We need to go over to see Greta and Paddy. It is the right thing to do," and in an Irish way, it was. We crossed the street.

The Mulgrew's house was full of people already, with cousins, other neighbours, Father Mike from the Church and Tommy, our old Football Manager, haven't seen either since I stopped going to mass. Mum and Greta wrapped arms around each to her and held each other as women who know the pain of another woman do.

Dad shook hands with Paddy, who patted his shoulder, and shook his head. My turn, I went to Paddy first. His eyes were full of tears. He shook my hand. "You are a soldier of the Republic," he said, and he hugged me. "Ramie died a hero, my boy," he went on and he broke down.

I went to Greta. She just wrapped her arms around me. I know she had been crying, but she was OK at that point. "Was he all right at the end, Joe?"

I nodded. "It all happened so fast he would never have known a thing."

It was the right thing to say. Greta would know that, apart from the family, I was the one who would suffer his loss most. Geraldine was standing by the mantelpiece.

We had a truce for a while, ever since she gained a steady boyfriend, a big Milkman called,' Sean somebody,' don't remember, but a "right lad" according to Ramie. She cried when I went over to her, and I would have cried too if I had any tears left.

"You don't look well Joe, you should go home," Geraldine whispered.

Beer and sandwiches and endless cups of tea were produced, and the conversations got louder. Then everyone fell silent. I turned; Pat entered the house. They all knew Pat was a high player in the stakes and had been for a number of years. It only dawned on us later, typical, closer to him than most, but the last to know or believe. Pat must have been conscious of the hostility, but he walked, well marched up to Paddy, I thought 'Good God, he's going to salute,' but he shook Paddy's hand moved towards Greta who, to be fair, let him give her a kiss and a hug but neither spoke. Geraldine turned her back on him, and he walked out as quickly as he came.

Was Pat to blame was it me, was it the clowns who partitioned Ireland? Last, there was Ramie's girlfriend Carmel, I went to speak to her. She was as ashen faced as me and also been crying. She was from a big Republican family further up the Falls and been though similar experiences. Two of her cousins were killed in action and another was doing life for killing a Policeman. I said how upset I was, and she nodded. "Too many sacrifices," she said, adding, "but it has to be done."

I agreed though at that moment, and other moments too, I would have had anyone other than Ramie and the Mulgrew's' paying the price and anyone other than me involved.

My Mother insisted I go home, and I went upstairs and collapsed into my bed half asleep, dreaming of soldiers shooting and Ramie, whom I would never see again.

## Reflection Pat

Joe, Ramie, and I were best buddies from when we were wee boys, although I hated football, which they loved. They were pals when my family moved to Belfast. We came from County Armagh.

My family were traditional Republicans. Both my grandfathers were active Republicans back in the 1920s. We came to Belfast because my dad's cousin owned a plumbing business, and he got a job there. I went to the Grammar School, and they went to St Peters which cut our contact a bit. I will never forget the night of the 'Falls Curfew.' My Mother was beaten, and my Dad arrested, leaving me upset and angry. From then on, I was the IRA's.

I was prepared to do anything to get these foreigners out. I will always be grateful to Ramie and his Mother for their kindness that night. When I became more involved, I was exasperated at Joe and Ramie just drifting along, thinking chucking a few stones at peelers was 'doing their bit.' Let them get more involved to see what the organisation was trying to achieve. Joe was a capable driver and Ramie an excellent shot, but there was something not right. When Ramie was killed, Joe went to pieces. He was a potential security risk.

# Chapter 6

# THE AFTERMATH

Ramie was killed on the 27 October 1975, two months beyond his 20th birthday. The next few days were a blur. The funeral was organised. Pat sent word I would be in the Colour Party. Mercifully, someone other than Pat was sent to coordinate the family and the IRA's role at the funeral. It was planned for a Wednesday and would be a very public affair with TV cameras and thousands of mourners, for that was our way. My Mother said Greta would have loved a private church affair, but that could not happen.

As the cortege headed to Milltown Cemetery, I walked, in uniform, with the obligatory beret and sunglasses, behind the coffin. I carried a large tricolour and marched in front of the immediate family. Eight members of the Cumman na mBan flanked the hearse. Another group of uniformed volunteers marched in advance to keep the crowds back. Crowds lined the road. We walked for half a mile, drove for about ten minutes, then got out and followed the hearse. Near Milltown, Ramie's coffin was removed from the hearse, a tricolour was placed over it, and volunteers carried the coffin along the road and into the cemetery. I continued to march behind Ramie's coffin.

There was a heavy police and army presence. They looked apprehensive. Trouble was unlikely to happen during the funeral, but as sure as night follows day, riots would break out afterwards. The soldiers looked on aggressively. Not much would have provoked them to get stuck into the crowd. At this stage there was a respectful silence despite the odd shouts of 'Brits go home 'or 'murderers.' You could have reached out and touched the tension. Most wanted a respectful funeral, but there were always those who wanted to fight. Once we got into the Cemetery and marched to the Republican Plot, it became calmer. Father Mike said the prayers at the graveside.

Our volunteers fired a volley of shots over Ramie's coffin. A senior Provisional spoke to the crowd, telling them Ramie died a soldier who laid his life down for Irish freedom and his death would be avenged. The speech allowed the shooters to disappear into the crowd, while overhead a helicopter filmed the event. I have seen this on other occasions as a member of a colour party. I left with my family, all of us except Eugene. The Mulgrew's walked in front. My flag was taken. I pocketed the beret and the sunglasses and as I walked out; the police were withdrawn up the Whiterock Road, no sign of the army; the tension reduced.

In the days after Ramie's funeral, I stayed in the house, didn't go out, didn't see anyone. I realised how much my social life revolved around Ramie. He 'left me' and he didn't need to. He took the last of my childhood with him. I ended up going out for walks with Carmel, nothing untoward. We both wanted to talk about him. After a couple of months, she drifted back to her own area further up the Road.

Pat told me I was to go to the club. In its back room, Delaney, Sean, and another person I did not recognise talked through the shooting. This tribunal quizzed Pat about what happened.

"Ramie failed to fire on the second signal. He claimed he had a target but through lack of experience, he miscalculated how effective the soldiers would be."

I was asked if I agreed. Pat glared at me. I kept my head down. I did not want to blame Ramie, but Pat was correct and when Sean dragged it out of me, he said. "That's it done."

He left before us but as he walked past me, he commented. "I believe you and Volunteer Mulgrew were friends from you were wee boys. I am sorry for your loss." He was almost human then; I suppose.

He was not at the funeral. He was one of the top five most wanted men in Belfast. If he attended, they would have tried to arrest him and that might cause loss of life. As happened sometimes through the 'Troubles,' both sides stepped away from a confrontation.

On our way back, Pat said, "The security forces will pull you in because they will know you were a close associate of Ramie. They may have helicopter footage of the shooting; they will have of the funeral. I will know nearer the time."

Now all this may seem obvious now, but it wasn't on my agenda back then. Even more worrying Pat added that there was concern within the organisation about whether I could handle the interrogation. Was I tough enough if harsh methods were involved? Was he talking about torture? Since Internment it was believed the Brits tortured prisoners, and no, I wouldn't be up to withstanding torture for sure. Who did I know, Pat of course, Sean whom if I was 'persuaded' I could name, Gerry also, Delaney, one or two others? For instance, I did not know the other guy involved in the betting shop raid and with the balaclavas on, I doubt if I would recognise him.

The training exercises began with a couple of ex-soldiers whose faces I would recognise, but we never got their names. Just the guy from Pat's school. This would not have been high calibre information unless I was prepared to testify against Pat, Sean, Colum, and Gerry. The intelligence services possessed plenty of information about their activities from their own sources and Informers. You could argue I shouldn't be around. That would make everyone involved more comfortable. Being 'not around' could vary from me being sent to Dublin or taken up a quiet back road and getting a 'two tap,' two bullets in the back of the head. Pat didn't mention the latter, and I was far too anxious. Such treatment was reserved for touts, but it focused the mind on not cracking under torture.

I let it sink in, I was sickened because of Ramie. I wasn't tough enough to be on operations, not disillusioned with the Cause, just my capacity to fight. Pat walked into his house although these days he stayed elsewhere most of the time. He muttered he would have more information for me within the next few weeks, all very mysterious. He sent me a message a while later. We agreed to meet about

1.00 pm down on the Road. Pat was late. I hung about trying to avoid speaking to people. Then he arrived.

"You will be picked up by the RUC at around 6.00 a.m. tomorrow morning. You will be interrogated by Special Branch and by Military Intelligence."

'Christ Pat, have you got a list of questions they will ask?' I wondered. But I just nodded. He continued, "Ask to see a solicitor, but they won't let you unless they charge you. They might be rough," he added, "our advice is 'say nothing.' try to fix on an object in the interrogation room, even a crack in the ceiling, remember say nothing."

'Pat,' I muttered to myself, 'sounds fine and thanks to the boys for their advice about the crack in the ceiling when the RUC is being rough, a euphemism for beating the living shit out of me.' The less Pat thought I would fold, the better. The 'boys' don't take to people folding!

I entered the house and asked Mammy and Daddy to sit down, a most un-Joe thing to do. The last time I did something similar I was eight, and it was to tell them if Celtic came calling, they would lose their eldest son to Glasgow. They took that well, less so this announcement.

Since the afternoon of Ramie's death, they saw me in a different light. It was as if I was a malevolent stranger who moved into their home. They were worried about me and my future. My parents experienced a little of the pain I had for the loss and grief of Ramie.

They were aware consequences would follow that would threaten me. We weren't a family who sat down and talked problems over. It wasn't our way. It may be nice to talk and share, but it was not our way.

I began, "Listen, what I am going to tell you is important. Tomorrow morning, I will be taken in for questioning by the RUC," my Mother gasped. "it is no big deal. I will be released in 24 hours, 48 at the most. It has to happen."

I added, "I don't want you involved. They may search the house they may not, don't get involved and don't let any of the neighbours get involved. It is only me they want."

We chatted for a bit and told the girls when they came in, Maeve worked for the DHSS and Nuala was still at school. Both were soon in tears. I ate my tea, and we all went for an early night. It was a shame, there was so much joy about Eugene's vocation and, in a smaller way, my two 'O' levels. These were a distance away now.

I got up at 4.30 am, slept little, made myself a cup of tea. I remained calm. When the police came, I would walk into the street and hand myself over. If I hurried, that might spook them and lead to shooting. This was to prevent them wrecking the house, which they often did out of spite. Dad told the neighbours on either side and across the street, including the Mulgrew's.

The Brits came about ten minutes early in two Land Rovers, one with four RUC men and one with about five soldiers who fanned out either side of the vehicles, weapons pointed. I came out the door straight into the arms of two big cops who threw me in the back of the Land Rover. It was over in seconds. There was no shouting, a quick in, grab the target and away. I left home with more fuss on my first day at Primary School.

We drove across Belfast to a large Police barracks. By this stage, I was both cuffed and blindfolded and I was searched. I made no struggle or protest. It must have been the easiest arrest these cops ever made of a 'dangerous terrorist.'

After an hour, I was still sitting handcuffed and blindfolded in the same chair they left me. Thank God I didn't want a pee. The room was bare, a lino floor, three chairs, the one I was in and the other two facing it. I was fine until I was put in the chair. The effect of the blindfold or the cuffs or the cops disappearing made me more nervous. I worried about who would appear next in this pantomime. What would they do to me?

I lost track of time, which was unnerving Two guys came in and removed the blindfold and the handcuffs. They might have been Special Branch; they were from Northern Ireland and neither wore a uniform. The first guy was friendly enough. He asked me if I would sign a form to say I had not been mistreated. I said "Sure." They were so surprised they did not have the form with them, and it was never produced. That wasn't what they expected, but no one told me about a form, and I didn't know the correct response. Apart from being cuffed, blindfolded, and stuck in a chair for an hour, I had not been mistreated. I finally remembered the catch all 'say nothing' phrase Pat told me would have covered their request. I concentrated a bit more.

One cop said, "Your parents must be distraught," true.

"If you cooperate with us, it will save you and your family much grief."

I said nothing. The other cop got involved. He had a distinct style. He slapped me across the face. It was as hard a blow as you could get without breaking the skin. He hauled me to my feet by the hair and kneed me in the groin. I felt the tears well up. I can still feel it today if I dwell on it. He propelled me back into the chair by lifting me by the hair. The two charmers both left the room; 'away for a cup of tea,' as the so called 'hard man' of the duo announced in cheerful tones.

I sat on alone for another hour and the door opened and this elderly gentleman wearing glasses popped his head around the door. It was like a hospital waiting room.

"Ah, Joe McFaul?" he muttered in an English accent.

I ignored him, but he didn't wait for a response, anyway.

"I am sorry to have been late, caught up, you know how it is."

Christ, you would think he was going to say 'stick your tongue out, or we were doing an interview for a lifestyle magazine.

'It's a shame about your friend, do you blame yourself for this entire business? 'was his theme, mixing sympathy with a little guilt, just enough to tickle the emotions. I felt exposed but this was the time saying nothing counted.

Throughout the entire conversation, which was one way, he never lost his soothing, reasonable tone, showed no sign of irritation at my failure to respond or constant glances at the ceiling to search for the elusive crack.

The KOG (Kindly Old Gentleman) continued. "So let me see, you have lived in Sevastopol Street all your life so you will know Pat Kane from number 4. You are the same age, you were at Primary School together, yes, you will know our Pat."

Well, 'our Pat' point made. I know a lot about you, and I am more interested in Pat than chicken feed like you, unspoken but quite clear, even to me.

"When did you first meet Sean O'Connell?"

So that was Sean's surname. I learned something. He continued.

"Of course, you will know Gerry McGivern. You were at Primary School with him too."

Still, I said nothing.

What about Colum?" he barked to catch me out.

I stared at him with a blank expression; it was only later I was aware he was talking about Colum Delaney. In a typical Irish way, we called the top guy by his surname. If he had said "Delaney" I would have known.

He continued, "Joe, I know you have been told to say nothing. I know the prospect of informing on comrades repulses you, but have you another route out? How will your family and your community get out of it if everything stays the same? My people are capable of give and take, but while shootings and bombings continue, we cannot ignore them. If you won't say anything to me, fine, but take one message back to your comrades. This has to end. At some point the process of talking to each other needs to start."

You know it might have been more convincing if I wasn't experiencing a sting in the face and a sore head from being pulled by the hair, plus the pain in my groin. Interrogating terrorists is a tricky business to get right, more so if it's not clear which ones are the terrorists, maybe we all were.

"Well, that's us done now. You can go. Out to the left, press the black button on the door, into the foyer and through the double doors."

I got to my feet unsteadily; this was an unexpected turn of events. I walked out of the interrogation room; I looked back at the be-speckled older guy, and he waved, "Speak again soon," was his final rejoinder.

I walked into the cold fresh air; it was about ten o'clock. None of the cops at the entrance to the police barracks, either inside or out, gave me a second glance. I approached a steel turnstile and was ushered through a pedestrian exit, again without comment. I wandered out to the street. There was a BP service station, opposite the station. After a couple of minutes, I recognised it. I used it to put fuel in Uncle Sean's car after I toured the Cregagh area, looking for Jess two lifetimes ago.

I was detained in Ladas Drive, a major facility for holding suspected terrorists and those arrested to be interrogated, although it doubled as a more conventional Police barracks. This was not the friendliest area for an IRA suspect to be turfed out into the street. Most guys from West Belfast would have no clue where the hell they were. I went to the Cregagh roundabout, up along by the big Ravenhill rugby grounds and past the Ormeau Park to the Ormeau Road. Much friendlier territory but a tougher journey than the same one I drove in my fruitless search for Jess two or three years earlier. I walked into town and got up home about noon.

My Mother was upset when I rolled in. "I will need to phone the Office," people who worked for the Post Office always referred to it as 'the Office,' "and tell your Dad."

After she finished on the phone, she made me lunch. For the first time in yonks, I was hungry.

I hung about the rest of the day, after all I had nowhere else to go, but the 'Organisation' would get round to speaking to me. It would be Pat who would contact me. When Dad came home, I ate my tea as well, much to my Mother's delight.

Once again, I asked them to go with me into our wee front room. We lived our life in the kitchen. The TV was there it was where we played as kids. The front room was for when visitors arrived or where my Mother went to sit and knit to get peace.

I sat on the green cloth settee beside my Mother, Dad sat on one of the matching chairs.

"Look," I began, "this business is not finished."

"Joe, what…?" my Mother interrupted, but I held up my hand.

"I know Dad talks about retiring from the office when he is 60, but the IRA doesn't work like that. Once you are in, you are a part of something, you know about events and people, you even know things you don't realise you know. Random facts like where people drink or meet, who is friendly with whom, who lives where ...."

I began again. "The Brits are interested in me. They are not sure what I can do for them, but they will pick me up again. The 'RA' will know this, and they will be nervous about it."

Dad had said nothing so far. "Tell me, son, do they believe you could become an informer, a 'tout'?"

"It is possible," I replied, "I hope not. The question is, can they take the risk? They are being exposed and undermined by Informers. Of course, to 'take out' someone whom no one considers is an Informer creates more trouble than it's worth. They will think through this right now. I know after what happened to Ramie, you want me to walk away from this."

"You have done your bit for their Cause.'

I ignored the 'their.'

"The safest thing I can do is to stay close to them,"

I added, I would not be allowed to go on an operation. The chance of me being allowed on even a decoy strike would be quite small. I finished by telling them one way or another I would be brought into custody. My Mother shivered, but she thought of poor Greta across the street who would give anything for Ramie to be in 'custody' rather than his cold, dark spot in the Republican Plot at Milltown Cemetery.

For the next few days, I wandered about the Road, sad but at peace. A car pulled up beside me. This was always a worrying sound because of 'drive by 'shootings. Pat got out. Two other guys were in the car, Sean was one. Pat asked me how I was.

The 'boys' were aware I did well during the interrogation, but he warned me that was just a softening-up process and Special Branch, or the intelligence people, would bring me in again. I was not a high value target, a minor player whom they would shake from time to time to see what fell out. Another comment he made unnerved me, although I know he was trying to put me on my guard.

If I didn't play well with the RUC or the Brits, they might tip off the UVF or the UFF I was an IRA activist, and I could become a potential target. The loyalists take out an IRA man who gives no information the Authorities do not lose an asset, just a stubborn wee Taig who wouldn't play ball. Great, say something to the authorities, result bullet in the head from the IRA, say nothing, result bullet in the head from the UVF. A 'no-win, no-win' scenario.

Looking back, I overreacted to all this. I had been involved in a traumatic experience where my best pal was killed in front of me. I felt guilty about involving him and I was interrogated, in a none too gentle way by the RUC. My anxiety, at least, was rational. Pat's parting shot was not in the least reassuring. "Best thing is to keep in touch with us and we will keep in touch with you."

I took that as a clear warning I should not disavow my IRA links. I stayed at home. I was not a reader then, so I watched TV, a few videos were lying on the coffee table. The waiting was unbearable. Who would make the first move?

It was a Tuesday, three weeks after I was first detained, I was walking near the Dunville Park for something to do and lost without my buddy. An Army Land Rover passed me. Was it looking for me? That was too random. I sat in the sun enjoying the heat and then headed home.

As I went to cross the Falls Road, a car stopped behind me. It happened in an instant. I heard them get out but running away was pointless. My arms were pinioned. Whoever grabbed me wasn't convinced I wouldn't do a runner. I sat still without speaking.

A blindfold was put over my face. Who was it? Loyalists, unlikely, the 'RA', the Brits. Right guess. I was taken into a house across the city and the old guy was standing in front of me. "Hi Joe," was a friendly enough greeting.

"Nice to see you again." I replied.

He muttered. "You have said more in ten seconds than in over an hour the last time we met."

Well, no one told me this time I should not speak. That might be true in a literal sense, but a standing order existed to say nothing to the Police, the Army, or Military Intelligence. I was convinced it was unlikely we had penetrated his circle. The first time we met, my impression was he was late 60s, but this time I could see he was younger, mid-50s? He was a senior person in whatever was his branch of the intelligence organisations. He talked in detail about the IRA, in the way Pat talked about the Army/Police.

Why didn't these guys talk to each other? They were both so penetrated they didn't need a minor character like me. He said his name was Clive Greenhalgh. Why is he telling me his name? He said few people knew it. Ah ha, so if it popped up in the future, it would have come from me, a trust game. I would not buy his deal, whatever it was, very odd? We soon got all pally again.

"Joe, we need you to help to contribute, bringing this conflict to an end. Your community is exhausted, and we have paid too much in lives and resources to continue. There are many who exploit innocent people because of a crazed ideology, and it's going nowhere."

"What happened in Ballymurphy, and Derry runs deep, what happens seven days a week runs deep, you shouldn't be here,"

Anger was rising. How dare he continue this pretence it was our fault? He held his hand up as I waxed lyrical. I didn't know where the words came from, but at least I found them convincing. He tried again." There are things we did. We were learning as we went along. Can you say there aren't actions your side took they shouldn't?"

Looking back, he was right, but in that situation, these seemed mealy mouthed words, he continued. "I told your government," He corrected himself, "The Stormont Government, when we first came in, they would have six weeks of an Army honeymoon to make an accord with the Nationalist community. They were hostage to their own fanatics and didn't face them down."

I couldn't make sense of this; it was all above my pay grade. If people wanted to talk turkey, they needed to go to the Army Council, not a volunteer with limited credibility. I made that point to him, but he said. "We have often, but at the moment we can't get any response through our usual channels. You are one of several routes we are using to make contact. We are going to release you. I want you to speak to Colum Delaney, Sean O'Connell, and Gerry McGivern. tell them what I have been saying."

No mention of Pat, not as big a shot as he considered himself. To my eternal shame, that pleased me.

The blindfold was put over my head. 20 minutes later we were going up Divis Street, and it was removed, and I was dropped off outside Dunville Park.

I have this abiding memory during those times; every hour in daylight a guy is driven through Belfast City centre with a blindfold over his head and no one admits to seeing it or does anything about it. I wouldn't be surprised if there weren't dozens of guys, at any one time in the mid/late 1970s, being driven around Belfast with blindfolds over their heads!

## Reflection Greta

I remember as if it was yesterday when the McFaul's moved into our street. We were impressed because Gabriel had a job. He was a Postman.

My Paddy got odd bits of work here and there. Bridie and I had our first children within six months of each other. We got on so well, supported each other through all our pregnancies, and became friends. It must have been for 44 years until poor Bridie died; may she rest in peace.

My Raymond and Joe took to each other ever since they were babies.

They never fell out; they were made to be best friends. Joe was brighter than Raymond, who had too much of his Father in him, if you ask me. Raymond was anxious when it came time to the move to Secondary School. He thought Joe would go to the "Brothers". He was relieved when Joe failed his 11 plus, Bridie was disappointed.

I have never recovered from Raymond's death. I took comfort knowing Joe was with him. If it couldn't have been me, it should have been Joe. I do not know why the boys joined the IRA, I guess it was the times. Neither of them was cut out for it. I suppose that is true of a lot of young men in the 'Troubles.' They inherited someone else's problem and became victims of it.

## Reflection Carmel

I liked Joe. We both were very upset over Ramie's death. He was quite depressed. Ramie thought the world of him, the big brother he didn't have. Geraldine used to be less complimentary when his name was raised. I thought he might have tried it on with her when they were younger. She never said, but she mellowed as she got older. I believe Ramie and I would have got married and been happy.

Joe and I clung on to each other for two or three months. It was all about our mutual loss of Ramie. There was no passion, just comfort. In the end, it was best to separate. I was still friendly with Geraldine, and she was happy to talk about Ramie anytime. She was a bridesmaid when I got married years later. A last thing about Joe, his depression did not lift, he was sure bad times lay ahead for him, which worried me.

# Chapter 7

# CONSEQUENCES

Over the next few months, 1975 became 1976, and I drifted along as usual, but now I realise I was depressed. Once more, I was debriefed in the club after the latest pickup. It was fine. I was informed 'tasks would be assigned to me.' Different lads instructed me to report to the club for wee jobs. I would be dispatched to low key, driving jobs. A combination of a taxi driver or messenger, using an old Ford car, which was not stolen, for operations. They were still evaluating me, seeing if I was committed and reliable.

Pat was no longer around. Someone told me he was in Dublin. For a few weeks I had been "seeing" Carmel, we went on walks. Though it was cold, we shared a few tear-filled walks, hugs and non-passionate kisses and pints. It petered out soon afterwards. It was part of the grieving process, along with not sleeping well or eating much. I thought about poor Ramie's body lying dead in the room we fired from and later in his coffin. I wanted to shout out at his wake, "Ramie, Ramie, it's me," but I kept it under control.

On a warm June morning, I went onto the Falls planning to walk up to Milltown and visit Ramie's grave. I hadn't been there alone since the funeral, but Carmel and I often walked up to it. It was a maudlin mood I was in; I expect that describes it. As I arrived onto the Road, one dude who hung around the club was rushing towards me. He slowed down and muttered in a side whisper. "THEY want to speak to you."

That sounded urgent and, to be honest, my heart fell. I didn't want to be deployed today.

As I reached the club, a guy I didn't recognise walked out.

"Joe," he declared," we need you to drive this car to Carrickfergus. Don't look in the boot and avoid any Army roadblocks."

He handed me two keys and pointed at an old blue Morris 1100.

"You must go by the Shore Road."

At first, I was reassured; it was a driving job. He gave me an address in Carrickfergus, a place I had never been to. "Under no circumstances, look in the boot," he commanded.

In case I was caught, there were items in the boot I was better off not knowing about. Reflecting on it on previous trips, there was usually a passenger or a verbal message to give to someone, which often made no sense to me. I have never been to Carrickfergus. It was not an Irish Republican stronghold, far from it. As I drove down towards the City Centre and I cut down towards the railway station and the Shore Road, It was most likely explosives, which was unsettling. What happens if they are sensitive and explode? I told myself to 'Catch yourself on', you are only a driver.' As I drove towards

Whitehouse, I turned around a slight bend. An RUC patrol was telling traffic to slow down. I felt sick, but they were not stopping cars, just getting them to slow, maybe it would be fine. There might be an accident ahead. The Army wasn't around, a positive sign. Nothing I could do anyway. I slowed down as I approached the cop and smiled amiably at him, as any Shore Road Loyalist would at one of his own. He smiled back and as I drew level with him; he motioned me to move into the side. I hesitated. He brought his gun up level with my head and three more armed officers appeared and surrounded the car. I moved in, conscious of other cars going past with folk craning out their windows to see what was happening.

I got out of the car.

The nearest cop put his hand on my shoulder and smiled affable enough. As if we knew each other, we chatted about the weather. As an afterthought, he spoke.

"Where are you going?" he asked.

Just a wee message up to Carrickfergus." I replied.

Stay cool, stay friendly, look relaxed. I did all of this. He nodded in response implying, 'OK,' but he added quietly.

"Open the boot."

Whatever the game was, it was up for me. I took the smaller key out of my pocket and opened the boot. There were three Garand US M1 carbines, one with the 20-shot magazine, the others were old eight cartridge versions, two Lee Enfields and a Thompson which had seen better days and seen them a long time ago! There were no Armalites or 45 automatics, just two old pistols. There was a quantity of something in a clear plastic bag. Looking at the amount, and I am no expert on explosives, it sufficed to devastate a garden shed. If I had had my wits about me, I could have tried the line, pointing at the very dated weapons.

'I am bringing these to the Ulster Museum for a Second World War exhibition,' although I was travelling in the wrong direction!

I was arrested, handcuffed, and thrown into the rear of the Land Rover. Two Army vehicles arrived while this was happening and retrieved the weapons and explosives. My guess is they were parked nearby. They drove me across the city to my new home from home at Ladas Drive. No blindfold was used. I was bundled into a room with a bag over my head. After a while, two cops arrived and took off the bag. They were a sergeant and an inspector.

The Sergeant read from a sheet, "Joe McFaul, on the 27 June 1976 you are charged with possession of firearms contrary to section," he rattled on. "So and so of the something, Act." I did not take much in.

"You are further charged with being in possession of explosives likely to cause injury or loss of life, "blah, blah, you are further charged with being a member of an organisation prohibited under," blah blah, and" you are charged with being in possession of a stolen motor vehicle and of driving without insurance."

That was the gist of it.

"Have you anything to say?"

I ignored him. He read aloud," noted the accused refused to respond to the charges."

The inspector looked at me, a big country man not unlike my uncles from the Glens; he declared, "Son, your friends are not as friendly to you as you were to them. You have been stupid."

Well, yes and no, this outcome might keep me alive. I will never find out. The RUC men left the room, after I demanded a solicitor with a--, "We'll see," the inspector tossed over his shoulder.

I sat back. The door opened again, and a familiar face popped his head around the door.

"Joe, they got you first," he suggested and chuckled, polishing his glasses. "You are looking at six to seven," he wasn't talking months, "I can make it all disappear, or most of it, depending on what you can tell me."

I refused to reply, "Where is Pat Kane?" he asked.

"Oh," I replied, I may get entertainment out of this. "I believe he left for the South of France on his holidays." That amused me.

"Joe, you are an insignificant little prick. I wasted too much on you, given your value. I was sorry for you and gave you a way out."

"Right," I responded, "I get it, you are Salvation Army, wanting to save me from myself." warming up for a long exchange.

But he ignored my quip, shrugged his shoulders, left, and I never met him again in Ireland. No doubt he considered himself a reasonable person dealing with a load of 'cultchies' with no brains who couldn't recognise they were being handed a lifeline. He could have been right.

Two hours afterward, I was taken to Crumlin Road prison and placed in a cell on my own. I was advised I would be in court (Diplock, no jury) the following morning. I was fed a cold stew. Later, a solicitor came to see me. I recognised him from TV as a lawyer who often defended Republicans charged with terrorist offences. We both knew I was setup. I am sure he neither knew nor cared why. At least I wasn't being hauled out of a ditch with a bullet in the back of my head. The solicitor was associated with the Republican movement, defended Officials, Provisionals, and loyalists too. Whether he was partial to either wing of the IRA, I do not know.

Later, he was wounded in a drive by at the Law Courts but survived. However, in the present, he was explicit about what would happen to me. A bit like a second-hand car salesman you bring your car to, and he goes, "Oh, it's the 1971 model, the 1970 is worth more," or "it's a shame it's silver, now if it had been white," you get the gist. The Solicitor said, "If you had been caught and found guilty and sentenced before 1 March 1976," only three months earlier, "you would be a political prisoner in the Cages in the Maze. You would wear your own clothes and you would be entitled to remission on your sentence."

I thought; mate, it is 1 July 1976 so deal in the here and now.

"You will serve between four and six years," he continued, "you will spend most of your sentence in the H blocks."

These were built to replace the old Nissan huts and opened 18 months earlier.

A few days later, I was in front of a judge. I refused to recognise the Court (Foreign Power and all that) and received a sentence of four years for my trouble. How did I feel about being 'set up' by my side? Well, I have this take on it. Ramie and I did not buy into the political issues around the 'Troubles.' We threw stones at the RUC and the Army. It was expected. We believed in a United Ireland and joined of our own free will for kudzus or because we had no reference points or achievements. But self-protection was an important reason for us. For others, it was something to do.

Pat believed we would be enlightened by the experience. We were willing, agreeable blokes, not ones you would put up for the most demanding mission but reliable for routine activities. Ramie proved a top marksman, which was valued, and I -- I was his mate! I am not being disloyal to Ramie; he delayed his second shot because he wished to hit a target. Those who had planned the operation were not interested in us hitting a target. Speed would be of the essence to ensure we escaped. It was the buzz "scoring" gave him that influenced Ramie. If he had fired with me, we would have been off ahead of any return fire. Even then, we were unlucky. Our first shots alerted the soldiers, my second revealed more about our position. While most of the soldiers dived for cover, one fired a shot. He may have been an expert sniper or lucky. Ramie fired late and was hit. The operation was botched then.

The IRA's campaigns during the 1970s were characterised by bad luck or botched actions leading to 'own goals.' This was where volunteers blew themselves up with their own explosives or failed to deliver adequate warnings because they did not factor a vandalised telephone box into the equation resulting in loss of life occurring when it wasn't intended. This led to bad publicity and anger within the Nationalist community.

The problem for me wasn't the botched nature of the operation, more down to Ramie than me, but my reaction to his death, which left me fragile and vulnerable to Security Forces pressure.

It is fashionable to portray 'terrorists' or 'freedom fighters' as these clever, cold, evil individuals in command of their actions and emotions. Many volunteers were like me and Ramie. We grew up in socially deprived areas, in a community without access to decent employment and housing opportunities over a few generations. Yes, we were bitter, scared, but we wanted something better for the world we understood, our parish, our community, people like us. We stood with those like us, while always facing Government and media misinformation. We trusted people from our communities who had a different narrative.

There were a few who would be happy to silence me, just in case. The IRA was struggling to hold the Nationalist population, who were fed up with an eight-year-old war, appalled at atrocities they did not want committed in their name and seeing concessions coming through that would have been unimaginable ten years ago. A huge groundswell of support in the North for a United Ireland did not exist, and it wasn't a favoured option in the Republic of Ireland. If I disavowed the organisation but went to jail, when I was released and then, a big THEN, choose to help the Brits, my knowledge would be out-of-date. A few years in jail might cement my allegiance, lead to an increased skill base, a tougher, more mature capacity. The latter was spot on, but not about the skill base or increased commitment to the 'Cause.' There were others who, after a stint in jail, had had enough. The IRA was reducing in size to prevent the successes of the informer network.

After my sentencing, there were a few days when I could think about everything that had happened. In fact, this reflective period turned out to be weeks before my transfer to the H Blocks. HM Crumlin Road jail was run by the IRA. The staff and the Loyalist prisoners there knew it. In a typical Irish way though, they would not concede it, the Loyalists made the best of it and used requests through the IRA command structure to get what they wanted. Its senior men negotiated with senior prison officials and the place ran smoothly. I would have been content to stay in Crumlin Road. Relationships were forged there that led you to believe these hard men from both sides could find accommodation.

When I first went in, I claimed political status. There were 250 Provisionals in A wing. Some Informers and British 'plants' were sent in on previous occasions, so our intelligence people interrogated new prisoners. At first, they were sceptical of my explanation of my detention. Others who were imprisoned were accused of being planted by the British, not all of whom were guilty, but some were plants. It changed without warning. Someone outside sent a message in confirming my story and indicating I was sound, if a bit 'shaky.' I suspect only Colum Delaney would have the status to do that.

When I moved to the Maze, I would be catapulted into a tense situation. The "Dirty Protest" was ongoing. The dispute was, there was a further driving charge to answer at Court that wasn't proceeded with and after leaving the Court, I was being driven to the Maze. During the journey, we returned to Crumlin Road. I am sure an escape was planned, but I wasn't briefed about it. I was not transferred for about another six months, which was unusual.

I just drifted through life. When I joined the Provisionals, or way back when I truanted from school, I reacted to events and people around me, no plans, incapable of making decisions. When Carmel and I were doing our little 'walking out,' she used to say, "And what will become of you Joe?" I would mumble in reply about achieving a few more O' levels but for what purpose, which was what they call in Scotland 'sore heid'stuff? It wasn't the Provisionals I needed to leave. I was only involved for a year. My trouble was Belfast, or my problem was me. I wasn't mature; I had no job or education which could be a route out of the benefits/unemployment trap. I had had no girlfriends because I became caught up in a fantasy about my first girlfriend, Jess. She liked me too, but she was unobtainable. Sometimes, I would fantasise about Jess. She seemed less out of reach when I was incarcerated and proved a dream I indulged. Leaving for England, or the United States, though attractive was scary, it needed a decision.

Look, I don't want this book to be about life in the cage. There is a book in there somewhere, but this isn't it. It was an important four years for me, and it is appropriate I share part of my experience with you. The Blanket protest was on, and I was there during the first hunger strike and part of the second fast when ten men died. It was all so important for us, but less so outside the jail. Guys inside never appreciated how little interest in their plight existed in the broader nationalist community until the deaths of the Hunger Strikers.

When I finally reached the Maze, or Long Kesh, as we still called it, I was in a hut with about 80 others. We were a company, and the entire place was a battalion.

In each cage there was a wing commander in charge, in our case Desmond (Dessie) Meely.

We reported to him in a traditional military fashion. Each cage had several huts who elected their own leader, who reported to the overall OIC. I tell you there were violent nutters there, though not as many as you might imagine. I conformed with the discipline. It made it easier to negotiate with the authorities and kept the nutters at bay. During most of my imprisonment, there were various power struggles taking place. The IRA outside was decimated, but among prisoners there was a pecking order and rumours of changes in the leadership. Dessie kept out of that debate. We knew what was going on inside the jail, but rarely what was happening outside. Many prisoners possessed contacts and held strong opinions, but I was oblivious to it all.

We had a strange relationship with the officers. During the time I was imprisoned, a number were murdered outside and their colleagues, using disguises, were violent. This upped many antes. Other prison officers kept in with us by, for example, bringing us books and saying, 'remember tell X,' a leading senior IRA man, 'I did this,' meaning. 'I am a decent family guy, so don't shoot me.' There was a Scottish prison officer who used to delight in showing his Rangers FC tattoo, which was emblazoned on his arm. We used to sing Celtic songs to him, especially when Celtic beat Rangers. If Rangers beat Celtic, he gave it back, but we were a virtual choir, even blokes who did not like football. It meant I learnt all the Celtic songs, though. As for me, I made no mark, avoided conflict, and followed orders.

The Blanket protest had been running for two years. It was growing, and I will never forget the stench. It was interesting when well-known Republican leaders were captured, sentenced, and put in confinement, they conformed to the authority of the OICs', who were serving longer sentences.

There were also Loyalist prisoners, though we separated from them and from the Officials. The Officials split into two and the breakaway group was called the INLA. They adopted a more militant approach and were in their own compound. The Provisionals related well enough to the INLA since they both hated the Officials. They were all three militant Irish republicans. Clever eh? To continue the confusion, the Officials had a working relationship with some Loyalist UVF, as they struggled to move from a sectarian conflict to a class war.

As you know I was from a traditional Official area. I spoke to an Official years later saying it was a shame guys with similar aspirations and backgrounds fought with each other. I knew him because his wee brother was three years behind me at secondary school. I added, "Ramie and I were never threatened."

He laughed," Well, the reason is we thought you were just sixteen, that you were in my brother's class."

We were seen only as message boys, small fry not worth attacking, and we saw ourselves as tough guys! They were not aware of our ages until Ramie was killed in action and I was in court, 'aged 20 of ... Sevastopol Street.'

My incarceration was the only period I was certain I belonged in the organisation, I chose a low profile, a loner who followed orders, not a humorous or particularly sociable person though in the education classes classmates actually commented how animated I became.

I felt safer and more relaxed there. Nights were the worst. I fantasised about Jess, occasionally other girls like Georgie, or ones I hardly knew but never about Carmel or Geraldine or any of the Cuman na Bhan.

The Provisionals considered the H block campaign distracted from the 'armed struggle.' That led to tensions with the INLA. Various political figures and Church people were involved and visited the prison. 'we' were talking to the British Government.

There is plenty written about all this, but the key point is there were several disparate groups representing a strand of Republicanism talking to the Brits but not talking to each other.

What started out as an insignificant matter was to occupy me in 1979. I had a run in with a Ballymurphy 'Provie'. He knew about Ramie and our botched operation and gave me a hard time over it. This was almost three years into my sentence in the late Spring of 1979, and this guy, Padraig O'Dade, who was a member of a big Republican family from Ballymurphy, he was a bully. He liked to throw his weight around, if he detected any weakness in an individual or if the mood took him. We were playing football outside the huts and O'Dade 'did me', leaving his foot in as I tried to go around him. My ankle hurt and I limped off. It was an informal kick about, so unnecessary, but O'Dade did not hide it. A few days later, a group of Provos from Ballymurphy were talking. I was beside them and they included me in the conversation about issues between us and the command outside. O'Dade came up and tried to join the group. One guy glanced at him with an implied, "Clear off," or "you are not reliable or trusted." As he walked away, he stared at me with pure hatred. His body language said, 'I have known these men my entire life and they are pushing me out. How dare they include you?' It was as if I turned them against him.

There were genuine hard men in the huts who protected others who were not tough. O'Dade found himself in situations that did not work out, he was kept under control up to a point. As bullies do, he worked his way around to me again. Over the next while, I tried to joke with him, then I ignored him. For a while, both approaches worked.

One day, I wasn't in the frame of mind to divert his unpleasantness, or he wasn't prepared to let go, but he raised Ramie's death with me, saying it was my fault. I explained his problem was he did not know if his parents were ever introduced. Now, for reasons that escape me, this sentimental and 'folksy' view of the O'Dade clan did not endear me to Padraig. He punched me hard, and I fell down. I contemplated feigning unconsciousness, knowing after a few kicks, the others would break it up. But I was too angry, as ever my temper saved me from feeling pain right then. I jumped up and launched myself at him with a flurry of accurate but not very telling blows. A punch from him propelled me back against the door as I went near it. I lifted the sole of my right foot against the door, steadied my balance and used it to propel my whole body forward at O'Dade catching him a superb head butt on the bridge of the nose, he went down like a sack of potatoes.

In self-defence, or Police training manuals, I bet there are sections on restraint, but on the Falls Road we had a different code. As he lay there, I kicked him six or seven times in the head and face, as you do. I was aware when he hit me again, a few of the other guys came forward to prevent a massacre. The head butt shocked them, and the kicking of our brave Padraig elicited limited sympathy, at least long enough for the six or seven kicks, and then I was pulled off him. O'Dade was removed to the infirmary for a few days.

The Prison authorities left internal disputes to the chain of command in the Blocks. I was hauled in front of Dessie and the quartermaster, whom I choose not to name, even after all these years. He was from Ballymurphy but detested all the O'Dades.

They were a family with a fair sprinkling of criminality prior to the Troubles. I would love to say Padraig respected me for standing up to him and as a result he and I became friends, which is not what happens in the real world. Each time I encountered him over the next eighteen months, it was all he could do not to attack me. If nobody else was around, he confronted me, sticking his face right up to mine so I could feel his breath. It was intended to intimidate me, but also make sure I could not deliver another head butt. He was warned to 'cut it out.' I believe if the command in the hut changed, he would have used the opportunity for revenge. If we clashed again, without a structure around us, he would take his revenge. There were other incidents over the period, but that one stood out.

Then a personal crisis intervened. My parents took it in turns to visit me as often as they could. It was agreed Maeve and Nuala would not and Eugene was away. In 1978, my Father retired from the Post Office early. He was about 57.

I expect my actions, combined with all the stuff going on in the city, created health problems for him. One morning in August 1979, I was summoned to the Deputy Governor's Office. There were many reasons for being summoned there, but it had never happened to me. It was usually a 'higher up' involved in negotiations to reduce tension.

I entered his office, marched up to his desk, flanked by two officers. He spoke to me: "I am sorry to have to tell you your Father died yesterday evening. I can arrange for the Chaplain to visit you."

A few other words were added, but I was reeling from his announcement; 'Daddy, dead?'

This is a time as a prisoner you feel most isolated and guilty about family matters. Of course, I could not attend the funeral, so I was denied even that moment to grieve with my family. I walked out of the Governor's office and was placed in a small office in the same corridor. I assumed it was something to do with the death, a procedure. An older Prison Officer came in, I recognised him; he was middle management but was not involved with our cage. He introduced himself as Billy Morton.

You will appreciate I was still in a state of shock, so I may not have remembered all the conversation. I wondered at first if he was an evangelical person trying to recruit me for God's army. I was a little right about his religious position.

"You don't know me, McFaul, do you? My last sight of you was out of my car window about six years ago. You knew my daughter, Jess."

'Jess's Dad, …. my Dad, what was going on?' I mumbled to myself.

"I told my daughter you were bad news and unsuited to her. It never occurred to me you would become a terrorist, but I have never regretted forbidding her from seeing you, although I did not know what would develop in Northern Ireland."

Why was he telling me this? I can only assume he got a measure of visceral pleasure out of telling people like me they were not right for his God-fearing daughter. It was bizarre, as Jess wasn't in my thoughts. The only thing in my mind was my Dad and my family. Was he aware of what I been told? Did he expect I would be vulnerable so he could score a point? Had he seized a chance away from prying eyes, or did he see an opportunity to…. I do not know, lord it over me, for having the temerity to date his daughter.

I was dazed and returned to the hut. Dessie Meely was informed and spoke in a sympathetic way to me. Overall, there was support from other prisoners. I was a lone wolf. I had no close friends in the Maze. Of course, it was my choice, but other prisoners did their best. My Mother couldn't visit for a while visit, due to the grieving for my Father. Maeve visited, and it was a bit of a tear-stained occasion. She hated me being in there; she was doing her own grieving, and she was helpless to assist me with mine. To add to the bad news, Maeve told me she was leaving the DHSS and Belfast in a few months. Daddy left money from his lump sum, and she was going to College in Liverpool to train as a Physiotherapist.

First Eugene, then me, and now Maeve all, for quite varied reasons, moved out of the home. The family was no longer there.

Nuala also moved away later, but that had not been mentioned to me. At night, my mind raced over all this McFaul family business. I was thinking about myself. I was determined after my release; I would somehow engineer a permanent move from Belfast.

One thing all prisoners, not only political prisoners, share, is taking refuge at night in their dreams and fantasies. Prisons are very noisy places through the night, lots of 'shout outs.' The night staff delighted in ruining the sleep of prisoners by staging impromptu searches or just going about shouting. It was part of the punishment. I have to say, Jess figured in both my daydreams and fantasies.

I told myself make-believe stories where we ran away together when we were younger, or we made love. The encounter with her father only made me daydream more about her. Was she married, did she have kids, was she happy, did she ever think of me?

On to more rational matters. I remember during the period I first moved to the Maze being involved in Education classes on Irish history and the Irish language.

We also trained on weapons with wooden 'guns' mimicking a range of new weapons the IRA had access to, these latter were classes run by the prisoners themselves. Later, proper educationalists were brought in to deal with academic subjects. I studied 'O' level standard history, politics, and economics, though I could not enrol for exams and our timetable was not the same as College or school one.

An English guy, who was employed by the Open University, came into the prison to teach politics and economic classes. He lifted the standards, he told me he would help me get to Ruskin College in Oxford after my release if I had a mind to do 'A' levels. He was not Republican minded but into 'prisoners' rights and how people in prison could use Education to change their lives. If I wanted to consider a degree, he mentioned I might qualify for Open University credits. He influenced me. It also allowed me to dream of education as a route out of Northern Ireland.

The combination of the blanket protest and the decision to start the original hunger strike accompanied by violence against officers led to a deteriorating situation. There was so much going on, the first cease fire fizzled out and almost immediately the second too. The government was digging in its heels. I was released a few months early, it was unexpected. Intended to influence the IRA to call off the Hunger Strikes, my release and others were part of that policy. Those released tended to be volunteers like me. It was all too little and too late to be influential. Inside the prison, the two hunger strikes were creating a grim atmosphere.

There was a sense of waiting for a dreadful event to happen. Guys who lost consciousness were pulled off the strike by their families. Others stopped, but ten died. Anyone who is prepared to make the supreme sacrifice for their beliefs is worthy of admiration, even if you don't share their views. I would have admired the Loyalists if they had been prepared to go as far, but they were never that committed. Big on rhetoric and banging drums, less so making the ultimate sacrifice.

I was released in April 1980; not that early. I was in custody for a month prior to my sentence. The atmosphere outside turned as toxic as in the prison. The IRA within the prison was unaware of the increasing lack of sympathy for them in the wide nationalist community. People were getting on with their lives. An upsurge of Loyalist violence or action by the authorities refusing to negotiate over the Hunger Strikes rallied support. Then followed the deaths.

There was an increasing momentum to politicise the 'armed struggle.' It needed to change from a military campaign to a movement working to bring change. The emergence of Sinn Fein reflected this movement. Both organisations insisted they were separate. The IRA referred to Sinn Fein as "the Party closest to our view." Tensions existed between individuals in both organisations, although how separate they were is doubtful.

When I was getting ready to leave, I was called in by Dessie. He asked if I intended to continue in the 'struggle.' It was an important question to get right. Dessie was not big on man management, but he knew me well enough during my sentence.

Something I alluded to earlier. Due to the problems arising from widespread informing within the Provisionals, it almost completed its plan, at least in Belfast, to restructure into small cells, active service units

(ASU). The rest of the volunteers were to be in broader lower-level company activity. I knew Dessie would want to steer me away from ACUs, if I was deluded enough to consider I might want to join one. I took a risk.

"Dessie, I have found this hard, and the events before I was captured," note captured by the enemy forces, not arrested, charged, and sentenced.

"I need to take space for myself; I have hardly seen my Mother since my Dad died" - I trailed off.

Dessie nodded; he was relieved. As a released prisoner, carrying status in the Falls community or at least among the more fervent Republican supporting elements in it, I could be a target for the security forces.

"You should, you should," he shook hands with me.

The issue that had been worrying me most throughout my imprisonment was receding. I worried the IRA would have a claim on me and have a role for me.

Then he said, "When you were told the news about your Father, you met Billy Morton."

I did not see that coming.

"Did he know your Dad?"

"No, no, it was personal."

Dessie gave me a look which said, 'you don't have personal territory.'

"Well, I used to go out with his daughter. He put a stop to it, it was long ago."

Dessie didn't know whether to laugh or cry, but I would never have informed despite my being vulnerable.

One more thing, "he added. "You are aware how much O'Dade hates you. Be careful,"

This remark was strange. It was done with, oh well. When I walked out of the Maze, I had been told transport was arranged, so I was shocked instead of the standard minibus or taxi to see Pat Kane standing beside a smart newish Volvo. I had mixed feelings when I saw him again. He and I were friends since I was seven. There was no contact since just after Ramie's funeral. He was living in Dublin; his parents having returned to Lurgan. Pat did not force me to join the Provisionals and I guess any role he had in my being set up for the Shore Road incident may have saved my life, given some nutters around. There was a guy with him called Leo somebody, one of those guys who never smiles and communicates with a nod or a grunt.

We shook hands, got in the car, Leo moved to the rear seat. We drove towards Belfast, Pat pulled in near Musgrave Park Hospital and turned off the engine and motioned Leo to step out of the car. For a moment I wondered if they were assigned to execute me. God knows what for. Doing time for the organisation, keeping my mouth closed, being a model prisoner as far as the RA was concerned. Do I sound paranoid? God damn right I was paranoid and also depressed. I believe I was depressed most of the four years since Ramie's death.

I never found my carefree attitude prior to it, but I suppose most people, when comparing adult life to their teenage years and childhood, are conscious of that loss of freedom. Life for me was moving into two parts, before Ramie died and after. We had a re-run of the same conversation Dessie and I had, although I was clearer with

Pat, I would not be involved in the struggle again. I added I will always support the cause.

"I guessed that." he said. He would report this back, and he needed a firm quote. What I was unsure of was the level of Pat's seniority in the organisation. He only appears once more in my story, so forgive me if I go into the future briefly.

When peace arrived through the Good Friday agreement (a truce, not the permanent agreement people pretended it was) in April 1998, a formal period of power sharing ensued.

All the Loyalist and all the Republicans whose actions conspired to bring down the original 1972, Power Sharing Agreement. were now power sharing's most fervent exponents.

If you have observed political groups from Northern Ireland being interviewed on the TV news, whether DUP or Sinn Fein, they always appear in a cluster around their leader. In any other country, a political figure speaks to camera on their own, but Northern Ireland politicians resemble a makeshift choir.

I was struck, when watching the national news among the two political groups there were people in this background ensemble who say nothing but nod gravely when their leader speaks. On the Sinn Fein side, and remember, no Sinn Fein politician ever admits to having served in the IRA, a figure fulfilling that role was… Pat Kane. Always in front of him was Colum Delaney. Over time, Pat moved from the rear of the group to closer to the leader. He was Deputy Education Minister at one stage and is today a Minister in the Northern Ireland Executive.

Having satisfied himself on my plans, in so much as they interested him, I raised a point which came into my mind from time-to-time. It surfaced on occasions, a nagging doubt. I asked Pat on the night we went to shoot Doyle why was I sent to scout the crowd as I was the driver.

Pat swallowed. "Sean and especially Gerry did not rate you and intended to drop you from any operational activity. Colum Delaney was sure you might have more violence in you." this was said in a tone implying the great man can be wrong sometimes. "However, they all recognised Ramie as a talent they needed to keep, and I was told to make sure Ramie would still be up for it if you were not part of a new team."

I wanted to ask, but Pat beat me to it.

"Ramie wasn't keen if you were not with him."

Pat could have lied to me, but I know Ramie would not have wanted me out and them bringing in a new person.

Thinking about my earlier anxiety about my position, I am certain there wasn't any risk to me. Much of my paranoia was related to the trauma of Ramie's death. My future in the organisation would be one of the errand boys, not on operations.

Pat drove me home. One last thing he continued, "I have dwelt on Ramie's death, every day since it happened." he added, "I have lost a lot of comrades, but Ramie's hurt the most."

After my arrest, he would visit Paddy and Greta, if Geraldine was in the house, she would make an excuse and leave. Geraldine blamed him for Ramie's death. He reminded me of the nights after the Falls Curfew back in 1970 when his Mother was taken to hospital and his Dad to jail. He was brought to the Mulgrew's by Greta. As a 14-year-old, he couldn't show how he was feeling when Greta put him to bed, but later, he cried his eyes out. At his age, it must have been traumatic to see your Mother lying in the street with blood pouring from her head and your father trying to get to her but being dragged away by armed soldiers.

He shared a bed with Ramie for a few days until both his parents were home, but he cried that night. Ramie held him and comforted him.

"I suppose he told you." he added.

"No, he didn't." I replied.

Ramie never mentioned it even when we 'took the piss' out of Pat behind his back.

My Mother had been informed I was being released, but she was unsure when. I walked into our house with a black plastic bag with all my worldly possessions in it and shouted up the stairs.

"Hi, Mammy, I'm home." as if I popped out for messages four years earlier. We are not demonstrative by nature, not at all tactile, but I received a firm hug, and she kissed my forehead. The last time my Mother kissed me was when I failed the 'Qualy' at 11. However, this was an Irish Mammy, and she went into 'Mammy-mode.' "I'll make you something to eat," she said.

These days we would call it an all-day breakfast, it tasted wonderful.

Halfway through consuming it Greta breezed in." I couldn't wait any longer," she announced, giving me a big hug and lots of kisses.

The Mulgrew's were into touch and kisses, well except Geraldine, but you have heard that story! Greta chatted nineteen to the dozen. My Mother looked pleased if a bit strained. Poor Paddy died a year after my Dad. I don't know for sure, but I believe Greta's grief for her husband's passing was not prolonged. Occasionally, when someone dies, members of their family, who had no time for them when they were alive, eulogise them, not Greta. Later, my Mother made the wise observation, "Apart from Ramie coming back, for Greta, your return was the nearest best thing," and I guess it was.

After Greta left, I went up to my bedroom, the room I shared with 'wee' Eugene about four lifetimes ago. This was the bedroom I first fantasized about, Jess. The same room I accepted Ramie was gone and I would never see him again. I was angry, though I am not sure at who. Pat, Sean, Delaney, O'Dade, the Brits, my Dad and losing him, Jess's Dad and losing her, God, all these.

Then I broke down and wept. It was the relief at being home, coupled with an emotional release and my physical release. In fact, it was all of these and the emotions stored in that room.

After four years in prison, I would like to explain how different I was. I was coming up to twenty when I went inside. The biggest event in my life was Ramie's loss. Did he come into my thoughts? Well, yes, he did and would do certainly if I remained in Belfast. There were memories of him everywhere, the street we grew up in, the Road, and people who knew us. Of course, I never forgot him; but I didn't, couldn't ... talk about Ramie or the loss he represented.


## Reflection Bridie

My life was not interesting. Gabriel was a fine person. Not exciting, quiet, too quiet. He was a decent provider and tried to be the best Dad he could be, but the job came first. Gabriel was intelligent, but he held himself back and didn't get promotions at work. He assumed he would not get a job because of his religion. I got frustrated because he would not even try. Gabriel died too young; he worried about so much. He worried himself to death, but I miss him.

I loved my children. Did I tell you my younger son was a priest? What do you think of that?

Our Maeve is a bright girl. She was always going to do well. Nuala could be a handful. She was clever but determined to go her own way; she was afraid of nothing.

Joe, Joe.... well, he was never at home. When he was young, he ate and slept there. When he got older, he just slept there. As a wee boy, it was out with Ramie Mulgrew from dawn to dusk. I never understood why they joined the IRA. A lot of youngsters who were affected by the violence either joined or went away. Those boys let the violence pass over their heads. I saw no signs of deep commitment to 'the cause.' Joe changed after Ramie was killed and, after his own spell in the Maze, he became more mature, more thoughtful.

I wish Gabriel had lived to see how they all turned out.

# Chapter 8

# HOME AND A JOB

I settled down to living with my Mother again. I needed to tell her I wanted to leave Northern Ireland, although it meant I was deserting her. All the others were gone, and I was living there because I needed her. I had nowhere else to go. But, as soon as I was on my feet, notice I don't say back on my feet, it was time for me to move on. One consolation, at least I was free of O'Dade.

One more family shock was to be shared. I never expected Nuala to visit me. I had not wanted Maeve to, but we were closer. Nuala was the family baby, only she wasn't. She was coming up to 21. A couple of days after I got home, we were sitting in the front parlour after tea.

"I am surprised our Nuala has not come over to see me. I know she has moved out, but she is not at University. You said something in passing about her having got a flat with girls nearer her work."

Travelling across Belfast was haphazard because of the murders, bombings, shootings, buses being set on fire, Army patrols searching people plus the Loyalist workers strikes. It would make sense for her to stay nearer work, in a quieter a part of Belfast.

My Mother spoke as if she had to get this over with as soon as possible. The torrent began, "Now you know our Nuala was accomplished, at most things she did. She was in the St Dominic's High School choir, played hockey for her school team, got 8 'O' levels and three 'A' levels. She didn't want to go to Queens and applied for a series of jobs and she got the post in the GP surgery on the Lisburn Road near Queen's University. She applied for, and got into, the Health Board Headquarters as a Trainee Administrator, which offered training in aspects of the Health Service. Though Nuala was only 20, she was already promoted. She moved into a flat with two of her colleagues. They used to go on nights out when the city was quiet. One night a colleague's brothers joined them."

I listened as my Mother gave me more of the background.

"This chap, Paul MacErlaine, well, he is, or was, married. He has a son, hails from Ardoyne, and his ex-wife lives there, as do other members of his family. They have been living together on the Lisburn Road for the past six months. I haven't met him, but I meet her for tea once a week. She wants me to meet him, but I am not ready."

I was shocked, but to buy time while I absorbed this news, I asked, "Is he a Catholic?"

"Well, yes, he was at St Malachy's College. He is twenty-seven."

I regretted asking that. What I was concerned about was the age difference, almost eight years, especially since she was only 20 and he was her first serious boyfriend. Now remember, I have come out of Prison after four years because I fired guns, not convincingly, at fellow

*Belfast: Out of the Shallows*

human beings. In fact, I was being lauded as a 'hero' of the 'armed struggle' because I had been imprisoned for it. In addition, my best friend was shot dead in front of my eyes by 'them'.

I needed to respond in a calculated and mature fashion, borrowing on all the worldly experiences I accumulated. I couldn't speak.

My Mother added, "I spoke to old Father Courtney, and he said she can't come to mass at St Peter's, as she is living in sin."

My Mother was devout, but in my last encounter with Father Courtney, he congratulated me for taking a 'stand in arms.' Fair enough, he was from an old Cork IRA family. My Mother had to talk to someone and the rest of us were not around.

I began, "Father Courtney is a celibate man in his 70s. His last interaction with me was to congratulate me for trying to kill British soldiers."

She would have been better talking to Father Mike, but he had been ill and in Rome for quite a while. She couldn't seek support in the neighbourhood, not even with Greta, because there was more and worse to come. I needed a pause, so I asked, "Do Maeve and Eugene know?"

"Yes," she replied. "Maeve and Nuala phone and write all the time. Eugene offered to talk to her. They have always been close. Eventually, Eugene met with them both. He said he liked the guy, but nothing else."

I tried to absorb all this. I wanted to see a positive for my Mother, but right now nothing is happening. Nothing was jumping out. She made tea; a cup of tea helped most problems. I sat there trying to assimilate all she said. My Mother fetched two mugs of tea and stood there as if preparing to make a speech.

'Christ,' I thought, 'there is more. Maybe Nuala's pregnant, at 20, to a married man.' However, it was worse than that, much, much worse.

"The thing is— this man is a member of the RUC; he is a sergeant!"

Whatever criticisms that can be aimed at me, being stuck for words is not one of them. I made the most articulate response I could get to in this moment of madness and disgrace.

"The RUC," I repeated. I was hoping she was confused and meant the RAC.

We chatted about nothing else for the next few days and we finally exhausted the topic. I said at the end, "Nuala is young, but she has taken a step in a direction she has to go in. You don't like the guy is married; I don't like he is RUC. By meeting her weekly, you are trying to be a loving Mother and not start a family feud." My Mother replied.

"I was so happy you were coming home, but this situation has been hanging over me. I dreaded telling you after everything you have been through."

"Thank goodness your Daddy isn't here to see it."

I considered this; Nuala may have made a life-changing choice. She was the same age I was when I made one and look at how that turned out. As the baby of the family, if any of us were his favourite, it was Nuala. She was a real Daddy's girl.

"I have a notion Nuala's decision would have upset him a lot less than mine."

She looked at me and raised an eyebrow.

"Funny," she said. "Maeve said something similar."

"What was Maeve's view?"

My Mother replied, "It's Nuala's choice and she won't be criticising her over it."

I should not underplay the seriousness of the situation. If I stayed in the fight, my life could be on the line for it, but Nuala didn't know I stepped away. There were those who would say it was my job to sort it out with a bullet, even if it meant another much longer sentence. That would have had ramifications for any future relationship with Nuala, Maeve, and Eugene. Even now, in my current situation, it was possible the organisation might ask me to befriend him to set him up. In Belfast in 1980, you could not declare a personal ceasefire. We agreed I would not try to meet Nuala.

All this, unexpected as it was, gave me the opportunity to share my future with my Mother.

To my surprise, she was pleased, as she said, "I just want you to be safe. If you had to be involved in the 'Cause' you have done your part, you must find a life away from Northern Ireland."

I reminded her I had two 'O' levels, I intended to sit two more O' levels, one in politics and economics and one in sociology, and an 'A' level in Modern History.

Through the TV and Distance Learning Programme, I was completing a foundation course in my Open University degree in Economic and Social Studies.

Thanks to input from the Lecturer who came into the Maze, I received extra credits, so the next stage was the first year proper of my Degree.

I needed a job to fill the blanks in my CV, give me money and get me references. My Dad left us some money and Mammy put it in a Post Office, Savings Account, where else!

I wanted her to keep it for herself. She smiled. "That is what all the others said, I have kept enough for me. Eugene has his and Maeve has spent hers on an excellent investment in her education. "She was in the final year of her course and on placement in a large Hospital in Liverpool.

The rest of the year passed. I studied hard, but I needed to find a job. My Uncle Sean, or one of my Dad's old buddies, could get me a job as a Postman. I could approach local 'friendly' employers. Whatever it is, I will need to stick at it and find something I enjoy doing? The only thing coming to mind was driving. I had the money in the Post Office, so I used a bit to begin an HGV licence course. It was late May 1981. The deaths of the ten hunger strikers brought a lot onto the streets, but I stayed home a fair bit of the time, studying.

Drift was my problem. Looking back, everything I did either happened by accident, or happened as a reaction to what someone else did. It needed thinking through. Did I need a job? Yes, I needed money, and I needed the sense of purpose regular working gives you for a start. It would be a major plank in getting out of Belfast and all the drawbacks living there brought. Let's bring the best and the bad about me to the table and see where it takes me.

I will get the bad out of the way first by looking at the obstacles to finding employment. First, I was just out of Prison after a four-year stretch for being a member of an illegal organisation. How many would-be employers would find me an asset? Second, I had no employment record, which should about take care of the rest. Third, I lived in a part of the city many prospective employers would feel negative towards.

My conclusion, after all this deliberation, was a driving job. In the first half of 1981, I approached local employers, taxi guys, but they said I needed my own cab. I also contacted a company doing house removals. "How far are you along with your HGV? Well, come back when that's finished."

I enrolled with Ritchie's, a firm that specialised in getting people through their Class 2 HGV test. I didn't fancy trying to drive an artic. I did my test, but the wee bastard failed me. He claimed as I was approaching a roundabout; my indicator was on, but there was a car in my wing mirror coming in beside me. I waited until it moved on and then turned. The Examiner said I should not have kept my indicator on, and I should have held more of the road so he could not overtake me on the inside. Pernickety or what? But when I told the instructor from Ritchie's, he told me not to be disheartened. I was ready, and I should apply again soon.

I got wee jobs driving people to Dublin and Shannon Airport. The big attraction of Shannon was you could go through US Immigration there rather than at the US end after a tiring 8-hour flight. It was reasonable money but unreliable as it did not offer regular income or an employment record, it was 'cash in hand.'

One morning in August 1981, I was dandering past a grocery shop on the front of the Road. I was conscious of a guy delivering vegetables from a van marked Brewster's Distribution and Commercial Transport. I wandered into the shop. The owner, Pete, and his daughter had known me over the years and, as I bought chocolate, I asked in a loud tone, "Do you know of any driving jobs going?".

"Sure Joe, you'd be a grand driver." said the daughter.

This elicited not the slightest bit of interest from the van driver, who was stacking empty crates and boxes to put in the van. He left boxes behind as he went out to load up, so I grabbed the rest and followed him out. He thanked me, and I went for the direct approach.

"Are they hiring any drivers at your place?"

He hesitated for a minute, "God, I hate this run all over West Belfast. I wish they would get someone local to do it."

He said the manager was a John O' Sullivan who managed the West Belfast Depot. His last comment was even more interesting.

"Big John is expanding our runs up County Antrim to Coleraine, Ballycastle and Portrush and moaning about the overtime, so he might just want an extra driver."

I got details of the Falls Depot, up near the top of the Grosvenor Road and headed there. This was exciting. The depot was a car park with a Portakabin in the corner. All the drivers had to take their vans home at night. Often, they were stolen or burnt out to be used as barricades. I often wondered how, in the middle of a riot, someone would drive a van into a burning bus to add to the stew that was a Belfast Street riot. It hadn't occurred to me they hijacked it from some poor guy from their own community.

I knocked at the door of the Portakabin, and an older woman and a young girl were sitting behind desks with typewriters. I explained I hoped to meet Mr O'Sullivan, but they said he was over at Head Office and wouldn't be back until after lunch, around 2.00 pm. So, I left and wandered up to the Falls Park and, let me see, it was two hours later, close to 1.15, when I returned. No sign of Mr O'Sullivan, so I asked if I could wait and was motioned to an easy chair near the door. I chatted to them and flirted a bit with them. The younger woman looked about 18. Both were happy to have a distraction.

When the boss came in about 2.15 pm, he was, at first, quite stressed by me being there. I later found out he was disorganised and often made appointments without telling the women in the office, then he forgot he made the appointments. He earned a row from both the women and from an angry would-be customer, which all ruined his day.

I found out the women ran the office and a positive first impression on them was a major bonus. The younger one brought in two cups of coffee, handing him one and saying.

"I am sure Joe would appreciate a cup of coffee after having to wait so long."

Poor Mr O'Sullivan was on the back foot. I came uninvited, no notice or appointment, ingratiating myself with the powers behind the throne, and was now sitting in his office centre stage and he did not know why I was there!

I went for it. I explained I was from the Falls Road; I was looking for a driving job and there was talk his firm was doing well, expanding up the coast and might want someone for the West Belfast runs. It all came out in a torrent, but to be fair to him, he sat and listened. He was a nice guy, a little out of his depth as a Manger because of the stress, but his branch performed well because Eileen, the older woman, was employed by the company for years and she ensured he made the right big decisions.

I mentioned my studying at the Tech, how I started an HGV course, but I needed to be straight with him. "I am not long out of the Maze, after a four-year sentence."

It was as if I had not spoken. He said he was dealing with overtime claims that meant an extra staff member would not bring additional costs. Another hassle his drivers moaned about doing the Falls, Ballymurphy, Mo yard, New Barnsley Turf Lodge runs, etc. Two of the drivers were from the Markets and he didn't say where the third driver was from. I suspect he wasn't Catholic, and they couldn't send him to Nationalist areas.

All so enlightened, but it restricted his choice for who would do this part of West Belfast.

It also meant John ended up doing runs himself if someone was sick or an unexpected delivery came in. The third driver covered the Shankill, Ballysillan and Crumlin Roads but was based at Head Office even though he was notionally part of our branch.

All the drivers did the Antrim Road, Shore Road, Rathcoole, and Newtownabbey areas, everywhere except Ardoyne, which only the Catholic drivers went to.

John O Sullivan sat back in his chair, and a period of silence ensued. I got my breath back and supped my, by now, cold coffee.

"Look," he said; "I appreciate your honesty and from what I have said, you will know l am wrestling with creating another post.

Our company was taken over by a big firm based in Luton about two years ago."

He hesitated then continued, "We used to just do cash and carry to grocery shops locally. Since the takeover we have expanded to moving larger commercial goods coming over from the UK. They arrive in containers at Belfast Docks or Dublin. If it needs moved, we do it. We expanded and merged with other smaller Belfast firms. The routes were drawn up by a whiz kid in the company headquarters in Luton. The closest he has been to any part of Ireland is that he likes a stout."

He paused for a minute, "One point in your favour is you are from The Falls, and you will be comfortable with the area and, to be honest, if you are stopped by, "he paused again, "folk intending to hijack your van, you might dissuade them.""

I doubted that but as it was helping me, I said nothing. He added they lost three vans in the previous 18 months.

"Given your background, the decision to take you on is above my pay grade. You will need to go over to Alex Peabody, the Regional Manager, at the Belfast Head Office."

My heart sank when I heard his name, not one I would have associated with offering an opportunity to a "retired" IRA man.

John saw my reaction to the name. "Alex is English," he said, hardly reassuring.

"He is alright is Alex. Head Office is at Boucher Road."

I made to get to my feet, but John laughed, "You cannot just drop in; Gillian would eat you alive."

Did all these guys need a woman to protect them? He phoned Head Office and spoke to Gillian.

"Can you tell Mr Peabody I have a candidate," me a candidate?

"If we decide to create a vacancy here, I would like Alex to see him. Tell him I will phone him tonight."

That would be for a more private discussion. An appointment was made for the following week. His last comment was, "No offence, but it is a job interview, look smart."

I felt my face reddening, but it was true. My old jeans and sweatshirt needed upgraded.

I went shopping and bought two pairs of serviceable trousers and four work shirts. I also bought a more formal interview/funeral shirt given I wouldn't be wearing a uniform anymore. I bought a pair of black fashionable trousers and a semi-formal jacket.

When I was in town shopping, I was sure I saw Jess with a toddler on Royal Avenue. I was certain it was Jess. I suppose there was no harm in saying hello, but I wasn't certain I should disturb her equilibrium just to impose myself. Jess was twenty-four. I had not seen her since 1973. A lot had happened to me in the past seven years.

My Mother said she was pleased to see me buy smarter gear. I lived either in jeans, t-shirts, and sweatshirts since I was kid, or prison clothes. Remember, I wasn't on the blanket.

A week later, having received full approval from the Mammy and a cheerful thumbs up from Greta through her curtains, I headed off to Boucher Road for my interview. I arrived on time, and Alex's secretary, Gillian, brought me into his office.

Gillian was also the Office Manager, and she proved a key player in communications about everything from decent street maps to tips about whom to speak to at the docks or the firms we were delivering to and who might swap a shift if you needed time off.

Alex Peabody was a small guy with tiny round glasses perched on the end of his nose. He was bald, except for a semicircle of grey hair running from the front of his head over both ears, almost monastic in appearance. Alex was planning to retire, and he and his wife had planned to travel when she died, suddenly. Her loss created a void, so he decided against taking early retirement. When the option of setting up the Northern Ireland part of the company arose, Alex volunteered for it to fill the gap in his life. He used to quote one of his colleagues who sounded imminently sensible, "All right, I get it. You want to keep on working, but sodding Belfast?"

Alex was sent to a massive complex in Glasgow for six months. The Depot Manager there suffered a heart attack. This delayed the integration of the five firms they acquired in Northern Ireland. As a result, branches there just went on doing what they did prior to the takeover, doing local van deliveries, while others focussed on long-distance lorry transport. Alex was breaking down these barriers but experienced problems working in Manchester and even Glasgow had not prepared him for Belfast. He used to recount his first meeting with John O' Sullivan when he suggested leaving three rigid and one articulated lorry at the Falls Depot.

"Just to emphasise we have moved from van deliveries to general transport."

John laughed so long he started coughing, couldn't speak, and Alex asked him if he was having a heart attack.

"And I take it there will be four new lorries each morning."

The vans at the Falls Depot were taken home at night, which appealed to me. Alex fired questions at me, the majority about my HGV experience.

He was amused when I told him about the first HGV test and was impressed by the studying, I was doing at the Tech. Then, into the meat of it, he was well briefed by John.

He began, "Our firm is keen we integrate with all parts of the community here. We also have a value stating wherever we are based, someone who served a Prison sentence, deserves an employment opportunity, all other things being equal. No one at Headquarters in Luton could advise me about your particular crime and sentence," he said.

I winced at the mention of crime. Alex went on, "Now, I don't pretend to understand this place. I don't know why people would join organisations to kill people over events from three hundred years ago, and I don't intend to get into that mindset."

Having dismissed centuries of Irish history, he told me to come outside and got me to climb behind the wheel of a lorry. What next? He bellowed, "Cecil," and this tall, very thin guy with glasses emerged from a workshop.

"See what you think of young Joe's driving in the yard?"

Cecil climbed into the lorry. He didn't either look or speak to me. The yard was huge, but there were about 9 vans of various sizes and four other lorries, including two artics, in it. Alex shouted, "Let's see you manoeuvre around this lot and make sure you reverse."

Ok, go for it, son. I drove the lorry around and I did an excellent piece of reverse parking. I got out to check how close to the line I was. You can do that in the test, and I did not need to move it closer. First time, 'well done me.' We drove back over to where Alex was standing.

"He failed his test last week,"

Cecil said, "He will pass next time."

That was it. I went back into the office with Alex.

"John wants you, you start in two weeks, pass your test. I need two references,"

I arranged a Lecturer from the Tech whom I knew from my first time there to give me a reference. He was impressed I picked up formal education again.

A friend of my Uncle Sean's, who knew my Dad well, also agreed to write me a reference. He was a janitor at a new amalgamated Secondary School on the Falls. I went home and shared the glad tidings.

There was an issue with my Tech classes because working full time, I couldn't attend during the day. The Tech was supportive of Adult Returners so, switching to evening classes and one Saturday one was far easier than I expected. I had just a couple more weeks in my existing classes. I was staying around the house and was more disciplined about my OU work. About a week later, a new girl joined my politics class. She was quite opinionated and asked lots of questions and tried to draw other students into wider discussions that irritated the Lecturer. I stayed out of the wrestling for power, but I thought neither of them would have lasted five minutes in some of the power struggles I witnessed in the Maze. She was a slim, not pretty, but quite attractive, brunette.

After a class I sat in the canteen drinking a coffee. I know, I now liked the stuff. It was between Lectures, and I was reading a recommended text, when the brunette asked if she could join me. The place was mobbed, so I wasn't unduly flattered. We chatted a little, "I am doing a politics class as a refresher, but also, I am doing a Law Degree at Queen's with a politics option. Sitting through a class in politics is quicker than time spent in the library. I help with a community newspaper."

I wasn't sure what she meant.

"I also work in a Women's Advice Centre so I don't spend as much time studying as I should, and the Law part of my Degree is demanding enough."

Another one of these fabled women multi-taskers, female excuses for not concentrating on the job at-hand, I thought. Well, I did not just think it, I told her. Her jaw dropped, and I pressed my advantage.

"I have seen you in our politics class and it's not an 'A' level class, it is an 'O' level one.'"

'Eh,' four years in prison had not diminished my ability to make an impression on an attractive woman. Next time I might go for a good impression! Her face turned scarlet, "Women as "fabled multi-taskers!" she thundered.

Other students looked over at this escalating dispute. It had been a few years since I received a slap in the face from a young woman, but I sensed the opportunity for another was looming. I was quite enjoying myself, so I continued, "When someone has done something stupid, they divert attention by starting a philosophical discussion on, for example, feminism."

She countered loudly. "So, you don't respect feminism?"

Too many late-nights and evenings discussing politics in the cages prepared me for all the tactics involved in debating. I might have gone into Prison with limited critical faculties, but they developed in that 'university of life.' I ignored the Feminist line and pressed my point. "It wasn't me who went to the wrong level of politics class."

Would you agree women don't mind being called stupid as long as you dress it up a bit? No, me neither. Her voice rose again, throwing various bits of jargon at me.

I only recall, 'unreconstructed,' 'bourgeois,' like I am from Sevastopol Street on the Falls Road, 'misogynist,' Is that even a word, or is it what teenage boys do under their blankets at night, or is that called something else? Finally, she said, with a defining flourish, delivering the worst insult of all, 'man.'

I smiled; letting it set in. I was conscious at surrounding tables people stopped eating or chatting and were staring at the scene with unbridled joy. A row you are not involved in is always fun. I produced my coup de gras.

"Oops — people think we are having a 'lovers 'tiff!' I whispered, peering around.

She rose in horror. "If you were the last man on earth, I wouldn't —,"

I waved my hand in dismissal. "If you were the last woman on earth, I would be the last man," game set and match!

No, I do not know what it meant either. She ignored the patronising hand wave. Not many people interrupted her in full flow. Few men anyway. She subsided to consider it all. People turned back to their own groups or their coffee.

Enough fun, so I stood, "you will be relieved I am moving to evening classes, so you won't have to put up with me for the rest of the year."

This was too unremarkable a comment from such a provocative MAN to elicit a response. It was time to go into the second part of "our "politics class, so I stood, "Nice chatting with you, bye."

I enjoyed the exchange, the sort of thing a would-be student should do. She came into the class and sat beside me, was subdued, and just said when the class was over. "I am heading up to Queens."

I don't know why, but I said; "I am going up there too."

Ok, I was attracted to her. We walked up Great Victoria Street, across Shaftsbury Square and up Bradbury Place and Dublin Road, chatting away. I took the opportunity to look at her. How would I describe her, about five feet seven inches, curly black hair, pale skin medium to skinny build? She didn't laugh much. The earlier exchange was forgiven. She asked what I did. Why was I doing 'O' levels at my age? Now, I am always guarded about events in my life since 1975, for obvious reasons. I read the community newspaper she mentioned when I was in the Maze. It tried to adopt a broad Republican line, but one guy said it was produced by the Irish Republican Socialist Party (IRSP), a political offshoot of the Irish National Liberation Army (INLA). She came over as a bright, committed political activist. She hailed from the Ardoyne in North Belfast.

I told her about my involvement and about being in the Maze.

We agreed to meet at the Students Union steps for a drink later than evening. I went home, spruced up, much to my Mum's amusement. I had not been involved with anyone since my release. I made a point of meeting with Carmel; she was still unattached, and we went for a drink, talked about Ramie, but we had both moved on. She was friendly, but there was nothing romantic from either of us.

It was strange being back in Queen's. I hadn't been in the Union bar since the night with Georgie, seven years ago, and to be honest, it looked as if the same faces were still sitting in the same places. Universities are a bit like that, I suspect. They are a safe environment, so people hang on there as long as they can. I have this theory expounded to the very serious Dolores Kelly, my new amour from the Ardoyne. She talked about herself, and knowing I was from the Falls, she was comfortable mentioning her two brothers were active republicans, one was in the fledgling Sinn Fein and the other in the IRSP.

"That's nice," I said, with only a hint of sarcasm. "They must have a lot to talk about,"

Not so," she explained, either taking me at face value or ignoring the political aspect of their different choices. "They hadn't spoken for about 18 months until our Mother got fed up and banged their heads together." Families uh!

Dolores talked almost nonstop about Northern Irish politics, only pausing when an acquaintance would pass by and chat. She was a well-known figure in the Students Union.

Just to say Dolores was a lower middle class/upper working-class Catholic. Jess was lower middle-class Protestant and Georgie was middle class Protestant. In Northern Ireland it's not just about religion, class is always there as well. I was brought up a working-class boy, simple as that.

According to her, I was a 'Working class hero,' fighting and being imprisoned for the 'cause.' It is like being an artist or a poet, it transcends stereotypes. Dolores lived nearby with a group of other girls who were at Queen's. I walked her home, and she invited me in for coffee.

Here you will find a sensitive, calculating Joe you have not encountered. I wanted to sleep with her and the invitation for coffee might offer more than coffee, but again, it might not.

I declined the offer, told her how much I enjoyed the evening, "Would you like to go out for a bite to eat on Friday night?" I ventured.

"I have an editorial board on Friday night, and I will stay at home in Ardoyne."

My face fell at this seeming rejection.

"However, I will be back at the flat on Saturday."

We agreed to meet at a low-cost student restaurant in Shaftsbury Square, near the Loyalist stronghold of Sandy Row on Saturday about 7.00 pm.

On Saturday, I had a bath, told Mum I was seeing friends and I mightn't be home that night. A triumph of hope over reality?

My Mother's take on it was if I was "dressing up" to go out it meant I was not falling into old habits, which was all she worried about. She asked if I was meeting a girl and I hummed and nodded, which she took to be 'yes.'

We enjoyed the meal. Dolores still did most of the talking. We walked back to her flat with her arm crooked through mine and went up to the lounge. The flat was a large four bed roomed one, though one bedroom was smaller than the rest and it was set in a large, terraced house.

One of her flatmates, Mary Cargill, was from County Armagh and went home to her boyfriend at the weekend. Dolores thought he might be a Policeman. She did not elaborate on why she thought that but made a face. Another flatmate, also called Mary. I never could remember her surname, was involved in a drama group, with a boyfriend whom she lived with most of the week. She took the small bedroom. That left Marianne. She was a fellow Law student from London who was 'politically aware', according to Dolores. Marianne offered to make us coffee. She was a blond, buxom, dare I say, a tad overweight young woman with a polite semi-Cockney/ Thames Estuary accent. She was also an outrageous flirt and after a few drinks, she kept laughing when I said "Dolores." I wondered was it my accent.

At one point Marianne said. "I take it Joe knows he has to sleep with all your flatmates to get accepted."

Dolores stuck out her tongue at Marianne, who was enjoying her own humour, but then went to bed. Dolores and I began kissing and cuddling. I am sure you can imagine the rest. I said to her, "Why did Marianne laugh when I called you "Dolores."

She made a face, "I hate the name. It was my grandmother's idea. I used to get teased at school and end up fighting half the girls in my class."

Oh, oh possessed of a temper. A warning light flashed.

"So, what do your friends call you?" an innocent enough question.

"Kelly, only my family and my Tutors call me Dolores,"

So "Kelly" it was. After more cuddling, we made our way to Kelly's bedroom. It was as if we made love all night, which is how I choose to remember it; I was selfish the first time, but she was forgiving, and patient and the second time was much more pleasurable for her.

I ended up telling her the full post-1975 story, the Provisionals, Ramie, and my Maze experience. It was the first time she listened to me. I was surprisingly keen to talk about it. Maybe because of this uncharacteristic sharing, our relationship became intense. It was too quick. I believe Kelly wanted to live her dreams of Republicanism through a partner who fought for the 'Cause 'and served time for it and might be a future hero. I couldn't convince her I was done with the 'Cause.' She considered I needed a break or could not share my innermost thoughts with her I was "up to." It all stimulated her. I am not sure if that is the right word, but it did wonders for our sex life. There was a film out about six years later called "A Fish Called Wanda "in which one of the male leads would talk Russian to excite his lady love. Well, any mention of the Maze got Kelly all "het" up.

I started at Brewster's towards the end of August 1981. Combined with the evening classes, plus overtime and trying to sustain the OU, I only saw "Kelly" at weekends.

That suited her due to her commitments at the Advice Centre, the community newspaper and, of course, Lectures etc. at the University.

Just before my first day at work, I met with Nuala at one of her regular 'get togethers' with our Mother. We gave each other a big hug; I was pleased to see her after so long.

At first, the conversation was simple. We talked about Maeve and Eugene, friends, and neighbours and we chatted about Dad. My Mother got quite upset, and so did Nuala and, you know, tears were starting to well up in me as well. I had not been involved in the funeral and missed the rituals which support during grieving. I had not been conscious of how much I had missed out on those. We also discussed my new job, the driving tests and Nuala said. "I gather you have a girlfriend."

"Well," I countered, "I have a friend who is a girl." I did not give too much away.

"She is much younger than me."

Kelly was three years younger than me, but I added, "It's early days." They both laughed. The one thing we did not discuss was Nuala's man. We talked about her job, her colleagues, that she was going to a Greek Island on holiday in September.

As she left, I gave her a big hug and whispered in her ear, "Stay happy." I got a big kiss; my Mother was pleased something she dreaded went so well.

Remember, I said I thought I saw Jess one Saturday shopping in Royal Avenue. Well, I went down to buy more fashionable casual gear as my pre-prison wardrobe was bang out-of-date. I wandered up and down Royal Avenue. I hoped I might bump into Jess. This time I resolved to speak to her. Half of Belfast passes through Royal Avenue on a Saturday afternoon, especially the female half, so it wasn't a shot in the dark. I crossed the street near the new shopping mall at Castle Court about 2.30 pm and Jess walked out, almost bumping into me. She was on her own. Apart from running away, I could not have avoided her.

"Hello Joe, how are you?" She asked it in a mature grown-up way, the smile was the same, not sure if the eyes still sparkled the same. Inside, I was excited at seeing her but unable to speak. If she was the shy teenager, I remembered we could have stood in silence for quite a while. This Jess was a mature wife and mum. She chatted away.

I wondered if her Father told her about our encounter in the Maze. I asked her about Robert. I said I thought I saw her a couple of weeks ago with a young boy. 'Was the child her son?'

"That was my wee boy, William." She added she had a daughter, Ann, as well. Robert was working for an engineering firm near Sydenham. I chatted about my driving job, my studying and mentioned I was seeing a girl who was doing Law at Queens. I hoped she might show she was jealous. How immature. I was trying to impress her and omitted minor details like four years in Prison. It was a nice friendly catch up. I longed to kiss her, but it would be inappropriate and, all too soon, she had to rush off, "Lovely to see you, Joe, take care."

I dwelt on this meeting with Jess for days. She was so different, matured yet she still had the same smile, and I sensed, or so I wanted to believe, I was a little special.

Did I imagine that? For the next four Saturdays I patrolled Royal Avenue, High Street, Ann Street, and I saw her again coming out of a store. She was on her own. I thought up a plan.

"Hi Jess, busy shopping? Have you time for a coffee?"

She smiled, paused for a minute. "Oh well, yes--. I suppose so."

Not brimming with enthusiasm, but affirmative at least. Possibly meeting an ex-boyfriend, albeit of seven years ago and having coffee was risqué! We drank our coffees. Jess chatted away about her kids, about her house, about Robert (damnit) and her parents. Her Mum had early dementia, but her Dad was managing fine. Why did Robert have to be such a decent husband, why did Billy Morton have to be one too?

At this stage, my plan was to tell Jess I was in love with her, had been since we first met, suggest we try to rekindle our relationship. Was I suggesting an affair despite her loving husband? Her kids, her home. The possibility of anything between us was silly.

I chatted about my sisters, my brother becoming a priest, my Dad's death, and my job, but I never mentioned my imprisonment. I even mentioned Kelly.

She took all this on board, politely, interested, then a glance at her watch and again she needed to rush. I got a peck on the cheek, very unexpected. Jess was gone. That meeting dealt with the lack of closure in our relationship.

Somehow seeing her and talking to her brought me out of the fantasy state, this was real adult life. I had matured. I thought I was over the childhood fantasy about Jess. It served its purpose in getting me through a few dark, lonely nights.

I joined the fight, but Ramie's loss was a heavy price, so was my time in Prison. I had a sense of entitlement about putting together a better life, one more wrapped around my own needs and aspirations.

I met with my sister Nuala on our own. I needed to reassure her that her choice as a partner was not an issue, it was she who was important. The first time we met after greeting her I said. "Gosh, I don't remember the last time we had a serious discussion."

"We have never had a serious adult discussion, Joe." she replied. She explained how I was not like a big brother, as she grew up, I was never around, never much involved in family "stuff." Maeve was, to her, the eldest sibling. I reminded her how upset she was when I told them I would be picked up by the Security Forces.

"Don't forget," she said, "I was still at school. I was in tears and upset because I saw how upset Mammy and Daddy were. I was sad for you as my brother, but you were in Prison from when I was 16 until I was 20, important years in anyone's life."

How differently my siblings perceived me? Maeve and I were closer, Eugene and I shared a room. He wrote when I was in Prison, so we interacted more. I said to myself, 'I don't want my little sister to be a stranger'

## Reflection Nuala

I suppose I wasn't supportive of Joe when he went to Prison. I was quite young, and I was closer to our Eugene, anyway. The whole Ramie grief thing hit us hard. Ramie was a friend growing up, Maeve and I played with his sister Geraldine since we were tots.

First Joe was sent to Prison, and the impact on my parents was awful. Then my Daddy died and, if I am honest, I blamed Joe at least a bit.

I did well at school, didn't fancy Uni and I got a super job. That brought me into a different, more religiously mixed circle. Most of my colleagues were aware I had a sister and a brother who was training to be a priest and I didn't mention Joe.

My Dad was keen Maeve, and I should not visit Joe, and I believe my brother was happy with that. Maeve wasn't and if she hadn't gone to study in England, she would have visited and perhaps after a while I would have too.

I met Paul, the love of my life. It didn't work out for him in his marriage, but we see a lot of his son, wee Paul and his wife, or ex-wife, is not hostile. Older members of Paul's family are not keen on me. I met Paul after they separated, though.

Over the next few years, Joe and I met up and our relationship grew closer.

# Chapter 9

# LEARNING THE ROPES AND BEING HUNG BY SOME OF THEM

It's odd that, so soon, I should acquire a girlfriend and a job. What could go wrong with life now? All this good fortune was the least I deserved after my problems. During the first weeks, I was based at Boucher Road to familiarise with the company, the staff there and the routes for the lorries. I went to the Docks, learned the procedures, and agreed, having got my HGV class 2, to do a Class 1 licence so I could drive the artics. Cecil was helpful without ever quite speaking to me. Our communication, as I reversed the big articulated lorry, was through grunts and raised eyes.

I spent a week accompanying other drivers on deliveries all over Ireland. I got experience of the main roads in the South. A few years later, Ireland's economy benefited as a member of the EU and the tax changes introduced to boost the Southern economy, but this was before the improvements. The M1 was still under construction, driving through Drogheda was the only way. Such a pain.

My first job on my own involved going to Larne to get a load and drive to Cork. I went to Galway to pick up bricks and bring them back to Belfast. Gillian was brilliant about sorting routes. I enjoyed the open road but the roads in the South were a nightmare. They do not believe in dual carriageways. I communicated via international sign language, involving one or two fingers with impatient car drivers. A truck with a twenty-foot container gave you a lot of say in a head-to-head.

When I got to the Falls depot, I undertook van deliveries around areas; I knew. I drove long distance at least weekly. Once to Salford near Manchester, my first time out of Ireland. John was never pleased if Head Office called me in for a job. None of his other drivers had a HGV, so when I was away, John deployed one of them to West Belfast. They were only doing it monthly, as opposed to once or twice a week. They should have limited their moaning, but that is not a driver's way.

Christmas 1982 passed with no major issues in our house. Kelly bought me a nice watch and I got her earrings which Nuala and I picked when we met, as we did sometimes, without Mammy. We both needed time on our own with her, and I agreed I would meet her Paul soon. A few times, I went to Kelly's home and met her brothers and her parents. She came to our house on Boxing Day. My Mother fussed around with enough home baking to feed the Army of occupation. She made a point of knocking on the front room door when she brought in tea.

Bringing a girl home for the first time as a man in my mid-twenties is the Irish way. Most Irish men wouldn't get married until they were 40, if left to their own devices.

Over the Christmas and New Year holiday period, Kelly and I went for walks in safe areas in South Belfast like Barnett's Park, Shawsbridge and the towpath by the Upper Lagan. We were studying and enjoyed exploring the world, encountering new ideas, and testing how they fitted with our earlier understanding of events. Access to new information and ways of thinking was challenging for me. I struggled to move past long held positions and prejudices. For Kelly, it was all about seeing what fitted the 'Struggle' narrative. If it did not, it was discarded.

The seriousness with which she met issues sometimes irritated me, and I know the levity I adopted provoked her. We would stomp back to her flat not speaking and end up in bed in passionate lovemaking that melted our differences away until the next time.

In January and March, I was away earning excellent money plus overtime and could buy a second-hand Ford Escort. Having a car meant going to work and Kelly's flat was less risky.

Despite my Mother's initial enthusiasm, she picked up from me that Kelly and I would not be a permanent item. It didn't end well; I still don't know how much of it was my fault. A woman might say, 'all of it.'

There was a party at Kelly's flat to celebrate Marianne's 21st birthday, early May 1982. I don't care for parties. I hoped Alex would produce a long trip to England, but no such luck. Trying to enjoy the event, I drank too much and got a warning hissed at me as I grew loud, so I drew back.

The students were pleasant, but many of Kelly's friends were intense. Now Marianne's friends were bad rascals, well, some of them, but very sociable and fun. People asked what I was studying. They were not being snobbish, and I was not sensitive. Remember, I was a taxpayer keeping the Universities going, also a lorry driver who was into his Open University Degree in Politics and Social Studies, with only five years to go, I could cope! If I needed to exert myself, I could say, "One night in the Maze…" or "One day we were shooting at the Army," but I didn't. Kelly and I went to bed about 2.30 am. The Mary from Armagh went to her bed and the other Mary left.

Most of the guests, except Marianne and this red-headed guy she was pursuing, also left. That left me and Kelly and Marianne and her victim. We discovered a friend of one of the Marys' who was drunk and asleep in the bath. It made it more demanding going down for the night. Doing your night-time ablutions with a member of the opposite sex, whose name you didn't know, snoring about two feet away was different. I intended to sleep late given the amount of drink I consumed, which meant I should not drive.

The flat's phone rang, turned out it was about 8.00 am and Marianne shouted in an irritated voice, "Kelly, it's for you."

Who in their right mind phones University students at 8.00 am on a Saturday? I rolled over and pretended I hadn't heard. Marianne might be annoyed because she was holding prisoner the red-haired boy she pursued! I did not know it, but he was also gone, Kelly whispered, "A woman I work with at the Advice Centre was abused. Her husband put her out of the house. She walked the streets half the night, and the cleaner found her at 6.30 am."

Way too much information. My head hurts," I grunted.

"I need to go there; her kids are with the husband; I have to get him out and her back into the house." This information was of no interest to me, but being Kelly, I got the entire story. I offered to drive her over, but she declined and said she would get a taxi.

I mumbled. "See you tonight. I need more sleep and I will go over home." I got back into a deep sleep.

After a while, I was conscious of Kelly getting back into bed. A hand went down my boxers and she yanked them off me. As I was coming to, I was quite aroused. Kelly never initiated sex in this way, and it was exciting. She hauled me onto my back and a large breast was thrust into my face. Kelly didn't have large breasts! It was Marianne, and by this time, she was astride me. I was almost awake, anxious, aroused, excited, all of those.

We shared a passionate coupling, I groaned, but Marianne hardly made a sound. Her hands were all over me. She held me tight, and her eyes were closed. Did she care or even realise she making love to her friend's partner?

I should have stopped her, but I just enjoyed it. I thought of this after Marianne climbed off and snuggled in for a cuddle. By a cuddle. I mean our bodies were entwined, but I did not put my arms around her. It was a gesture to the absent Kelly. Pathetic I know. The strangest thoughts come into your head in this situation. Years ago, we had a priest at confession who used to ask us, "And did you entertain any impure thoughts, my son?"

I said to Ramie, we were only 13, "I replied, 'Father, I don't know if I entertained them, but they sure as hell entertained me."

Ramie knew there wasn't a chance in hell I responded like that. He loved the story though, often telling it when we were in company. Not sure why that came into my head.

During the love making, Marianne and I didn't exchange a word. She moaned enough for anyone else in the flat to hear, I suspect. Marianne returned to her own room. I experienced a sinking sensation that there would be a reckoning for these moments of pleasure. I needed to escape.

I put on my boxers, crept to the bathroom, checking if the refugee from last night was not still in the bath. She wasn't, thank God. A quick wash at the sink, put on my "best" jeans and t-shirt and slid into the Escort. There was no sign of Marianne. I hoped Mary Cargill would have carried out her plan and leave for home early, maybe when Kelly was leaving.

I was disappointed to see her coat still hung up at the front door of the flat. She would be gone by this evening leaving only the judge and prosecutor, no jury.

As I drove towards the Falls, my mind was reeling. I needed one of my plans to cover any eventualities. I only had Marianne and Kelly to face. Somehow, this did not represent a tremendous advantage. I went home, got something to eat and wandered onto the Road. It was like my court appearance hanging over my head. The time I was on remand was my only similar experience and I got four years. I am sure the judge considered me the Laurel or Hardy of urban terrorism. The opponent this time, did not take prisoners.

My Mother liked to know if there would be a key in the door after midnight. My first instinct was: I will be home early tonight. I examined the various scenarios in my mind. Marianne might declare undying love for me with all due reference to what happened between us in Kelly's bed. Second, Kelly and I would have a massive row, followed by a passionate making up to blow a whole new impetus into our relationship. Third, Kelly borrowed a gun. I believe she would have a fair number of sources and just shot me. Finally, fourthly, what if Kelly tearfully conceded Marianne won the battle for my heart and she and I took up together in a short-lived but passionate fling?

Right, marks out of a hundred for likelihood, number four, me, and Marianne got three out of a hundred, Kelly shooting me got seven, she might cope with giving up her Law career but not volunteering at the Advice Centre. Number two, us making up, it scored ten out of a hundred. All that was left was getting home early following a right "doing" from Kelly. It got 80. "I will be home early tonight, Mum," I shouted as I headed out about 7.00pm.

I put on my new t-shirt, a Christmas present from Maeve, and my best trousers. Something about a condemned man? I read King Charles 1 wore two shirts on his way to his execution in case he shivered in the cold and people believed he was afraid. Me, I was terrified. Despite having two sisters, I wasn't equipped for war with women. I saw them in action against each other and it was scary. When war broke out between Maeve and Nuala, I headed for the door. As I drove across Belfast two further alternatives occurred: just keep driving, don't face the consequences, at least not tonight. I had no other links to Queen's, apart from Kelly. The evening classes at the Tech meant our paths would not cross or, if she waited for me, at least there would be witnesses.

Perhaps Marianne said nothing. They were flat mates rather than friends, were tied together until the Summer under the same roof. A few weeks earlier, there was a conversation about sharing again next year. Mary from Armagh decided she would travel daily next term. She would be in her final year and the last few months would be about studying and the library rather than Lectures and Tutorials. As I parked the car, I felt more cheerful.

I rang the bell, the door clicked, and I went upstairs. As I reached out to the flat door, it opened and Marianne swept out, blanking me with the air of an aggrieved woman. Bang goes any hope the matter was not aired. Did that mean she and Kelly fell out? Would the minor role I played in the contretemps result in a modicum of forgiveness? Kelly was sitting on the settee in front of the fireplace writing a card.

For a second, I thought it might be a sympathy card. 'Dear Mrs McFaul, I am sorry I had to shoot that bastard son of yours. Love Dolores Kelly x"

'Get a grip, man, it's no laughing matter.'

Kelly was subdued. I knew she had been crying. The look the latter gave me as she left also eliminated undying love from her. I stood awkwardly. Kelly fixed me with a stare, difficult to describe, anger, pain, and some… I don't know. She said nothing, didn't ask me to sit. I stood between the settee and the door.

To break the tension, I ventured, nodding at the card, "Someone's birthday,"

She replied in measured tones, "Mary Cargill has appendicitis. Her sister was in touch, and she won't be back for a month. She might not be back this term. She will be lucky to sit her exams in June."

I was sympathetic for Mary, but I thought, 'she could have stopped could have that mad bitch Marianne from taking advantage of me when I was half asleep and very drunk, or at least revealed Marianne crept into me' Mary could be scarier than Kelly if provoked. Somehow the phrase, 'apart from all that did you enjoy it?' leapt into my mind. Before I could get a word out, Kelly waved her hand dismissively. I wonder from who she learned that.

"Why Joe, why? Did you just wait for an opportunity to impose yourself on poor Marianne, who drank too much?" Kelly's voice rose." Don't start telling me you were drunk and don't remember a thing. Marianne told me everything."

"Everything," I blurted out, "like how she…" but the dismissive gesture reappeared.

"I considered you a good guy with decent values who was putting his life together, building an education base. I could see you as a community leader, or a future Sinn

Fein politician. But you are a pathetic, immoral, cowardly excuse for a man. I never, ever want to see you again. GET OUT."

I tried to reply. Kelly turned her back, and I slumped towards the door. I was hoping she would ask me to stay on the one hand though dreading it if she did. When I got over home, I was at once relieved and regretful. I expected when Kelly and I broke up there might be emotion, and I would feel guilty. The relationship should not have ended like that, but my immediate sense was of relief. I reasoned Kelly was not serious about me, nor did she plan our future together.

I had no inkling Marianne fancied me. It was a response to her failed pursuit of the red-headed guy at the party. Instead of going into the house, I did what any self-respecting man does following grief from a woman and went to the pub. The effects of last night's drinking took its toll. I staggered home, more drunk than I ever had been in my life. I slept from about 11 o'clock on Saturday night to 5.00 pm on Sunday night. My Mother wisely said nothing. She had a fair idea Kelly and I split.

Next week Alec produced the England trip I hoped for before the party. Too damn late. I went to Birmingham, taking farm equipment via Cairnryan to farms near Dumfries. I drove the empty lorry down to Birmingham, which maddened Alec, because he couldn't get another contract from Southwest Scotland to the Midlands. I filled the lorry and went back to Preston, unloaded half the Birmingham cargo, and took on a new half load.

Waiting over-night in Liverpool to get the boat to Belfast meant seeing Maeve. We had only met twice since my release. We all knew she was seeing a Liverpool guy, Graham. He was a canny lad. He was a Liverpool FC supporter, and he said I must come back and go to Anfield with him. Graham worked for an insurance firm and was doing various exams to qualify as an Accountant. Like me, he worked out, after he left school, qualifications were important. He liked football and cars, so we got on well.

We went out to dinner and, to make a foursome, Maeve invited a close pal of hers, a Scouser called Angela. She was a nurse whose Mother was from Trinidad. She was a beautiful looking black girl and brilliant company. Nothing transpired between us except a brief kiss and cuddle. She was seeing a Doctor from the Hospital, not regularly. It is a Hospital tradition Doctors have first pick of the best-looking Nurses.

The public, you, and me, were always second in this part of the grand selection race! I was pleased to see Maeve, and that she was settled in a career and with Graham. We would meet in August at Eugene's ordination to the priesthood.

I went back to Belfast, van driving. I would prefer to be away from the city during the 'Twelfth Fortnight.' It was always a tense time in Northern Ireland.

The better-off Catholics headed to Donegal or Spain, the rest of us tried to survive the sense of intimidation and negativity hanging over the city.

I was heading up the Springfield Road towards Turf Lodge in a one ton flat-back full of bricks and arrived next to Fort Monagh Army base. I saw a crowd on the road.

The local denizens sallied forth to attack the base, a regular ritual, and they were well armed with stones, iron bars, hurley sticks but no petrol bombs, at least yet. I started a three-point turn to get out of there when they charged past me. They realised I was carrying a load of bricks. Two jumped on and threw bricks onto the road for their mates.

Before they nicked too many, a patrol of soldiers supported by RUC arrived to disperse them. I was in no-man's-land between the two. As the youths retreated, the army and police advanced. I sat there, unable to move while the two groups fought. The soldiers fired baton rounds and stones and bricks were hurled in their direction by their opponents. My cab door was opened, and I was hauled out and back down towards the base by a big cop. I thought if I timed it right, I could get my vehicle away and save the load, but before I could do anything, I was 'rescued.'

My would-be rescuer said, "Sit tight you."

He was put out by my assertion I had it under control, now I might lose the truck and my load. I am sure he was irritated, 'there's gratitude for you!' I appealed to the Army Officer standing nearby. The soldiers were Gordon Highlanders, the same regiment present when I was arrested on the Shore Road, but not the worst Scottish Regiment Belfast experienced.

I shouted, "tell me when you are going to charge, I can get the lorry away, and they will have less ammunition. Just make sure your guys don't shoot when I jump into the lorry."

The cop said, "Listen son, you just stay here."

The Army guy could see the advantage of the bricks being removed. He didn't fancy one of his soldiers jumping in the truck. He would have been an easy target if an IRA sniper took advantage of the melee. The officer barked orders into his radio. Two minutes later, the soldiers and the Police, led by yours truly, charged the crowd. I veered left and jumped into the cab, completing my turn, and headed back down the Springfield Road to safety.

It was years later when the humour surfaced of a former IRA detainee leading a British army and RUC charge against a crowd of Republican youths in Turf Lodge, just to safeguard a lorry load of bricks. I had not reckoned with a TV crew, or else film from the Army being given to TV, but it was featured on the late evening news. I didn't appear, but the Brewster's flat top did as I drove it away. Big John wanted to nominate me for employee of the year until I pointed out I might end up with a Belfast knighthood as an added but unwanted honour. A Belfast Knighthood is, 'you pick the night we bring the hood, bang bang.' Big John told Alex my actions reflected well on their appointing me. He doubted any other employee would have been so unfazed by the riot to have driven the truck to safety — he had a point.

I will gloss over Eugene's ordination in Dalgan except to say it was a happy McFaul event, though we were all conscious our Dad wasn't there. Maeve and Graham, Nuala, but not her partner, and I attended. The sad bit for my Mother was that Eugene was off to Brazil for two years. His second mass, a few days after the Ordination, was in St Peters Pro-Cathedral and the neighbours and far-flung relatives attended. The Brennan's from Coatbridge, Tommy, and Laura also came. I had such fond memories but not seen them since I was a wee boy. Tommy made me a Celtic supporter and any man who dispensed half-crowns as Tommy did was bound to be alright.

There was a meal afterwards. My sisters claimed, after a few drinks, I went around saying, "Ah ha, one of the McFaul boys made good at last. The other became a Priest!"

Just what devout people attending a celebratory Mass would find amusing! Maeve told me to cool it.

"It's just a wee joke," I moaned.

"Yes, and it might have been funny if you said it once and only to the younger ones," she hissed back.

My second year at Brewster's passed without incident. l was caught between the van driving and lorry driving. A driver from the Markets left and John appointed another Falls Road guy. I ended up being based at Boucher Road more and travelling further afield, this infuriated John.

There was a regular trip bringing farm equipment from Ballymena to Sligo, Galway area and around Limerick, I often stayed over and became friendly with a girl called Denise from Limerick. We had a quick fling, but I would never be around enough to give her a half decent social life. I gained two further 'O' levels and was into the second year of my OU Degree proper. There was a clock ticking in my mind. After two years at Brewster's, I had an employer's reference, four 'O' levels and an 'A' level, time for me to move across the water.

One Friday, in early September 1982, I went to the Tech to enrol for the second year of my 'A' level history and Kelly was standing near the door of the main building. Her eyes caught mine, and she smiled. I waved and hesitated, went over to speak to her. I could greet her with 'I have forgiven you for being angry because one of your friends took advantage of me,' but decided a toned-down approach would be proper! A' Hi, how are you? By the time I crossed the crowded room, Kelly was getting into a black taxi and driving away. I was satisfied with how my education was progressing. I still needed to complete the final year A level history, but I could concentrate on my Degree. Kelly and I needed a more civilised discussion. Undoubtedly, some grovelling would ensue, but also a better closure to our relationship.

On a Tuesday in October, I got home at the usual time, parked up and breezed into the house, hearing female voices coming from the wee kitchen. Gosh had Nuala come over home? She hadn't done that since I got back or a surprise trip home from Maeve. I leaned in the door with a big smile on my face. Our kitchen wouldn't fit three adults and I gaped.

It was Kelly, drying plates. She said 'Hi' as if we parted the earlier with an arrangement for her to visit.

Mum pushed us into the front room, and I sat down uneasily. Kelly mentioned she saw me at the Tech in an apologetic tone. She realised I was coming over to speak, but she was late for a meeting at the Advice Centre. This was interesting. The first night since she threw me out of the flat was beginning with Kelly apologising! My Mother brought in tea and biscuits. Kelly told Mum before I arrived, she could not stay for the evening meal.

I said to her. "I should apologise to you for..." What were the right words I should use to describe what happened between me and Marianne?

Kelly, of course, cut in, "Sleeping with my flatmate," she suggested.

I flushed and nodded. "I am sorry..." Kelly was entitled to her apology but was taking all this too cheerfully. She laughed.

"When Mary Cargill recovered, we spoke at the start of term. She knew, of course, we split. She wasn't keen on getting drawn in, but she said she heard Marianne go to you in my room."

There was a certain justice that Marianne didn't deserve to get off Scot free.

"Mary knew I was going to end our relationship, but I was leaving it until after the party. Marianne was privy to those discussions too."

Everybody was but me! The Saturday night drama's temperature might have been lower if she had mentioned it earlier. She wasn't sharing with Marianne next term.

Mary Cargill was travelling from home and the other Mary had moved in with her boyfriend, Kelly lived in a flat on the Lisburn Road.

I asked about her course, the newspaper, the Advice Centre, and her family.

"Not all of my family and friends consider you a total waste of space," she said in a reassuring tone of voice. The inference was most of them did.

It was the least intense conversation I ever had with Kelly. I drove her over to her flat in the old Escort. She asked about my work. I got a perfunctory peck on the cheek and that was that.

In November 1982, on one of by now, rare trips around West Belfast, I had an unpleasant experience. I finished delivering to various small businesses. These were contracts Alec wanted us to drop, and John insisted we keep, out of loyalty to old customers.

I came down the top of the Glen Road and spotted a roadblock ahead. It was manned by a group of guys in balaclavas armed only with hurleys. The IRA did this as a visible way to emphasise their claim of 'policing' the nationalist areas and I was in the past one of the 'blockers'.

Blocks targeted local 'ne'er-do-wells' rather than the security forces. The RUC would be informed by the patrolling helicopter and would drive up towards the roadblocks. Bins were sounded to give warning, and the guys would disappear into the alleyways and streets of the local housing estates. I encountered these sorts of street events often, they caused me much less anxiety than the

Army and RUC blocks. If a soldier had been killed from the Regiment stopping you, they could be brutal if given the remotest excuse. The RUC was not as unpredictable, but they possessed intelligence which was often outdated or inaccurate. There was also the haunting memory of the Shore Road incident, I pulled in as instructed. They asked where I was going, where I came from and what my business was. They instructed me to open the rear of the van. That could be more sinister. It was possible they were looking for a van to carry a device. I had been on those kinds of fishing trips. But even if that were the case, they would say, 'We know where you live make myself scarce.'

As I stood at the rear of the van, I was conscious one guy standing at the side of the road was staring at me through his mask. It was Padraig O'Dade. He walked over, grabbed me, knocked me down and started kicking me, shouting 'the bastard's a tout.' In comradely fashion, his mates lined up to get in a few kicks.

"What are we going to do with him?" One guy asked. By this time, I rolled myself into a ball to limit the damage from the kicks and protect my head. The last time this happened to me was in the Maze. Prison Officers in disguise attacked us after one of their colleagues was shot. We knew to lie in a way which limited the damage, but it only worked if the 'kickers' were not trying to kill you.

A voice commanded, "STOP"

I looked up past the ugly grinning face of my old sparring partner O'Dade. He removed his balaclava. I suspect he wanted me to be sure I knew it was him. The guy who shouted, as far as I could judge, was older and in charge, but I could not see his face. Other guys, but not O' Dade, explained I was a tout. He, the older guy, asked my name, which meant nothing to him, but I needed to move this on, or I would be taken away for interrogation.

I spoke, "So, who claims I'm a tout except big nose O' Dade?" The latter scowled.

The guy in charge said. "Anyone else know this guy?" meaning me; "or anything about him?"

They had been happy kicking me two minutes before, but they agreed they did not know why apart from the 'tout' accusation. The guy in charge scratched his head, unsure what he should do. Time was passing, and the RUC would soon be arriving. He asked, "Why did you call him Big Nose?"

O'Dade's nose, while not huge, was prominent where the bones had not knitted following my butt and kicks a few years ago. Not that big a nose but a nose you might stare at fascinated by the imperfection but trying not to focus on it.

"I was in the cage with him," I replied.

"Did you do that to his nose?"

I nodded. By this time, O'Dade was subdued, and the rest were shifting nervously. Too much time was passing.

Their Commander needed to decide. Did he let a 'tout' go and an enquiry would result and disciplinary action?

If they hung around much longer and any of his guys were caught, he would also face an enquiry and disciplinary action, not much of a choice. I could tell he blamed O'Dade for the whole thing. I chose then to play my trump card. "If you have any reservations about me, you can ask. "And here I mentioned the name of the quartermaster who attended my disciplinary hearing after the original incident with O'Dade.

Again, I reserve the right to not mention his name. The incident now, as I pointed out; 'Immersed in legend as the 'Battle of O'Dade's nose,' like Rourke's Drift, but with more blood!'

The older guy showed his teeth under his hood, so he was smiling. I guess not an O'Dade fan. I was told to go and as I got into my van, Police poured out from unmarked vehicles and an Army patrol materialised. The roadblock party scattered in lots of different directions.

I hoped O'Dade would be caught, I would not have born witness against him to the authorities but to another tribunal. The blows he administered to me might mitigate the 'Battle of O'Dade's nose,' and if we were to meet again, his grudge might diminish. Not much hope of that.

Someday I was going to have to face up to the feud.

An RUC man growled. "Wait there."

After a few minutes, the Army patrol re-emerged. Their only capture was a familiar older guy. The rest scattered to the four winds.

The Police brought the guy over." Is this the man who stopped your vehicle?" They said he was a leading local Republican.

"No," I said, "Never saw him before in my life, nothing personal, mate," I added, nodding in the prisoner's direction," but they were a lot younger."

The RUC let him go reluctantly. As I watched him leave, Without thinking it through and I later regretted it, I muttered to one of the RUC that I recognised one man on the roadblock as a fellah named O'Dade.

Quick as a flash, he asked. "Which O'Dade?"

"He is called Paddy, Patrick... I am not sure."

He nodded and said, "Thanks." Payback time for the beating and I thought no more of it.

The RUC took my details, phoned John O' Sullivan and allowed me to return to the depot. Once more a conquering hero, albeit one sporting a blackening eye and a few bruised ribs. Eileen fussed over me while Maureen made welcome tea and Jim phoned Alec demanding I should receive an award from the company and a bonus given it was the second company vehicle I saved.

Twice was enough, it was time to leave. I told my mother after New Year about both incidents.

I had not mentioned either to her. "I need to get out of Belfast. "I told my Mother. She was alarmed enough to insist I should leave as soon as possible. Back at work, I arranged to see Alec. I told him I was intending to leave Northern Ireland as soon as possible. John knew this and he must have mentioned it to Alec, so it was no surprise. He looked at me very deliberately, took off his glasses and cleaned them. I had not seen him before without his glasses, made him look younger.

"Would it be possible for me to transfer within the company to the London or Birmingham depots?"

"Offhand Joe, I don't know about vacancies. The company has an excellent reputation as employers, which results in minimum turnover." Alec added, "Give me a few days to make enquiries."

The following week, he phoned and invited me over late in the day. The office was empty.

He began, "Joe, I hoped when John retired in a couple of years, you would take over the Falls depot. It has potential if the community calmed down. You could get our integration developed because you have worked both sides of our customer model."

So that's what it was, a customer model. Christ, somebody was planning the company's activities! Try being around locked docks at 1.00 am when no messages about a delivery got through and drivers slept in their cabs all night.

Alec continued, "I spoke to a partner, told him about your heroics over the two incidents and how you saved our vehicles. I know the Glasgow depot, its Manager and most of the guys working there. Unless you are set on going South, We believe you would fit in and settle in Glasgow."

I needed time to consider Glasgow and promised to get back to him later. I phoned Maeve, who was aware I was moving to the mainland. She was disappointed I would not be nearer her, but suggested I contact Tommy Brennan in Coatbridge for his advice. I had not seen him since Eugene's ordination, but he and his wife were friendly with Maeve after they attended Dad's funeral. When they were over in Belfast visiting relatives, Tommy called with Mum and his wife Laura phoned her from time to time. Anyway, Maeve called to say Tommy had invited me to base myself with them in Coatbridge until I was settled.

The next week I told Alec I would go to Glasgow; I phoned Tommy, and he assured me of a warm Irish welcome in Coatbridge. I packed my stuff and had a tearful parting from my Mother. This was difficult, sad for her, but she was relieved I would be safer.

"You have put an awful lot behind you son, a fresh start is the right way forward."

Too right. I loaded my car and, armed with Tommy's directions, went to Larne, over to Stranraer and up the A77 towards Glasgow. I got lost in East Kilbride, as you do, but finally made it to Tommy and Laura.

## Reflection Dolores (Kelly)

The time I first met Joe, he was annoying, a typical male chauvinist. After a while I found I liked him. I was impressed he had been in the Maze. I admired how he got into Education. He could speak well, despite being quiet, though he was witty, in a dry way. Joe could have a political future in the 'Armed Struggle.'

What happened with Marianne disappointed me. She was aware the relationship was finishing. just not when. I knew her. She never kept a boyfriend. They passed through the flat like I don't know what. She claimed she fancied Joe, but she only fancied him because he was with me. After the party the other fellah she pursued took fright and escaped. Mary told me Marianne went to my room, Joe did not go to hers.

Why did I want to finish with Joe? Well, he lost interest in the Cause. He was only interested in extracting himself. That meant leaving everybody else stuck in the Northern Ireland quagmire. Joe might become a Social Studies Teacher in a Secondary School, if he was lucky, or a minor clerk in the Civil Service if he wasn't.

# Chapter 10

# SCOTLAND AND A CHANGE OF CAREER

I may not have understood the ins-and-outs of grief and mourning then, but I missed my Dad. He died when I was in the false bubble of the Maze. After I came home, it was as if I expected to see him about the house. In Coatbridge, Tommy wanted to talk about my Dad a lot, and it was emotional as we talked about him as a young man. We also chatted about the girls. The family position was Nuala doing a 'line,' with a fellah from Ardoyne and doing well in her career. The Brennan's wouldn't have a problem with her relationship with a Police Officer, Laura would struggle with him being divorced. Anyway, our family approach was based on a 'need to know' principle. They were aware I was involved with the IRA. There is something very 'Belfast' and Catholic that I could talk about my time in the IRA, but not mention my sister was living with a divorced Policeman! One thing I would have to get used to is the different perception of the Police in Scotland, although the impact of the Miner's Strike was to change that. The only one of Tommy and Laura's children still at home was their youngest Gabriel, named after my Dad, who was a student at Strathclyde University and stayed in the Halls of Residence.

The Brennan's were in regular contact with both Maeve and Eugene. Laura was a kind person but also a devout woman and my mass attendance went through the roof in the four months I stayed with them, much to my Mother's delight. I struggled with my religion through teenage angst, and a lack of forgiveness for God being posted missing when Ramie was killed. Someone was to blame, anybody but me.

During my first weekend, Tommy took me and Gabriel to my first match at Celtic Park. Not only was it my first time seeing Celtic, I sang all the songs, of course, but it was my first time at a match with a crowd of over fifty thousand. Tommy suggested I phone Alistair McDonald, my new boss, and I did on the Thursday. He asked after Alec and instructed me to report to the Cambuslang Depot. 12 miles from Coatbridge, on Monday at 8.00 am. On Sunday afternoon, I drove to the depot, giving Tommy and Laura space and taking the opportunity to familiarise myself with the route. Alec and I discussed whether I should mention my imprisonment with Mr McDonald. Alec counselled me against it. "You are going there because you have a fine two-year record as a company employee, and because I recommended you. If something which creates an issue arises, Alastair is off the hook. He can point back to me, better that way."

I agreed to say nothing. The next morning, I arrived at the Depot just after 7.30am. A security man at the gate advised me to park behind two massive warehouses. He pointed out the driver's lounge or 'saloon,' as he called it. There were three older guys sitting around on settees reading the papers. They greeted me in a friendly enough fashion. Later, more drivers drifted into the room. At the Falls Depot, there were four drivers, ten at Boucher Road, but Cambuslang had 50 drivers. They weren't all at the same time. A few were away on weekend trips, others were abroad. These drivers were Glaswegians who vied with each other as who was the biggest comedian.

The banter started. "So, you are from Ireland, North or South?"

"North."

"Ah, so you are one of us."

I was from the North but not one of him. This was well received by some, not others, but it was all banter.

In Northern Ireland, in those rare mixed workplaces, you never ask someone about their religion. Identifying signs were where people lived or their school or their name.

It was a topic avoided in public, but these guys just shouted it around in mock abusive tones with no real hint of hostility towards each other.

For a guy with a sheltered upbringing about religion, it was an eye opener. A small, rotund figure stuck his head around the door. He was wearing a dark suit, shirt and tie, management. The volume dropped. He surveyed what can best be described as the carnage that was the drivers rest room with dismay.

"Is that lazy wee sod Douglas in there? I'm not coming in," he added. "I might catch something."

There was a chorus of boos and one guy shouted out, "Now come on Ally, if you were married to that wee honey, you wouldn't be in early either." cue laughs.

"Don't call me Ally, hmm, I will pass on to the good Mrs McDonald your views on her not making it to the top of the honey stakes shall I, McLeod?"

This led to more laughs. I was sitting beside McLeod and there was a sharp intake of breath from him. I was to learn Mrs McDonald, who had no role or authority within the company, used her status as an Edinburgh born wife of the Depot Manager, to reduce to bits and pieces any Glaswegian malcontent who called her husband Ally. He also never referred to his wife as anything other than 'Mrs McDonald.' Alastair called me to come out and shouted back over his shoulder.

"Has the Union called strike action? Have you lot any intention of doing any work today?"

Grumbles from the masses about late night deliveries, the company didn't allow a proper Union, and gripes about failure to pay overtime were met with, "If you used the company routes, you wouldn't get lost, and if there was a proper Union, I couldn't fire at will whichever one of your faces I don't like."

We walked away to the sound of applause. It was to the company offices, a two-storey old but solid building, a far cry from Boucher Road's Portacabins. On the way through the offices, I was introduced to Debbie, the full-time receptionist We went to the general admin office where time sheets and expenses claims were to be submitted "ON TIME" Alistair and the supervisor, Erica, chorused together. On to Accounts, which dealt with invoices and customers. When I entered the Planner's office, there were three guys and a woman. Their role was to allocate jobs and price contracts. The real money was made in long distance, but the firm did a lot of business in Central Scotland.

I followed him to his office. His PA, Jane, offered to make me a coffee, and hissed in my ear, when Mr Mac Donald headed on into his office, "Don't let the drivers con you into calling him Ally. He hates it, but Alastair is ok."

I went into the boss's office. It was a large room comprising a huge old table and twelve chairs. At the top was a big wooden desk, behind which Alistair was enveloped in a massive swivel chair. He motioned me to one seat at the table and he began.

"I worked for Alec Peabody twenty years ago. I was his number two for four years and he covered for me here when I was off with my heart attack. Whatever I learned about management, I learned from him. He holds you in high regard, which got you in the door. But your progress in this branch is down to how well you do, how efficient and how reliable you are. Also, how well you work with other employees even, God help us, that unruly crew of drivers. I am trying to transform this place and change the culture. All new employees go through a period of induction. The one group who resists the change is the drivers. Only two other drivers completed the induction, they joined in the past three years. The rest resist change."

No surprise, I know drivers only too well. As he drew breath, I wanted to say something, but an intelligent question would not surface, so I complimented him on his office.

"Ah yes, it's the old company boardroom."

"Was this depot a company?"

"Yes, they had five depots in Scotland. They were taken over by a UK company from Luton, which was acquired by a Hong Kong-based conglomerate.

God knows who the Board is now or where they are based or who owns the company. It has strong and developing links with similar companies all over the world. We get rebranded regularly, it costs an absolute fortune."

Now all this information beyond the English takeover was new to me. Alastair added, he was prone to do this, showing an in-depth knowledge when he came over as disinterested in detail.

"Of course, you are doing an Open University Degree in Economics, so all this will be meat and drink to you."

I nodded sagely. The door knocked, and a slight figure with reddish hair stuck his head in the door. He looked to be two years older than me, walked around the table, nodded affably at me, and shook hands. First handshake, I noted. Alastair said," Ah Gavin, meet Joe from Belfast, who is our latest recruit. He will go out with you for a week. He does all the drives from Wednesday with you riding shotgun. He has been on the one-dollar tour with me. Give him the ten dollar one and put him wise to the real ins-and-outs of the place."

As we went to walk out, a figure crashed through the door. What a sight. He was average height, Asian in appearance, and hadn't shaved for a few days. He appeared quite striking at first, but when I got closer to him, his suit needed a dry clean, his tie was undone, and coffee stains on his shirt. Was he a rough sleeper, someone who fell on hard times and tried to get a few bob from Alastair.

The latter looked at him and spoke. "Well timed Karim. This is Joe, our latest recruit from Ireland."

The guy looked at me, gave a perfunctory nod, then said. "Sorry, Alistair got tied up at home."

He had a home! His accent sounded South of England, not cockney, but well spoken.

He turned back to me and gazed in amazement while Alastair said, "This is Karim Jatri, he is my deputy, so anything you need just ask Karim."

Gavin propelled me out the door. As we left, he and Jane exchanged looks and Gavin made a motion of cupping one of his hands together and taking a swig. Jane nodded, but neither said a thing. Gavin took me through the offices at a more leisurely pace. He didn't do formal introductions but stopped at a few desks of people with whom he was friendly, and we chatted. They all had Irish stories, or relatives or holidays there

We returned to the driver's lounge. Gavin got his paperwork, so we jumped into his cab and drove to Aberdeen. The first week was like that, Inverness, Carlisle, Port of Leith, and Friday was St Andrews, a delivery to the Old Course Hotel. We parked, went for a dander around the town and grabbed lunch in a cafe. I loved St Andrews. It made an instant impression on me.

Within the week, Gavin briefed me about the personalities in the Depot, who to avoid, among the drivers who wanted a new drinking partner and who was the right person to see about what, as opposed to who, was the designated person. He said Alistair was a good gaffer, and Jane, the PA, a decent sort, the supervisor, Erica who ran the general office, could be an absolute nightmare.

"Under no account, allow yourself to be alone with Debbie, the receptionist, at the end of a night out if she has had a drink." He warned.

He then described two Christmas Parties where he ended up alone with Debbie, the second one just after he became engaged, what he revealed of the first Christmas 'do', he should have seen the second one coming.

We got on well. He married Lynn three months previously. They lived together for a few years but now intended to start a family. In return for the information he gave, he wanted my story.

I suspected Jane and others we met in the offices were curious about the new driver. Gavin acknowledged as much. That was fair enough, but certain territory I wouldn't cross. I talked about my family, football, mentioning I was a late convert to education.

Mention of studying would lead to banter from the drivers. I reckoned, as a diversion, which would be a price worth paying to avoid getting drawn into drinking circles or talking about my knowledge of the 'Troubles.' Over the years, drivers would explain to me how easy it would be to sort the troubles in Ireland. British Government propaganda allowed them to argue with no recourse to facts or evidence that the problem would be solved by a lot of killing. This was an odd way to bring peace. Funny how many people in a country proud of its own history cannot grasp the significance of another country's history.

The more mundane information would be the best currency in the gossip market that was the Cambuslang Depot. I was well prepared. Did I have a partner? Was I gay? Was I running from a failed marriage or romance? Tell all. I mentioned about being in a relationship with Kelly and about it not working out. I said I fell in love when I was about 17.

"Didn't we all" Gavin interjected.

I told him I didn't take to the Deputy Manager one bit.

"Ah Karim," he went, "well, there's a story there."

He was born in North London. His parents were well-to-do Pakistani shop keepers and owned a dozen shops. They set up a property business, buying and refurbishing houses they bought at auctions. Karim's elder brother took over the property business. It was intended Karim would manage the shops. Karim put off this plan by pursuing higher education, he went to Manchester University. If there were any abuses Karim didn't indulge at Uni, they must have been invented after he left.

"Apart from being almost an alcoholic, using drugs and not being able to keep it in his trousers, Karim is alright."

That was a peculiar recommendation. Gavin explained Karim was married to the beautiful daughter of a Ugandan Asian immigrant who had been a judge there before Adi Amin expelled the Asians. Karim was terrified of his wife. Gavin suggested she only joined him in Scotland because her father insisted.

"But never forget, if you have any problem, just go to Karim. I don't know of anything large or small he can't sort. Alastair relies on him in a crisis which is why he tolerates the state he is often in. He is approachable and very bright."

There was one other thought I wished to sew with Gavin.

"I am living with an aunt and uncle. I want to move, get a room of my own, if you hear of anything, let me know. I intend to save and buy a flat in a couple of years.

Gavin and I were football fans and persuaded me to play again in unusual circumstances. He had a brother and a sister; his brother Callum was 22 and had a learning disability. As he grew older, Gavin's parents were determined Gavin and his sister would not end up having to look after Callum full time. They arranged, or lobbied might be better, for him to be admitted to a Council residential hostel in Motherwell. Callum was distressed when he first went there, but after a number of months settled. The family's plan was he should live in familiar surroundings and when his parents were no longer alive it would be his home. He attended a Day Centre in the town and went with Gavin to see their local team, Motherwell. Callum could be distressed by the noise.

"Noise at Motherwell, you mean the sound of the sweetie papers being unwrapped."

I could not resist it. Oh, how Gavin laughed or didn't. Despite the Celtic Rangers thing, the most deranged football supporters in Scotland were Motherwell fans, although Greenock Morton ones could give them a run for their money.

Gavin, Callum, and other hostel residents went to a nearby High School on a Monday night and played football on school pitches with the approval of the school and the lady janitor. They obtained the key to the changing room from her.

Younger staff members would join them if they were on duty. Later they came in their own time. Word got around the day centre and a couple of Social Workers brought five or six guys they were supervising. Gavin said if I was free on a Monday night, I should join them. Not all the residents were at the same level due to their disabilities.

They spent all of Tuesday trying to impress the staff or their girlfriends at the centre on their football prowess! Most in the hostel were brought up in institutional care, long-stay hospitals. The move into the community expanded their worlds, but they could revert to the institutional culture. Callum and two others were brought up by their parents and found the young men from the Hospital background intimidating. They could be quite physical.

Our Monday sessions began with shooting goal, which was focussed on the more disabled guys having time to score goals. All the 'staff,' we were all staff to them, even a volunteer like me, played. A group of the abler residents sat it out until this opening bit finished. They didn't enter the spirit that everyone should get something out of the evening and were waiting for the proper match to begin. The two top dogs were wee Geordie and Angus. Geordie was a pacey wee forward with skill and courage, while

Angus was a big bruiser of a midfielder come defender. Both lived at home and attended the Centre. Prior to turning sixteen, they spent many years in a long stay Hospital. They stayed there from about the age of 10 or 11 because they were too difficult for their parents to manage. Simply how things used to be. When they became old enough to claim their own benefits, their parents relented and brought them home.

Angus was a tough character. He spent his formative years fighting with his three older brothers. In the Hospital, he could handle himself. Geordie's back story I do not know. Angus and Geordie had a history on the wards. This transferred to the Day Centre and to our football games. Fights between them broke out. At other times, they could be friendly. If they were picking the teams, they always chose each other first, even ahead of 'staff', many of whom were talented players. Eventually, they would fall out, a fight would have to be stopped. Geordie was emotional, difficult to get to disengage, Angus tended to calm down first.

Those Monday nights were among my happiest days. The guys with Down's Syndrome were overweight. Each one needed to 'get a goal' they could brag about to their friends at the Centre. When we were playing the matches proper, they would run around shouting for the ball, encouraging their pals. Although the athleticism was beyond them, they loved being involved, telling staff and relatives they played football on a Monday night. We drove the boys back to the hostel and were invited in for a coffee, later for soup and a pizza.

One issue was preventing those who didn't go to the football and who had their tea earlier getting seconds. I learned if you were brought up in an institution, access to food was important. The hostel was managed by Jack Smith. He was a legendary figure in Lanarkshire, Learning Disability circles. Jack was about 5'9", ruddy complexion, enjoyed his dram and he could multi-task like no one else. Whether it was overseeing a resident washing their hair, bellowing a menu to the staff, making the tea, and relaying a message to a Social Worker on the phone, he did it all at the same time. He ruled the hostel on a combination of charisma and humour.

I lived with the Brennan's three months longer than expected. One night as we left the hostel Gavin, and I were chatting.

"Lynn is pregnant. We have a two bedroomed flat with a boxroom for the nursery. We are petty strapped for cash. Would you be interested in moving into our spare room?"

I jumped at it and stayed for two years, including the stress around wee Bella's birth. Do you know what it is like to sleep with earplugs in or creep out for an early shift at 5.30 am while your landlady paddles past you in a nightie covered in breast milk? I shared the kitchen and the bathroom, had my tea out most nights and went to study in the Mitchell Library in Glasgow City Centre.

I was asked to be Bella's Godfather, a role I shared with Callum. On occasions, I went to the Brennan's at weekends, Tommy and I still went to Celtic together when I was not driving abroad or down in Liverpool. I did a terrific deal on the car. The battered Escort was replaced with a six-month-old Cortina. The new Sierra came out, so I made what I thought was an excellent deal. There were only seven thousand miles on it, belonged to a salesman. It was in mint condition and cheap for a car, less than a year old.

I remained with Gavin and Lynn for two years, becoming a dab hand as a babysitter. I also increased my income. One Friday I received a call from Gavin to say he was doing a 'sleep over' at the hostel because staff were involved in industrial action. Jack asked if I could come in for the Sunday night. I was happy to, as it got me out of the way of the Douglas family. Bella was two months and up a lot at night. Gavin was a friend who was reliable and sensible, but we were not close like Ramie and me.

I had not thought about Ramie for ages. When he came into my mind, I was at first morose, missing our closeness. Then I got angry with him. Why hadn't he just done what I did, followed orders? Mind you, I would still have left Belfast. We would have drifted apart. But when I was visiting the family, we would have met up, sank a few pints, reminisced about us as lads, laughed at our daftness. From the time I spent with Carmel, I knew she didn't resent our friendship; she recognised he needed to move on to…. to a more adult life. We would have talked about Carmel and his kids; I would have shared my Scottish experiences. I guess Ramie was just Ramie, a quick shot often paid off for him…... just not that time, on Leeson Street.

The industrial action was only on weekends. It was not about the hostel but wider Council issues. Jack lived in an adjacent property and staff came in at 7.00 am, easiest £30.00 I ever made. Jack could pay me as a sessional worker, and I did it at least once a month. Jack said if I came in on Saturday or Sunday at 3.00 pm, which ever night I was sleeping over, I could be paid for a full shift plus the sleep over allowance. It went towards my payments on the new car.

Two or three years passed, football, played and watched, accompanied by much studying. Lynn couldn't figure me out, as with Carmel, she never once produced a girlfriend or a cousin I should date, very telling about me. I saved for a deposit on a modern two-bedroomed flat in Dennistoun, near Gavin and Lynn. I moved in on the second week in April 1984. Two bedrooms, it was as well there were fitted wardrobes because the spare bedroom would only take a single bed and a bedside cabinet. The flat came with white goods supplied, smaller than the ones you would buy in, say Curry's. My Mother insisted I buy a new bed, mattress, and bedding. I bought a double bed, no harm in hoping! One night after the game, we were sitting in the hostel and my new flat was raised. I mentioned I bought a bed. Jack suggested, "Joe, if you have no problem with second-hand furniture, there is a store with furniture donated for an earlier Hospital closure programme."

I picked up a decent settee and matching easy chair, a coffee table, and a kitchen table with three kitchen chairs, four would have been better, but one was broken, A Social

Worker said his wife's Mother bought a new TV and I would be welcome to her old one if I collected it. It was a colour TV and sat well on that coffee table.

Welcome news from Liverpool, a new generation of McFaul's. Graham and Maeve had a little daughter, Charlotte (Lottie). Life was quiet. I enjoyed driving.

My degree was nearing its completion, and I wanted to see how I could use it. I briefly dated a girl who was friendly with a woman in the general office, but there wasn't much spark between us. It just suited us both for the summer.

I was planning to go to Belfast because Eugene had returned home, and Maeve was visiting too. Just when my life is on an even keel, something rears up and puts the kibosh on my tranquillity.


In Belfast Padraig O'Dade went to see his cousin Dermot, who was planning to buy a car in New Barnsley, Padraig claimed to know about car engines. His Auntie Mona told Padraig, "Our Dermot will be back in twenty minutes. Do you want a cup of tea?"

She always felt sorry for those four boys, a waster of a father and their Mother dying a few years ago. Padraig went into the living room and supped the tea.

An Irish News was lying on the settee. He read the football, the GAA sports, and the betting, still no sign of Dermot. Padraig read the front political pages, our ones,' he surmised, 'are as bad as their ones.'

As he skimmed through the other pages, his eye was caught by a photo of a family group around a Priest and the heading 'The McFaul family of Sevastopol Street welcome Father Eugene back from Brazil.' The photo was taken from Fr Eugene's ordination a couple of years ago but there was the hated Joe McFaul smiling out with an arm around each of his sisters, always pretending to be everybody's pal. Padraig was livid. First the incident in the Maze McFaul caused, then informing on him after the roadblock. He overheard a cop say the driver recognised him. Also, the trouble he got into encouraging his colleagues to give McFaul a kicking. 'I hate Joe McFaul.' he said to himself and resolved he would 'get' McFaul.

One Wednesday in October 1984, I was in the workshop as there was a problem with my lorry. I was due to go to Inverness. Alastair regarded any fault with a lorry as being the drivers. I was going to start and finish late with no overtime. A message from the general office said there was a phone call for me. I never got calls. I went upstairs and took the phone.

"Hello," a female voice said, "Is that Joe McFaul?"

"Yes," I replied, mystified.

"This is Vicky Campbell of the Sunday." mentioning one of Scotland's leading Sunday tabloids. "I understand you were imprisoned for atrocities when you were in the IRA in Belfast? We are running a story on Sunday, and I wished to give you the opportunity to comment?"

I went weak at the knees and hung up. Jane was standing beside me, "Bad news Joe, are you alright, here, grab a seat?"

I collapsed into a chair. Everything was spinning around me about my new life in Scotland, the Brennan's who knew a bit, Gavin, Alastair, and Jack who know nothing. My colleagues were all going to read about me and "atrocities." What atrocity? Was my entire world built on a lie? I turned to Jane, "I need to see Alastair, it's urgent."

"Right, I will see how his meeting is going and bring you a coffee."

She came back with a mug of coffee and said the meeting would last awhile and disappeared down the corridor. She returned, took my arm, and said Karim wanted to see me. I just let myself be led into Karim's office.

Gavin described Karim as a problem solver. I changed my mind about him. I observed how he dealt with disputes between drivers and the office, or the planners and also between customers and the firm. Any of us in the chain could get something wrong. It was known that with larger problems, Alistair used Karim as his first and last line of defence. He was a fixer. Gavin heard, via Jane, Karim's wife read the riot act and telling him unless he sharpened up, she and the children would return to London. She would make sure the wrath of the judge was directed his way. Karim liked Glasgow and being 400 hundred miles from his controlling parents and his intimidating father-in-law. It resulted in a much sprucer, more sober, and reliable Karim.

When I went in, he motioned me to one of two soft chairs beside the small conference table in his office. I muttered something about 'trouble at home.' I meant Ireland, but I didn't want to say any more. We weren't close, but I respected him.

He began, "Joe, I have no intention of prying into personal grief. If you can assure me this has nothing that will impact on the firm, we can leave it."

It was going public at the weekend. Adverse publicity had implications for my employers. It was easier to talk to a relative stranger. There were no other agendas. I told Karim about the phone call. He was listening intently but said nothing. I gave him a potted history of Ramie and me, the various IRA operations, and the outcome, including the 4-year sentence.

I told him about my time at the Belfast branch and stated I was not involved with the organisation since my release in April 1980.

Throughout this, Karim sat in silence listening, said nothing, and then he fired questions at me. "Why has this come up now?" "Is there someone in Belfast with a grudge against you?" "Who passed the information to a Scottish Sunday newspaper?" Why?" "What was the atrocity?"

"That's the weirdest thing about the allegations. I was not involved in any atrocity." I asserted.

The organisation would have changed, and the current players would not know or else remember anything about someone as insignificant as me, who was only active during 1975/76. The only name he could drag out of me who might hold a personal grudge was Padraig O'Dade. I told him about Padraig and the O'Dades.

"Why would O'Dade do it now? Is there anything you or your family have done which might attract publicity now?"

"Nothing." I repeated 'nothing' twice more. Then I remembered.

"Well, about a week ago, my Mother phoned. She mentioned that the Irish News, the main nationalist daily newspaper, carried a splash on Eugene's return from Brazil. There was a picture of his ordination. The whole family was in it, including me. Before I got drunk, though, she didn't say that."

He probed further. "Would this guy O'Dade have access to the newspaper?"

"Yes. "I replied with more confidence than I felt, I wasn't sure O'Dade could even read.

Karim sat back. We must have sat in silence for ten minutes. He phoned an acquaintance somewhere in the media, or was it the police, anyway he chatted to him. He told me to bring my chair around to his desk, gave me a notepad and pen, and instructed, "Listen to the conversation I am going to have with the Newspaper, scribble a note to correct me if anything I say makes little sense."

I watched him in action, a master class. He got hold of Vicky Campbell, introduced himself, though I could not make out what name he gave but heard him say he was an advocate acting on behalf of Joe McFaul who would be today seeking an interdict to prevent the paper publishing a foul and scurrilous story about his client.

"Though between you and me, I hope you publish the story." I winced.

"Because this McFaul chappie,"

I winced again at 'chappie,'

"--Seems a decent cove, and he will make a considerable amount of money from this, your money. Not only is the story false in every respect, but you are putting my client's life at risk with para-military groups in Northern Ireland."

I gave him a thumbs up and he pursued this line.

"I will hold you, and your paper, responsible for any threats or violence my client is subject to. You and the paper, not my client, will become the next story."

He adopted a more reasonable tone. "Can you tell me who your informant was?"

Vicky Campbell was not for backing down and refused to disclose her sources.

Karim continued. "I understand that, but if it's one Padraig O'Dade. I suggest you check the source and indeed the whole O'Dade family of Ballymurphy. You will have colleagues in Northern Ireland who have links with the RUC, and I recommend you contact them. Anyway, can you tell me the nature of the atrocity my client was allegedly involved in? If there was any truth in it and we refute my client's involvement in any atrocity, again, your colleagues in Northern Ireland and the RUC would have plenty of information.

It is a matter for you and the paper, but my client would prefer not to have the publicity because of the risk you would create for him. Good day Ms McClure."

Karim hung up, impressively.

Karim knew the paper was burnt by some fake stories from tip-offs and these ended up in Court. They had to check their facts. He told me to go for a walk and come back later. He would get a replacement for my run or rearrange the delivery. I thanked him. He nodded and moved on to another problem. Karim was a risk taker. He said he was advocating for me, but mentioning advocate and 'interdict,' implied he was my lawyer. That could have come back to bite.

Later, I came back to the office. We agreed he shouldn't phone back pretending to be the advocate, so I phoned Ms Campbell. She was in a meeting but passed a on message saying they were consulting with sources in Belfast and, if I wanted to issue a statement, to contact her the following day. Karim's advice put the ball in their court and if they were checking it, he believed it would go away and it did. This experience marked a high and a low for me in my time with the company. The euphoria, when it vanished, took as much out of me as the devastation when it surfaced.

I thanked Karim, he grunted, "Ireland, compared with Kashmir, a doddle."

No idea what he meant, but I will always be grateful for the speed and effectiveness of Karim's response. He was not a man for the safe option. One other disturbing issue was my Mother said on the phone a few weeks later a friend of mine, who was in the Maze with me, called to say he wanted to get in touch.

"He said his name was Patrick, seemed a friendly lad from further up the road. He heard you worked for

Brewster's, but when he contacted the firm, they wouldn't or couldn't give a forwarding address."

She didn't give my address, but said I was in the Glasgow Branch of Brewster's. O'Dade saw my photograph at our Eugene's ordination. I was going to have to deal with the Padraig O'Dade problem, although I didn't know how it would end. One thing for sure: it was not going away. The grudge was more personal and intense than it should have been. I had a contact, an acquaintance who was still active and close to the leadership in Ballymurphy. He told me after the roadblock incident, O'Dade was lifted. I guess O'Dade assumed, correctly, I grassed on him. Apart from that little reminder of Belfast, events moved on in Scotland.

## Reflection Karim

I didn't know Joe well during his time in our depot. He was well liked by the other drivers, but not especially popular. When folk were going on a night out, you were pleased he was in the company, but he wasn't the first person you invited. Of course, he was studying hard for his degree, which I admired. Without being disparaging, it wasn't easy for a guy with his background to get into higher education. I missed a lot of lectures at Manchester and did the minimum reading for tutorials, yet I got a 2-1 and with a little more effort it would have been a First. Joe always held himself back and I, who knew him hardly at all, found out why.

# Chapter 11

# RESURRECTION

Jack and I discussed the possibility of me going into Social Care a few times. The hours weren't attractive, with evening and weekend shifts. The pay was poor, but with my degree imminent, I would have career opportunities. He got me a Regional Council application form which had 1974 legislation covering offences, including possession of firearms and terrorism. I told him.

"Jack, I was in the IRA in Belfast. I served four years in prison."

Then it was his turn.

"I was in the Argyll and Sutherland Highlanders, then I came into Social Work. I did two tours in Ireland, near Crossmaglen. It was a grim experience. I lost comrades. All behind me, I've moved on. Is it behind you?"

I admit, I saw this career crashing and burning in flames before it started. I told Jack the rest of my story and he was impressed. Whatever my political beliefs and how they were expressed, my life was changing. I will always be grateful to Jack. He could have walked away. He owed me nothing. But he sought advice from a senior figure at District Headquarters, and I was advised to submit the form. There would have an interview at Regional headquarters in Glasgow to assess my suitability as a

Council employee. If I passed this, a further interview would be held at District level for a post in the hostel Jack managed. Jack was required to put in a formal report about me based on the three years he knew me.

The whole bureaucracy appeared designed to keep me out. Anyhow, I went for the interview. There were two senior managers from Social Work and a representative from the Legal Department. They gave me a grilling, but no blows to the head were administered. I was up front about my complete story. They didn't ask at any point about my current political beliefs but focused on my understanding that Council employees had to adhere to the Law of Scotland. I learned Scotland possessed its own legal system, which I did not know, though I knew Northern Ireland had a separate system from the mainland. Bang goes the segment of my Degree on the Legal System of England and Wales. There is a clue, if I had looked for it. They told me, if I was appointed, there might be a special insert in my contract.

The Regional meeting concluded with even the Council Solicitor friendly. They didn't keep me waiting long. Five days later, I was told I could go forward for an interview. I met one of the Senior Social Work blokes at a seminar a few years later and he remembered me. He said, the year I was approved, there was a guy who did 12 years for murder when he was 18. We both proved valuable and committed workers. He went on to say the Region needed to practice what it preached about rehabilitation. The District interview was a doddle. Jack wanted me. I put in my notice to Brewster's, nice send off with a meal and the pub, avoided Debbie, just, and started a Social Care career in February 1985.

I stayed with Nuala during the Christmas season. I met her Paul again. He got his divorce, and they were planning to a marry in a Registry Office. I promised I would attend. Paul was an Inspector by this time. He and I didn't talk about his work, but he was interested in mine and especially the newspaper incident. I was advised by Paul to get it out in the open. At dinner one night, my sister was talking about me and girlfriends. Kelly's name came up, and he rolled his eyes.

Being from Ardoyne, of course, he knew of her and her family.

I said if we were still an item, she would have been at the table with us for dinner and he made a motion of drawing his finger over his throat and Nuala slapped his hand and said, "our Mother liked her." Paul and I got on well.

I stayed working in the hostel for over two years; I did training courses and was promoted to Shift Leader, and temporarily, Jack's Deputy, so my career was going well.

The football continued, and I met Gavin for a drink from time-to-time and was a babysitter for my goddaughter. I was later promoted, for a temporary period, to an Assistant Training Officer at District, which I enjoyed. I wrote a couple of papers which were shared in the Council, and one was published in a journal on the efficacy of bringing long-stay patients with disabilities into the community.

I was offered the training post permanently. My role involved setting up and running courses on Learning Disability and Mental Health. Additionally, I developed lifestyle training videos for service for users and staff. As a result, I was promoted to a Regional Training position. I contributed in a teaching and tutoring capacity to courses. Arising from this, Glasgow University asked me to take on a tutoring role with student Social Workers. My Manager suggested, in 1987, I should do a one-year postgraduate course, qualifying me as a Social Worker. The Council was keen I should do it, so in September I went to Moray House in Edinburgh. I read, not just for exams, but for enjoyment. I was far from the best student on the course. There were serious students, and a few rascals, who were funny. I took a low profile, but I gradually emerged more with my Belfast stories and my driver stories. I fitted in as a social member. My nephew Dominic was born around this time to Maeve and Graham.

Alongside the academic part of my course, I was required to complete two long supervised practice placements. One was in learning disability, which was my field, and one in childcare, 'real social work'. I did a shorter placement working with adult offenders. I was well warned childcare was a nightmare of child abuse cases, lack of fostering placements, children caught in dreadful cycles, workers swimming against the tide. There was no escape. After Christmas in my second term. I returned to Glasgow, to Easterhouse, to do the childcare placement. It involved visiting families on the Department's 'books, 'and help run a group for teenagers. The young people

223

were brilliant. My role included supporting a few families with children on the "At Risk Register" with my placement supervisor, Matt Connelly. Matt was a big Grenockian, with all the Greenock wisecracking and hard approach coupled with huge warmth and commitment to disadvantaged families.

We did an interview with a Mum, Dallas, who lived in a high rise but, halfway through the interview, it was interrupted by the return of "the man of the house." He was father to the two youngest of the six children, had drink taken and took over the interview. He at once fell out with Matt, "Pick a window you're leaving."

Matt crossed the room in a flash, stood over the 'lord and master.'

"And who would do that?"

Himself subsided in his chair but as he sat back down the lady of the house, who, until then all sweetness and light, also crossed the room and punched her paramour in the face, proclaiming 'ARSE' at the top of her voice. The children watched this exchange with a look of weary familiarity. Matt then engaged with the family in a productive discussion. He showed to me how a Social Worker should intervene sensitively in the lives of a family whose future, like their present, was grim.

After we left, Matt chatted over the events. 'No, he did not' believe the children were at risk of, what he termed, 'undue violence.'

"Their Mother would discipline them physically but might kill anyone else who threatened to harm her brood."

He had an interesting take on the exchange with her partner.

"I have known Dallas for years, two of her brothers were under my supervision ten years ago. She is from a physical family whose communication is limited. Disputes are not settled by verbal exchanges; you know what I mean?"

"Come on, I am from Belfast. Working class West of Scotland families are no different from their counterparts, just a few miles across the sea."

I hadn't witnessed that level of familial violence. I wasn't shocked, taken aback maybe. Attack was the best form of defence.

"Could the whole thing not have been kicked off by you confronting Jimmy or whatever his name was?"

"Nah, I know Dallas. He was in trouble before we arrived. The ante went up when he came in drunk and went up further when he threatened me. I defused it and saved him from more punishment."

"But he might attack her now we have left?" I countered.

Three reasons he won't. First, she is more violent than him, he is all mouth. Second, her four brothers are petty gangsters. Despite my efforts as a young Social Worker, not all have liberty, but they have friends. As a final point, did you see the angelic little blond girl who was sitting beside Dallas? Well, her Teacher gave Dallas a mild row for allowing the child to miss school for no reason. Dallas got upset and the wee girl bit the Teacher so hard she needed four stitches. We will be at the Panel next week and Dallas always gets tense there. Any hint her children might be taken from her, even a threat, all hell will break loose."

The next week we were at the Panel. This is a forum in Scotland which holds what is called a Hearing where children supervised by the Social Work Department have their cases reviewed by Panel members, volunteers especially recruited and trained. Three of the children under supervision attended the Hearing with their Mother. The Panel members were excellent with Dallas. They were familiar with her and knew she would be on a knife's edge. Matt had them well warned. The Reporter to the Children's Panel, this was the title of an independent official who oversees the legality in the Children's Hearing, is a key player. He wasn't the regular Reporter who dealt with this family and Matt warned me he could be officious.

"If he gets it wrong with her, Dallas will give him one slap, "muttered Matt gloomily, "and I will have to wade in."

The Chair of the Panel made sure there was no confrontation. The Panel members, two women and a guy, were ordinary folk, with no airs, and graces. Matt was whispering to me through the Hearing explaining what was going on and, from a learning perspective, what was really happening. Dallas agreed she would make sure the children attended school and she would work with the family's Social Worker. Matt said two years ago they never went, now they go at least three, sometimes four days a week. He added during his predecessor's time, the Social

Worker was held hostage by Dallas and a different partner and there were three or four Police vehicles outside the flats. The situation was calmed by the Social Worker's Manager just as the Police were about to go in heavy-handed. I asked him, "Should the children be removed to give them a better future?

"Goodness knows we used to, but the children gravitate home as soon as they are able. Research shows the period away from family creates greater problems for children in the future. When would they have the security of living with someone who would die for them and likely kill for them, too?"

The placement finished all too soon, but two other matters need to be aired. Then I am done with this part of my story: one work related, the other personal.

I visited another family for a few months. Matt worked with the Halligan's, who also lived in a high rise. It was not a straightforward case, but none of the volatility of Dallas. The Mother was a drug user and her reliability as a parent was a source of concern.

The removal of her children was always on the cards. I spoke to her at length about their safety and she guessed we would move them to their Grandmother's home under an Order. I assessed the maternal Grandmother, prepare a report for the Children's Hearing, but because the Gran lived nearby, I did not have to do a school transfer.

This offered stability for both their Grandmother and the children. Matt and I told the Mother the following week we would bring the kids to their Grandmother's.

I went to bed on the Friday night with the air of a righteous man who proved to be a competent 'child saver,' as the original Social Workers in Victorian times were called. The phone rang. In those days, remember houses had phones, people didn't have phones. I was groggy as I grunted into the receiver. It was Matt, three sheets to the wind. The Out of Hours, Emergency Duty Social Work Team (EDT) were called out by the Police to the Halligan's. The Mother took an overdose, and the children were running loose in the flats. Neighbours were wakened and phoned the Police and an ambulance. The Police contacted the EDT. They suggested someone familiar with the case should come and my name was recorded but no contact number, normal procedure for a student.

I had had a few pints. I picked Matt up and went up to the flats. Matt slept the whole way. The ambulance left for the Hospital with Mrs H; the EDT returned to the comfort of their base. According to Matt, they possessed a manual "100 Tips to Avoid a Piece of Work." The neighbours were sitting with the children but wanted back to their beds and the Police wanted away as well. I left Matt and two cops to persuade the kids to settle down, went to their Grandmother's house and wakened her. She was quite happy, even relieved to take the children, but less concerned about her daughter's wellbeing. I went back for the children and Matt, and I brought them over to their Grandmother's. They were all quite tired by then.

Matt and I headed home. It was about 6.00 am and I ate late and consumed too much beer. I was awakened at 4.00 am, sped into work mode after a tiring week and I was feeling sick. You know the sensation you are going to throw up, but you fight it. The only thing in my mind was, 'please let me get Matt dropped off at his flat, get to mine, go into the loo and have a conversation, 'Huey, Huey' with Mr Cruikshank, and get to my pit.'

As I was going down the hill, Matt was dozing. There is a lot of wind around high-rise flats, so I opened the car window to let in fresh air. A dog walker with a wee west highland terrier was sauntering along, whistling tunelessly without a care in the world. I drove a little way past him. I pulled into the side of the road, wound the window down and I threw up over the footpath. The guy with the wee dog nodded cheerfully at me as he wandered past, still whistling. I guess he saw much worse on his early morning walks around there. Matt opened one eye and spoke.

"Hey Jo Jo." He always called me Jo Jo. "How do you do that?"

"Do what?"

"Whistle and puke at the same time?"

I dumped Matt and went to a car wash because the wind blew last night's meal all over the side of the car. Childcare in Glasgow had its moments. If I added in stories shared on the Criminal Justice placement, they would fill a book. I passed my placements and the exams, returning fully qualified to Regional Headquarters. There was so much exciting and engaging about the course, especially the other students, most of whom were older learners. I missed the stimulation, the staff and, above all the other students, but I was glad to get back to a more familiar routine.

Alright, alright, something a bit more personal. I know I promised. On my first day, I spent two hours with Matt trying to work out the childcare experiences which would help me. It was a course requirement for certain boxes to be ticked for his final placement report, though I wasn't going to work in childcare. To Matt, childcare was Social Work and everything else social care. I didn't share his hierarchy of the caring professions, but hard-bitten twenty-year time-served childcare workers hold that view. Paratroopers and infantry, marines, and sailors.

In a world where newspapers described everyone who helped an old dear across the road was a Social Worker, I understood his cynical dismissal of those who hadn't trod his path. It was much more difficult than helping.

Childcare proved tough and not rewarding in the way the hostel was. Matt showed me to my desk in a large open plan office. I gaped at the desk opposite mine, which was unoccupied.

You could not see the desk because it was piled high with rubbish or what looked like rubbish which spilled onto my desk. One of the other workers, Pete, a big guy I had just been introduced to, looked over, grinned, "Don't worry, Lisa is back tomorrow." He laughed, "The rubbish will be tided, although it will be replaced with another lot."

The next morning, a small young woman with a cascade of dark red curls down below her shoulders swept into the office. She was welcomed with a chorus of shouts, "How was the holiday, Lisa?" "Meet a nice man?"

"No such species."

"Well, how about the one sitting just opposite you?"

Lisa flounced up to the desk, eyeing me suspiciously. I tried to remember what Matt said about her, but it went right out of my mind. It was something like.

"Your desk is opposite Lisa O' Neill's. She is a terrific Social Worker, skilful, but eh, a little eccentric."

He might have added, she cannot speak until she drank a strong black coffee and smoked a cigarette first thing at her desk, never got to the office before 9.30 am, never went home much before 8.00 pm. She had a negative perception of men, men older than her, male students, male student Social Workers and, for all I knew, Irishmen as well. I gazed at her and needed to say something devastatingly witty and memorable.

"Hello, I am Joe McFaul, I am a student from Moray House on placement with Matt," was the best I could manage under the intimidating gaze of this fierce young woman. This suggestion was received with a look which made me wonder if I suggested carnal relations on top of the desk in front of everyone. I went for it. 'What the hell.'

"When you are making the coffee, no sugar in mine, please, just a dash of milk."

After a pause, she responded, "milk," as if I said rum mixed with cocaine. In response, she buried her head in her hands.

"Hey," I said, too cheerfully and too loudly," never mind, I'll get the coffees."

No one was doing any work as the drama unfolded. They gazed on with a mixture of horror and anticipation. Let the records show the new student lasted until 9.40 am on his second day, then he was devoured by Lisa. I brought the coffees back, put them on my desk and brought a semblance of order to hers, at least enough room to get her coffee onto the desk. She gazed at me with what can only be described as unrelenting hostility, so, 'what the heck?'

"Your turn tomorrow."

The Team Manager arrived to introduce herself to me and welcome Lisa back, though I thought she skirted around Lisa:

"I realise you are busy, Lisa, but I know you will help Joe if Matt isn't around the office."

Lisa consumed most of her coffee and almost transformed into a normal human being. A general air of disappointment from the rest of the office descended once the entertainment subsided. I went on with my files and got lost in case histories. It must have been about 11.00 am when a mug of coffee appeared on my desk. I thanked Lisa, and we chatted about the course and one or two of the families in my files she knew through office duty, but in one case, co-working with Matt.

Each day started much the same, but I took a low-key approach, ignoring Lisa until she took her first sips of coffee and the fag halfway smoked. Later, if I were in first thing, I would get up as soon as I heard her charge through the office.

You heard Lisa before you saw her, and the coffee arrived at her desk at roughly the same time as she did. In 14 weeks, she made a point of never saying thanks once.

A seriously pretty girl, Lisa, but she could be volatile, confident, but not aggressive. Another thing about her, she dressed to the 'nines.' She possessed a lot of clothes. Her mother used to buy her a lot, and she was always well-groomed and fashionable, according to female colleagues.

Lisa and I got on well, but at lunch time, or in mid-morning people, would gather for a coffee in the Team Manager's office or a little makeshift kitchen/staff rest room.

I avoided it, if Lisa was there. She was more and more helpful, but I didn't want her to feel I was hanging around her. I learned a lot from Matt and Lisa. Despite distinctive styles at the core of their interventions, but they shared a huge personal commitment to disadvantaged people.

Matt used his humour to communicate and Lisa her intellect, for someone on a singular path prior to this, my Social Work horizon expanded.

On a Friday after work, most of the office would decamp to a local pub to deal with the stresses of the week. Matt led, and I was always invited. I appreciated the invitation, but I wasn't too sure how the dynamic of an 'newbie', and a temporary one at that would fit in, I made excuses. As the end of my placement approached, I became more comfortable with the wider group, so one Friday I agreed to go. I left my car at my flat. The group sat together but seamlessly divided into two. The noisiest group was male and was an audience for, or with,

Matt. He fired his one-liners in an unending stream, coupled with a range of stories based in and around 20 years in Social Work full of comments like 'back in the old Glasgow Corporation days.' They were all about rat catchers, what happened up closes and the activities of Glasgow City 'Polis.' There was the odd cross discussion. The other group, totally female, was quieter and focused on work-related issues and technicalities about improving Social Work practice. As a student, that's where I would get useful experiences. I went with Matt!

When they discussed everyone else, attention turned to me. People assumed I worked in Social Work in Belfast. I did not want to bring my extracurricular activities up in this forum, although politically, it might have attracted more respect than elsewhere. Most Social Workers had major reservations about the unfairness of society and fighting to overthrow it would have been welcomed, at least by Pete, a confirmed Socialist Workers Party member, 'Big Red Pete' as Matt described him.

The effects of the drink sank in. I made sure I bought an early round and a second one towards the end of the evening. It was a long night. As the night wore on, people drifted home. Only Matt, Lisa, and I were left. Matt staggered out, leaving me and Lisa. Neither of us were sober. We headed outside for a taxi. A sticking point was Lisa lived in the West End, and I lived in the East End. As the cool air hit us, it refreshed me. Lisa curled her arm into mine, hanging on to me. We hailed a taxi, and I intended to put her in it, but she hung onto me, and I got in with her. We arrived at her flat. After an eternity of rummaging in her enormous bag, she found the door keys, and we entered. It was an untidy version of her desk. I spotted a couch in front of a fireplace with an ornamental gas fire in it. We fell onto the couch together. Gosh, she was pretty, and I noticed how big and green her eyes were. It was the alcohol? We sat there and discussed having a coffee and we kissed. One thing led to another, and we ended up in bed. We caressed each other. I undid her bra and took off her blouse and my pants. She was a passionate woman more a Marianne than a Kelly. Oh God, what brought Kelly into my head, worse Marianne? Lisa had beautiful full breasts and was demanding but also gentle, a rare combination.

"Now like this," she commanded, guiding me.

We made love, no mean achievement in our state, though Lisa seemed more and more energetic. We slept until about 10.00 am. I wakened Lisa at one stage to find out where her bathroom was.

Months later, I asked her when she was first attracted to me. Of course, she replied, "Hasn't happened yet."

The next day, she revealed she took "a shine" to me the first time we met. She said she loved seeing me sitting with the coffees and took it as a sign she was special to me. She felt hurt because I avoided her around the office, especially at informal gatherings such as lunch or coffee breaks. No one knew if I had a partner, but she got a pal to phone another friend at District Headquarters HR, who confirmed there was no Mrs McFaul. She said it made her happy to hear this.

She added. "I got it into my head you were gay, I have gay friends and I couldn't see any tell-tale signs, but, as an Irish Catholic, I thought you might be very guarded. You are holding back. Was it a tragic love affair?"

This was the opportunity and I told her about Ramie, the operations we went on, and my time in the Maze. I described the unrelenting fear, always part of my everyday existence from 1975 to 1980. I believed it was due to my pretending to be something I couldn't be. The disclosure made us closer. Those early days of our relationship were passionate. I was happy to go along with Lisa's ways. I was content, almost fulfilled.

She came over to Nuala's and met my Mother. We stayed at Nuala's. My Mother couldn't cope with an unmarried couple. Paul took to this live wire bundle of red-haired Scottish dynamism. We went down to Maeve's twice and Graham brought us to the football at Anfield. Maeve's daughter Lottie enjoyed playing with her new auntie. It was the easiest way to describe her to a four-year-old.

Once back at the Region, I was drawn into planning changes to Criminal Justice Social Work Services involving its funding and the service delivery. I enjoyed this challenge of contributing to creating what was a new service.

In October, Lisa and I went to Corfu. We stayed in a hotel near Corfu town and used this as a base. We hired a scooter and went up around the coast to Sidari and Palaiokastritsa, staying overnight in local tavernas. If you ever want a tan, go around a Greek island on a motor scooter. Because of her colouring, Lisa wisely covered herself in one of my t-shirts. She claimed I was like a blond Adonis if it was not for the face. You don't realise how much sun you are getting on a bike. As the second week began, we woke up to clouds. Gone were the clear blue skies we enjoyed. The rain started about 11.00 am. It came down in stair-rods. It poured and poured, non-stop.

Lisa and I ate breakfast; went back to bed; played cards and read. I was happy to engage in political, even philosophical, issues, because there were no other distractions. We argued about whether being trapped in a hotel in Corfu during a virtual monsoon was relaxing and helping us recharge our batteries, Lisa's view, or a sodding miserable blight on a wonderful holiday, mine. Our usual dispute about Lisa's smoking raised its head. We had our first blazing row, but the passion when we made up was brilliant. It was as if the taps were turned off at 6.00 pm. As suddenly as it started, the clouds and the rain were gone, and the sun came blazing out. We went across the road with our towels to the beach and lay in the warm evening sun. The rain disappeared from the streets, Corfu in October.

We kept our own flats and didn't move in together. We both preferred our independence, and our relationship was based around weekends and any joint arrangements, such as going to my sisters or Lisa's Mum or the Brennan's. Lisa was my first proper relationship since Kelly, but a different person. I didn't have a type. She was gentle and kind, where Kelly was tough and combative. I treaded softly as I sometimes upset her with my robust humour.

We went out for a meal on either a Tuesday or Wednesday, which became 'our thing' because January to April, we met at work daily, but the pattern continued after my placement finished; I didn't think about it. At weekends, we would go to Largs or the Ayrshire coast, or I would insist on St Andrews or other parts of the East Neuk that called me. We would walk along beaches, and we discussed buying a dog.

"You could keep it at yours," I suggested.

"Why mine?".

"Well," I replied, "the dog can't stay in a flat all day."

"Obviously." agreed Lisa.

"So, you could bring it to your office, and don't look at me like that. You know your office would be a lot more flexible than headquarters."

I pronounced, "You are out-and-about; the dog could help engage with children. It wouldn't work trying to engage Greater Glasgow Health Board pedants and martinets."

Game set and match. We never got a dog.

We stayed with Lisa's Mum in the Borders a few times. Her Dad died when she was a teenager, and he was a distant figure in her life. I suspected the marriage only continued because he became ill for a few years prior to his death. Lisa's Mum, what can I say?

She had been a childcare officer in London and Edinburgh, then finishing her career as a Social Worker in the Borders. She was tiny, with oodles of curly grey hair. She dressed like, well, a Cherokee squaw. It was a 1960s thing. Long flowery dresses and braids in her hair.

It was strange how she would buy Lisa coats and dresses which were the height of fashion while she remained in the 1960s. She was kind, but honestly, wacky. She was a vegetarian. God help me. We used to eat these bean shoots and fruit for dessert and went down to the pub for pie and chips. Lisa just rolled her eyes. She regarded staying with her Mum as an opportunity to purify her body after excesses.

"Purifying your body isn't high on my list of priorities." Lisa rolled her eyes.

I don't know why this happened, but as a reaction to Lisa's Mum's lifestyle, when we stayed in the Borders, on a Sunday, I went to mass. Lisa could not believe it.

"You are just trying to provoke my Mother," she said in an exasperated tone.

"Look, "I said, "I don't mind your Mother worshipping the garden gnomes or the Sun God or whatever, so why should she have a problem with me following the faith I was brought up in?"

"One, you haven't practiced since at least 1969, "Lisa pointed out.

She had a point. I enjoyed winding her up by saying with a name like O'Neill, she possessed a few Catholic skeletons in her cupboard. Lisa made a face at me, very mature. I found the old church atmosphere and the service peaceful; I am not a fan of "happy clappy." There was something oddly reassuring in the old familiar rituals, although I never went when we came back to Glasgow. Mrs O'Neill never commented on it, although I am sure at dawn, I heard her incanting to the Sun!

We went to Liverpool for Christmas 1989, and Lisa enjoyed the time there with Maeve, Graham, Lottie and Dominic, the latest addition. My Mother spent Christmas at Nuala's. Paul was always kind to her. In Liverpool, unexpectedly, Eugene came up from London. There was much scurrying around, and he ended up staying with Graham's parents. The whole family thing was overwhelming for me, but Lisa loved it. For four days we went to different people's houses. We ate and drank too much.

There is a bit of the old Irish priest in our Eugene. So pleased was he to get leave to join his family for Christmas it never occurred to him other plans, like accommodating Lisa and me, might be in place. With no sense of huff, we agreed we would move to a local Hotel, but Graham said nonsense and his parents were lovely, though having a Catholic Priest in the house was a novel experience. Graham said he did not think his father worried about his swearing because he was unaware his every third word was a swear word.

Two days after Christmas, Eugene and I ended up in Maeve's kitchen. We cleared the tables, did the dishes, and sat down for a drink. This was our first proper conversation since he left home to study for the priesthood in 1975, almost 14 years earlier. We saw each other at his ordination. During a period, he was based in Ireland teaching at his old college; he visited Nuala's, and we met there.

He talked about Brazil and how he longed to return. Another option would be for him to teach at the College in Ireland. His role in London was administrative, but someone in the Order had to do it. He applied to be seconded part time to a Parish in Kilburn. The Parish was a Priest short and if the Diocese and the Order could agree; he wanted to go there. We talked about Nuala and Paul. Our Mother wanted it to go away as a religious obstacle, but of course, it could not. Eugene's take was we supported our sister.

As a couple, they were happy, and an annulment was unlikely. Nothing could be done from the Church's point of view. Eugene was not able to attend the wedding, but our Mother attended, as did Maeve, Graham, little Lottie, and me.

We argued about religion, my lack of faith, "Where was God when Ramie was shot?" getting shot. Back and forth like a tennis match we went.

"Protecting the soldier Ramie might have killed. Do you not believe in God?"

"Where's the evidence?"

"All around you. Do you think beauty, love for others, partners, children, parents, poetry, music, art came from a gas explosion?"

"I have you there. Science has proved the bible wrong."

"Not so, it has proved wrong those who think it a literal account in a seven-day framework."

"What about the big bang?"

"Who, or what, caused the 'Big bang.' Oh yes, it just happened, and the human race came from it, but it didn't happen on any other planet. Anyway, have you thought God may have created the 'Big Bang'?"

'Our God is not an interventionist God', it is about faith hope and charity, and you cannot have hope without faith. etc. We argued what did free will mean? On and on it went. My time in prison, my studying and especially my Social Work course left me better able to debate serious matters. Values, customs, traditions, morals, and God's existence all entered the debate. I held my own. Funny thing, we were two brothers having a serious discussion, and I felt as if I was the 'wee' brother.

After the Christmas break, Lisa became moodier than her normal self. I let it go, putting it down to any of a range of probable reasons or a combination of all of them. I should have seen this coming, but one Friday we were eating a takeaway at my flat when Lisa said.

"Well Joe, where are we going?"

A little piece of advice; If you are ever asked that question by a partner, I suspect you need to go down on one knee and say, 'Will you marry me?' My response would set the future for our relationship.

"I like what you and I have. It suits me… how we have arranged it."

The hesitation before I uttered a word spoke volumes.

"We have only been seeing each other for a year, goodness I lived with a man for three years and couldn't wait to get away. I like what we have, Joe, but it is not enough. Sometimes it's as if you are somewhere else. You do not take me for granted exactly, but in emotional terms, we are no longer growing. We are just… I don't know, marking time. I am not sure what for and you will not tell me, or you don't know either. I feel unsettled. We should take a break from this."

She wanted more, and I wanted to give it, but couldn't, and I didn't know why. Am I "selfish", "damaged," "scared of commitment," all these and more said to me by friends of hers and of mine? Even my sisters took Lisa's part. They thought the world of Lisa and believed we were well suited. It all unravelled quickly. There were no scenes, no tears, we met up in the pub when I went on the odd Friday night.

I missed Lisa, but not the intensity of analysing every little thing, wrapping a context around it. Sometimes you just need to chill. I was not interested in seeing anyone else.

We packed a lot into the ten months we were together. I was coming up to 35 and Lisa 26. Everyone, including me, knew I let something precious slip through my fingers. I did not have the sense of relief I felt when Kelly and I finished and any guilt over her lasted a couple of days at most. This was different.

A few times, I wanted to phone Lisa and suggest we go for a drink but put it off. Two days before her birthday on 2 April, I rang, and suggested dinner and she agreed.

Last year, I didn't know it was her birthday. We had only been going out for a few weeks. I was tipped-off in time to buy a card and a delicate perfume, and we went for a meal. I vowed I would make it up the next year and we bought each other nice presents at Christmas.

I booked a well-regarded restaurant in the City Centre. Lisa would come dressed to the nines; it would be a 'look what you lost' statement.

At first, I was going to treat myself to a haircut, a new shirt, but I knew better than to get into a competition, one I could not win. I settled for a shower, my favourite designer navy blue suit she bought me and a nice present.

I decided on a silver bracelet. The jeweller assumed it was a pre-proposal present to be followed by a ring. I did not want to disappoint him about a future sale, but it was nice.

Lisa was fashionably late. I suspect I was supposed to be on tenterhooks but to tell you the truth, I half wanted her not to show and send a message 'no point in our meeting, sorry. It was not to be.'

Lisa swept in, showering the restaurant in clouds of glory. As she walked to our table smiling, I thought how gorgeous she looked, 'punching well above your weight, Joe.'

A peck on the cheek and Lisa arranged herself at the table, looking quizzically at me. Well, I issued the invitation so I suppose I should sketch the parameters. Funny how you think in managerial terms.

"It's nice to see you Lisa," I began, "you look a million dollars."

"I know.".

"It's really nice to see you on your birthday," handing over her present and a card. She took both with a smile but didn't open either.

We chatted about friends, her Mother and mine, my family. I asked about Matt, Pete, and the rest. We ordered the starter and the main course. For all the world it was like a first date with the guy trying to impress with a gift and the girl flashing her eyes and laughing at his jokes, if only. We got to coffee without touching on anything intimate or important. Lisa moved up a gear.

"Joe, I know you will reflect on our relationship and believe you failed me or yourself. I bet your family gave you a bad time."

"Dead right there, Lisa,"

"It just wasn't meant to be. It could have been, but there you go. Remember I told you, I explored the possibility of going to Australia a few years ago."

Yes, I did, it was before we met. She got her Social Work qualification approved, as far as it could be, under their requirements and was looking at working in a secondary role until she could be approved as fully qualified under Australian Regulations. The prospect of starting over again when she was qualified in Scottish regulatory terms, acted as a disincentive.

"I am leaving for Adelaide in July," she finished.

It wasn't Lisa's only surprise for me.

"I hope you meet someone who lives up to the pedestal you put JESS on."

Until then I was Mr Cool throughout the whole evening, that knocked me right back. A smile of triumph appeared in Lisa's eyes.

"Jess," I spluttered.

"Yes, the 'Jess' you shouted out the second or third time we made love, the "Jess" you murmured in my ear the time we were at my Mum's cottage. She went to bed, and we lay, almost dozing, beside the smouldering embers of the log fire until 3.00 am. I assumed it was a girlfriend you hadn't mentioned. The more we talked, a Jess did not seem to fit in,

I asked Maeve at Christmas and all she could remember was a girl you met when you were a teenager. She couldn't remember her name but said you only went out with her briefly."

All of this was new to me, but Lisa didn't invent it. She was not a vindictive person; she was straightforward; she finished by saying:

"I don't know what you want from a relationship, Joe. I don't even know if you want a relationship with anyone. You are an adult. It's up to you. We should stay in touch by email when I go. I will let you know the dates."

She stood up, we hugged briefly, and she swept out as I called for the bill. A few days later, she phoned to thank me for the lovely bracelet, card, and meal. She was pleased her Australian plans were proceeding apace. She sounded so warm and friendly and just for a second, I wondered if I should say, 'could we try again?' but that would be unfair. I loved being with Lisa. She was so funny, so sincere, and so gorgeous, but I didn't love her.

I phoned my Mother, although she already heard from the girls. It was a more difficult conversation than any we had, except for the night Ramie was shot or the revelations about Nuala. I joined the IRA, went on operations, got a four-year prison sentence and I didn't consider the impact on her, she was never anything but supportive and loyal to me. She believed breaking up with Lisa was, a mistake. I later learned she and my sisters were to discuss it ad nauseam for months afterwards. She liked Lisa, and she took the cue from her daughters, Joe met a lovely girl and was going to settle down at last.

Lisa went to Australia on 17 July. I was invited to her 'leaving do,' but it would be too awkward for everyone, it was Lisa's night not a 'will they, won't they' occasion? I loved Lisa… a bit. That was the problem. It was just 'a bit' and she wouldn't settle for second best. I intended to see her before she left, but life was busy, and it never happened. We phoned each other once or twice, and she promised to let me know how it all went.

## Reflection Lisa

Joe McFaul, we could have made it as a couple if there was more give and take, especially from him. Joe was a guy with decent values. OK, he wasn't as committed a Social Worker as, say, Matt or me, but he did want to help people improve their lives.

I could, and should, have waited before springing the lack of commitment on him. I think he was committed to me in the present world, it's just he wasn't always in the present world. If I waited, I could have dropped hints I wanted something more permanent. If he went along with that, we could have moved to having one nice flat. We might eventually have talked about having a child but being me, it was in my mind and came out in a torrent. I regret the way it turned out.

There was a dark side to Joe. I sensed anger within him, but I am not sure what about. I suspect if he admitted it, Ramie's death. He always came over as the misfit, the guy who did not have it in him to fight a war. I never detected genuine regret, more a sense he failed, not because he did not want to kill, but because he did not do it well. He was relieved he was away from Belfast, at the same time he regretted more he was a poor volunteer. I may have overcooked it, but Joe needs to resolve issues within himself One last thing, whatever lies ahead for Joe, and I hope he finds whatever he wants, he will never have a better-looking female partner than me.

# Chapter 12

# SCOTLAND PASTURES NEW

I got emails from Lisa two or three times a year after she moved to Australia. They petered out, as it should. I treated myself to a Honda car, gone up in the world since my Escort. I travelled to various European cities, Amsterdam, Barcelona and Rome, loving city breaks.

In 1995, Local Government in Scotland was to change. My colleagues debated at length what would happen to our employing Authority. Preparing for the future led to me seeking to develop my academic credentials and, as luck would have it, a new University, Glasgow Caledonian, opened and I embarked on a master's degree in Community Care Planning

In late 1993, I travelled to a hotel in Argyll because I was writing a policy document on developing services for offenders. I needed a break from the grind to concentrate. The first two days I walked and thought, ate dinner about 6.30 pm, a drink, then went off to my room to summarise my day.

As I sat in the bar, this scruffy looking English guy chatted to me. He was on his own but needed company more than I did. He was on a walking holiday throughout the West of Scotland and the Islands and hadn't taken a break for two years. I wondered if he was close to a breakdown. He was a Londoner called Kevin Linness. We enjoyed a few whiskeys. He worked in the Chief Executive Department of Fife Region. I knew a few senior Social Work people there, so we name tagged a few mutual acquaintances. He spent an hour selling me on the benefits of moving to the East coast. He was savvy about the politics within the Council.

Was it the drink, or the time, 1.00 am, but I sensed Glasgow was losing its attraction. If I had been a footballer, I would have signed a transfer form at the end of the evening. When I got up next morning, my new pal was gone. I finished my paper and returned to Glasgow, quite refreshed.

A few weeks later I was phoned by a woman named Fiona Gray, a senior manager in Fife Social Work Department and tipped to be their next Director after Reorganisation. She mentioned the Authority would advertise a vacancy for an Assistant Director for Adult Training and if I were interested, I should apply. I took this as a recruiting initiative for fresh talent, so I sent for the papers. The job was like mine and, although it paid less, it was of higher status, and I applied. The larger the Authority's population, the higher posts were graded. Fife would be the third biggest, but without boundary changes, something to consider.

I talked it over with colleagues, unusual for me as I preferred to play things close to my chest and submitted the form; there would be opportunities when my Authority disaggregated, but I should consider a move.

I drove over to Glenrothes and met Fiona, who briefed me about the Department and future developments. I liked her, a straightforward woman. It all happened in a short period, I reached the initial stage of the interview process, an assessment centre, they called it. We did tasks and presentations, working as teams and on our own, quite a tiring process and quite unlike anything I was aware of, never mind experienced. The Council's existing Human Resources and a private sector company organised the process. I was shortlisted to the first set of interviews. Fiona was not involved, and the interview was rigorous.

Fife HR phoned and told me that, me, and two internal candidates, would go to the final interview with Elected Members who would make the appointment.

In Scotland, Elected Members or Local Councillors liked to promote from within their own Authority. They preferred a loyal employee who was committed to their community, as opposed to an outsider.

They favoured a combination of the reward notion filtering down to improve morale and creating future career opportunities for high achieving employees. Internal appointments did not always go down easily with existing Managers.

I was last in. Most of the 14 councillors asked a question. At the end I was told to wait out in reception. I chatted with the other candidates. One claimed at least three of the Councillors present hated him for the past five years. Fiona and the current Director sat in on the interview but did not ask questions. After about twenty minutes, I saw Fiona and the Human Resources (HR) person who organised the interviews stride up the corridor. The HR person made straight for the people she knew, the internal candidates, and guided them aside as Fiona spoke to me, "Congratulations Joe, you have been appointed Assistant Director Training and the Councillors want you to pop back in so they can congratulate you."

I know what you are thinking. What about my involvement in the IRA and incarceration? I did not fail to mention it. It sounds weird, but it was almost 20 years earlier. Did it come up in my forms? You bet it did and I recorded it there. I forgot about it in the stress of the interviews, but more about that later.

Unlike Councillors, Strategic Managers welcomed fresh blood. It enabled moribund services to be reignited or folk cruising in their comfort zone to be challenged and, if they responded, fine or if they didn't, they could be moved on or into retirement. My experience of Local Government suggested employees were unlikely to be dismissed. People were transferred from office to office within a service or to another service. The emphasis was on limiting the damage, not on protecting the service users! I recall in Brewster's, two drivers got sacked, one for involvement in theft from a lorry and the other for driving under the influence, not a Brewster's lorry, but his own car.

Anyway, once the euphoria of the appointment was over, I realised my conviction or sentence was not mentioned. I phoned Fiona, not sounding at all clever, although I fulfilled my formal requirements on paper. She was guarded in her response. I could understand why.

There was an almighty row within the Authority because HR saw the form but did not advise the Councillors. I do not know if it was the correct decision, but it did me no harm. Ten years unblemished employment record with Strathclyde Regional Council and it was over thirteen years since I was released and, after a brief delay, I received my formal appointment letter.

The politics in Fife are odd. The northeast was Liberal Democrat. The big mining areas were staunch Labour, but within living memory, a Communist MP, and Communist Councillors served on the Council. Staff and local people valued them as committed community politicians.

There was a party for my leaving, old pals turned up, Jack Smith and Gavin, whom I kept in touch with, but not as much as I should have. Two of my colleagues did a joint speech, taking the piss unmercifully. One doing the worst Irish accent ever, which attracted too many laughs, and I went to Fife after New Year.

As an incoming worker, I got a flat in Glenrothes, 'new' town where the Authority was based. Kevin soon adopted me, although my primary concern was to avoid being recruited as his drinking buddy. He was very amusing company and knew his way around the Authority. Kevin had this fragility, no doubt because he worked so long and drank so hard. Nobody wanted to lose him, neither Elected Members nor Senior Managers. He was a bright guy. One night he raised my flat saying there were better quality ones to buy. I told him I dreamed of living in St Andrews. Kevin shook his head. "It would be hard to buy a house or flat in St Andrews. It will leave you no money for anything else. Kirkcaldy is a better bet if you enjoy the sea."

I viewed properties in Kirkcaldy and Dunfermline. One Sunday driving out of St Andrews having looked at houses there, I accepted Kevin was right. The ones I liked were outside my price range. Cheaper ones existed, but they were box like and not in keeping with what I wished.

I made money on the sale of my Glasgow flat and although my salary wasn't increasing because Strathclyde paid more, aspects of living in Fife were cheaper than in the city.

Also, as I was staying in the Glenrothes flat paying a nominal rent compared with my Glasgow mortgage, I saved a bit there as well. On the drive down the coast, I stopped in Crail, in the East Neuk, for a snack. I headed down towards Anstruthter and Lower Largo but for no real reason took a right and drove inland two or three miles. Realising the road was getting narrower, I made a turn in a driveway beside a cottage. I saw a For Sale sign in the garden. I noted the Estate Agent's number. I glanced up from scribbling it on a scrap of paper. What a shock! A face appeared at my car window. An older lady was hopping up and down. Presumably, she was not pleased at me using her gateway to reverse. I wound down the window, making profuse apologies.

"Are you the McClellan's?" she demanded?

I was about to quip I am not even 'one of them,' but replied, "No, my name is McFaul."

She mused for a second or so. "McFaul, I don't remember your name. Anyway, come in and park your car over there," she commanded.

I parked up and was ushered inside to coffee and scones. The owner, a Mrs Hepburn, she was either not baptised or didn't consider she should share her Christian name with me, was expecting two viewings, the McClellan's had not showed. The other couple said the cottage was small.

"What part of a small two bedroomed cottage did they not understand?" She sniffed.

She and her late husband retired there from Edinburgh, where Mr Hepburn had been in business. This man needs to be funny. I wanted to say, 'massage parlours or just the brothels.' I know, I know, but at least I only thought it.

"My husband died last year."

I expressed my sympathy, which she acknowledged with a little inclination of her head. Her daughters lived in Edinburgh and there were several grandchildren, so she wanted to return there. They renovated the cottage, with its lovely gardens, small at the front with the gravel driveway but large at the rear. there was a fair-sized lawn with shrubs, bushes, plants, and flowers and three trees they planted.

"If you buy Mr McFaul, you need to watch those trees don't grow too large and obscure the view."

It was magnificent. Fields full of crops for miles and that line on the horizon where the sea meets the sky:

"It can be windy and wet in the winter, but we never have snow," as if she decreed it so.

The kitchen needed modernising, but there was a new bathroom, including a proper shower and a bath.

"Mr Hepburn liked a shower."

One bedroom was enormous, the other smaller. It could double as a spare for visitors and a study. The lounge was spacious with a big open fire and the house had central heating and double glazing. I loved it. She told me she bought a modern flat, again a faint sniff of disapproval. It was 'almost' in Morningside. I needed to know that and acknowledge it, and I did. We got on well and I drove home excited but not sure if the price was in my range. Mrs Hepburn decided the cottage was for me.

In Scotland, a purchaser has to have a Solicitor to take the process forward. Mine put in an offer I could afford and told me through the Estate Agent there were higher offers.

He suggested I raise my offer by about four thousand pounds, with no guarantee the other bidders would not raise theirs.

I thought for a minute or two. "To go up several thousand pounds is too much on my budget."

Even if the offer was rejected, a plan was emerging to fulfil my hopes. A more dilapidated cottage needing a bit of work in the general area would be in my budget range.

The Agent agreed and said he would make enquiries and I should keep looking. I put the phone down. Thirty minutes later another call, "Joe, brace yourself, the seller has insisted your offer is accepted."

I wanted to put her decision down to my Irish charm and boyish good looks, but it transpired a rival bidder started to 'hmm and haw' over dates and changes they wanted done before they completed their offer. Another revealed they were in a chain which was holding up the sale of their existing property despite having denied being in one at an earlier stage.

"Oh, we thought they sold and could complete on ours," just what happens when you are in a chain. The other two bidders did not know she acquired her flat, 'near Morningside,' do not forget that.

Now I was the proud owner of a rural cottage two miles from the North Sea or, as Bill Connelly called it, the Arctic Ocean.

Gavin and Kevin volunteered to help me. Graham arrived complete with family, though he dumped them in a caravan site nearer St Andrews. A team like that helps you get a move sorted out and a plentiful supply of beer kept the workforce content. I stayed sober and drove Kevin home to Glenrothes. Gavin stayed the night, and I poured Graham into the caravan in a state of intoxication. He wakened not only the kids but most of the site with his scouse rendering of "You'll never walk alone." Maeve hadn't been this angry with me since I broke her favourite doll when I was six and she was about four and a half. The doll was taken prisoner and, despite extensive torture, refused to divulge any secrets. Dolls are like that; they clam up under torture.

The major Local Authority change took place on the 1 April 1996. Fife was affected, but to a lesser extent than most other Councils. We changed from Fife Region to Fife Council (Unitary Authority).

I settled into the training role and enjoyed more of being my boss, in as much as you can working within a Local Government structure. The team was talented, and

I enjoyed working with them. My job involved budgets and, as with all Senior Managers, I was involved more with Councillors. I built decent relationships there and with Civil Servants as we prepared for Scottish Devolution.

Arising from my job, the conferences over the 1996 changes and the looming planning around Devolution, I spent time in top class hotels. I was often away and Eugene, when he could, Paul and Nuala and my Mother enjoyed breaks in my cottage. My Mother was not keen on flying. This was not based on experience. Her gaze travelled from a plane in the sky and then the distance to the ground. To allay her fears, I suggested, "Don't worry about falling. You will be dead long before you hit the ground."

I haven't changed, and this brought no reassurance. As a result, I drove to Belfast via Stranraer to pick her up and leave her back. Later, Nuala would leave her on the boat, and I would meet her at Stranraer or Cairnryan.

Eugene loved getting out of London and Maeve and her tribe, despite the noisy night and her husband's tuneless vocals, took to mobile home life in the East Neuk, or my cottage if I was elsewhere.

Maeve contacted me on a Thursday night in May 1998 to say Mum was unwell. She was attending the hospital for tests for bowel cancer and Greta insisted she tell the family. She phoned Maeve, who contacted me, and she called Nuala, who phoned Eugene. I left the office at lunchtime on Friday and drove to Cairnryan. When I visited Mum, she looked so wee and old in the hospital bed.

The spirit I so associated with her was absent instead there was a resigned air. I stayed over the weekend and on Monday, Maeve and Graham arrived. All of us were relieved to see her rally on the Monday. She responded to treatment and was discharged home about ten days later. On the Tuesday I was preparing to head home in better spirits but, as I loaded up my car, the "Superintendent" as I called him because he was by then, Paul, came out to help me with my bags:

"Well, Paul," I suggested, "a better outcome than I was expecting."

"Look, the girls won't thank me for saying this and neither will you, but Bridie is not out of the woods. This rally may only last a few weeks.

The consultant was less specific. He explained there was only so much the treatment could do but they would continue to monitor her. Paul was aware there was more behind the comment. I resolved to return and did so twice over the next two months.

Nuala phoned late on Tuesday night 13 August and said Mum was 'incredibly low.' Paul suggested I come over at once. It is stupid what you think about in this situation. I had two critical commitments that week, one on the Wednesday was a presentation to Senior Councillors, and a meeting on the Thursday in the diary for months. Any other week but this. I phoned Fiona, and she went right to the point. "Go to Ireland. Everything else can be sorted out here or postponed."

She was right. I headed again to Cairnryan and got a sailing about 4.00 am. When I reached the hospital, Paul was sitting dozing in my Mother's room. Nuala went home for some sleep and Maeve's flight was due in at 8.00 am. I remained with her, and Paul headed straight to the airport. He was a source of strength to us all. No drama, he did what had to be done and he did it with kindness and without fuss. Eugene was on his way home, too.

My Mother died on Thursday 15 August, "the Feast of the Assumption," as Greta observed. Eugene celebrated the Requiem Mass. We were all there. Greta and other neighbours, Geraldine, Mother of four, the milkman clearly was more successful than me! My cousin, 'baby,' Ann, now a mother of three, and the children of cousins of my Mother's from the Glens whom I knew all my life. The familiar ritual was, at times, reassuring. It wasn't a case I no longer believed in God, more I just drifted away from attending Mass and the sacraments. I attended from time-to-time, including when I was in the Maze but, as I said, just drifted away.

It was a celebration of Bridie's life, and bits were nice, albeit emersed in all the sadness. Families should gather for a party at intervals otherwise the nice bits as a family only happen at funerals.

Nothing is ever all straight forward in my life. I was shaking hands with my cousins, trying to persuade them to come to a local pub for what the Scots call 'the purvey,' when a figure wandered out of the side of the church, approached me, and whispered. "Buried your Mother, McFaul. You won't be long after her."

I wasn't in the mood for a fight and anyway; I was wearing my best suit! O'Dade vanished as quickly as he came.

I stayed with Nuala and Paul for a week on compassionate and annual leave. I needed space to think. They put my quietness down to the grieving process. It was up to a point, but I could not believe O'Dade went to all that trouble and still needed to square matters with me at my Mother's funeral. He implied he was going to kill me. Despite my mood and the sadness, his appearance and threat preyed on my mind.

Anyone who held on to a grudge in that way was dangerous. I headed to the Falls Road and through an Advice Centre there I arranged to see Pat. We shook hands. I had not seen him since my release eighteen years earlier. His grip was firm, and he looked me straight in the eye. In earlier times, Pat always had a furtive look. Even as a teenager, he carried a lot of secrets.

He knew a lot about my life which I did not expect.

"You have done well, got an education and a career. I married a girl from Lurgan, Breda Rogan. you'll have heard of her oldest brother Paddy who played in an All-Ireland final for Down?"

"Sorry, I don't follow Gaelic football to much extent anymore."

Then, as a retort, for the success in my career, he added. "I may stand for Parliament next May, as an absentee MP, of course, but I will be elected in South Armagh."

"Gone back to your family roots, Pat." He laughed. The usual chat the Irish have.

I explained the O'Dade's history. To be fair, Pat was annoyed on my behalf that an incident from so long ago was carried to the steps of my Mother's funeral.

He apologised for not attending because of commitments. A better politician would understand how important it is to be seen at funerals. It was fine. We had not kept in contact. What most annoyed him was when I described the Sunday newspaper incident.

" Easier to bring those people (journalists) in than to get rid of them. Someone needs a wee word with your pal O'Dade, and I will contact the right person, Leo."

Leo who? Pat did not enlighten me. He took my mobile number. It was a Council phone. I hope they did not call it in and examine it. Even the average Local Authority's Chief Executive's Department would struggle to justify the call I might get.

"And it wasn't in line with Authority business when you and this 'Leo' discussed shooting 'Big Nose O'Dade.' You haven't claimed expenses, have you." A more serious infraction in Local Government circles?"

"Leave it with me, "Pat added.

Two days afterward, I got a phone call, "Joe McFaul?
"Er…. yes."

"This is Leo. We met the day you were liberated."

Liberated like a prisoner of war because that's what we considered ourselves.

"Pat asked me to phone you. The minor matter that is troubling you, you and I need to speak to Mr O'Dade."

Of course, we met before. Leo was with Pat the day I was released. I did not want drawn back in, but he was insistent it could not be done without me. He picked me up near Dunville Park, where I was 'lifted' and blindfolded by the security forces so many years ago.

We drove up to Turf Lodge and entered a house. If it was O'Dade's house, I worried we would have to deal with his Mother, wife, kids, whatever. I did not want to be there. A young guy took us into the kitchen. There was not anyone else in the house except Padraig. He was tied to a chair, with blood from a gash on the side of his head, bruising on his cheeks under his eyes, and one leg was twisted at an unnatural angle. A hammer lay beside the chair. Two shaven headed young guys stood near him, clones of the guy who let us in. Leo, who in the drive up hardly spoke and appeared mild-mannered, grabbed O'Dade by the hair and kicked his 'bad' leg, only bad because of the hammer used on it.

O'Dade screamed with pain and Leo brought out an automatic pistol and placed it in O'Dade's mouth. I stared into Padraig's eyes. He was terrified, and he thought, as I thought, this was his last moment.

Leo's tome was menacing. "If you contact McFaul again or if you approach a newspaper again the next time I will pull the trigger, nod if you understand."

O'Dade nodded; I nodded too, due to the level of tension. The beating and the threat were real. Leo dropped me off in the City Centre where I could get a bus to Nuala's. He gave me his mobile number, "just in case." It has been sorted." Was his final comment.

That was it, Leo, and Karim, quite different problem solvers, reflecting their different training and lifestyles, I guess. I was pleased to have O'Dade out of my hair. He made too much of something not that significant and suffered for it.

This latest O'Dade incident surprised me. Pat could either have someone warn O'Dade or leave it and hope it would go away. If the Police raided, my career in Scotland was ruined, I would be an accessory. Pat would claim he facilitated a meeting because of a dispute within the Republican movement and Leo would have backed him. It's what they do. It was a scary event.

I could now lay to rest a few ghosts, which haunted me in Belfast. Issues such as my dad dying while I was in prison, and of course Ramie, poor Ramie. I thought Ramie and I would always be mates. We would have lost touch when I left Belfast. Then we would be reunited at something like Bridie's funeral and be the same old pals, sharing drinks and memories.

Despite the reappearance of O'Dade, after my Mother's death, I could leave Belfast emotionally as well as physically.

I returned home, and I confess I experienced one of those lonely times, the sort we all have when we lose a much-loved parent. A part of you has gone forever, and I didn't have anyone with whom I could share my feelings. At this point, Lisa would have chipped in.

"Joe, when did you ever share your feelings?"

She heard about my Mother, through pals, and sent me a lovely letter and a nice memoriam card. She was living outside Sydney, married with a little daughter.

I loved visiting St Andrews. I often drove to the town for an evening meal, especially if the girls visited, with or without their spouses. Once they visited together, I offered to sleep on the couch, but they were pleased to share a room for a few days, reliving their childhood.

The girls brought minor improvements, such as soft furnishings, to the cottage. I was comfortable in my lifestyle. I was over forty, with quite enough excitement in my life to-date. In fifteen years, I could afford to retire, and my mortgage would be settled. Security becomes important as you get older.

One evening in September 1999, I headed to St Andrews after work, ate a meal and about seven o'clock I decide to walk around the Old Course and onto the beach. It was one of those hot Indian summer September days, the evening was warm with little wind. I walked over the narrow bridge built between the road and the beach to protect the dunes. I noticed a guy walking towards me, supporting a small older gentleman. They were chatting, so I stepped aside to let them pass. The younger man grunted his thanks and continued walking. The old boy went past staring at me with the continual smile older guys have when they meet another male but want to emphasise they are avoiding challenge. I smiled back as I went to pass him, and he kept staring and smiling, there was a flicker of recognition, and he grabbed my arm.

"Joe;" I did not know who he was.

His younger companion saw him grab me and came back muttering apologetically.

"Joe," the elderly man repeated, "the last time we met was in the Spring of 1975 in Ladas Drive Police Barracks. You asked if I was in the Salvation Army!"

I gazed, then I recognised him. It was the old MI5 guy. I could not remember his name.

"Clive Greenhaugh," he anticipated.

By this point, the younger man joined us.

"This is my grandson Gareth; he is a student at the University. Gareth, can you give me a chance for a quick word with an old....," I waited to see how he would describe me, an ex-prisoner, terrorist, stroppy rebel, but he said, 'acquaintance.'

Gareth shook hands and made off for the car park. I suspect this wasn't his first experience of that type with his grandfather.

Clive, my 'mate' Clive, enquired about my current life, where I was working now, and why I left Belfast. His interest was genuine enough, and we chatted about the Good Friday Agreement and the Peace Process in Northern Ireland or, as I pointed out, 'the Truce' because only a fool believed it was done in Northern Ireland. They all got tired fighting although a new generation would take up the cudgels. Partition was such a crude solution, a total cop out.

Clive could not help his old habits and slipped in a question about decommissioning. He would enjoy phoning his former colleagues and giving them an address where a stash of weapons could be located. He remembered I got a prison sentence:

"Only four years, not the six or seven you predicted," I reminded him.

"It was only a negotiating position."

We discussed my 'conversion' to education and career moves, including coming to Scotland. He was impressed at the relative seniority of my position; he was meant to be.

Never miss an opportunity to remind a Brit the Irish are from a land of saints and scholars. In that debate, I list the impressive Irish born literary giants: Jonathan Swift, Oscar Wilde, WB Yeats, George Bernard Shaw, Daniel Defoe, Sean O'Casey, Bram Stoker, James Joyce, Samuel Beckett, and Seamus Heaney.

"I recall you hailed from a decent family. I hoped you could influence characters around you. Every time we got your guys, or the Unionists or our guys, to agree, a faction within the group would pressurise it to walk away without an agreement. I suppose they arrived there in the end. I am writing a book about that dance. Would you mind if I quoted you in it anonymised, I promise?"

It was getting colder; Fife's Indian summer was fading. He dabbed at moist eyes.

"I wished to show what your generation could achieve and what others might have achieved if there had been more commitment from all sides. I can send you a copy. Do you have an address?"

"Ah… I am moving house," I lied. "Send it to Fife Council in Glenrothes."

Do you want the intelligence services knowing where you live, though they probably know anyway?

It must have been at least two years later when a package arrived at the office. It was Clive's book with a short-handwritten note from Gareth saying his grandfather had died earlier in the year, shortly after Clive's book was published. He promised him he would send me a copy but lost the scrap of paper with the address. It appeared later when he was clearing some papers.

I scanned the book. There was a reference to me on page 48 as 'Volunteer Eight,' whom he was certain was not cut out for the IRA. He wrote, 'Volunteer eight might contact influential people within the IRA to get them to resume talks, which stalled again.' Clive also mentioned me in the penultimate chapter as 'former Volunteer Eight' who got an education and was now a respected and senior person in British public services. He egged it a bit, but it was fine. I chuckled to myself. There could well be others somewhere in the United Kingdom living low key respectable lives now worried their past was returning to haunt them!

I visited my sisters. I travelled down to London several times to visit Eugene and met more Priests than you can rattle a stick at! A little perk of my job developed. I began an attachment to a college in Dunfermline as an Honorary Lecturer in aspects of Social Care with adults. I used the College for the Council's internal training, various external Social Work and Social Care professional bodies conferences and I contributed to the College's own courses. They would ask me to set up and/or contribute to courses and conferences.

Scots had unrealistic hopes for this brave new world. One implication for the Authority was ensuring first-line Managers and staff were aware of the different structures and funding streams emerging. Add in grants and initiatives from the European Union and disseminating detailed information with many new partnerships and alliances emerging.

I chaired plenary sessions, talked about research in moving long-stay patients into the community, reintegrating offenders, and the challenges of working in a fast-changing political environment. Under Council regulations I could not be paid for this, but the Authority was keen I did it as part of its support for the College.

Then there was an odd experience at a conference. There were three delegates from Northern Ireland and about nine from England interested in our Hospital closure programme and residential strategy with ex-offenders. My slot was before the coffee break and another after with questions to a panel. At the break, this young woman, dark-haired, pleasant smile, came up to speak. She appeared familiar.

"Hi, my name's Ann. I was surprised to hear a Belfast accent here. The link you made with Prisons interested me, my Grandad Billy," (to distinguish him from her other grandad, Sammy) "was in the Prison Service in Northern Ireland, though in different times," she added.

Lots of Prison Officers were called Billy. In fact, most of them were called Billy, but I could only remember one, so I responded with a merry quip." I suppose your Mother is called Jess and your dad, Robert?"

It was a spontaneous comment arising from her reference to a Prison Officer called Billy. She paled, stammered, looked unwell, "Are you OK?" I asked.

"Fine, fine," she murmured, heading for the coffee.

Through the next session, the only face I saw in the room of about ninety people was Ann's staring at me. She was bound to come up at the conclusion.

"How did you know my parent's names?" she asked.

"I am so sorry. I didn't realise you were from the same family. It was just a random comment. But I was friendly with your parents when we were young. I also knew your Grandfather was a Prison Officer and his name was Billy."

I did not explain how I knew that. Ann mentioned her parents liked Scotland and, when she and her brother were wee, they often came to the Trossachs, the Borders or the Highlands on holiday.

My comment was a shot in the dark. An unfortunate phrase given my history, although I did not tell her about my incarceration. In fact, I was only thinking aloud. She mentioned a Prison Officer called Billy. Jess came to mind, and I expected her to respond, 'no their names are Doreen and John' or something.

She was quite relieved I possessed no psychic powers, and we parted friends.

I hoped she would go home, tell her parents and her Grandad. I enjoyed the thought of Billy Morton choking on his semolina at the prospect of Joe McFaul lording it over a conference his granddaughter attended across the water, not living in a wee terrace on the Falls Road depending on British benefits. Yes, that pleased me.

The Principal told me once, "If we were a University, we would make you an Honorary Professor!"

Well, they were not, but at a summer graduation for the full-time students, the College made me an Honorary

Fellow. A Belfast boy who is also a 'Fellow,' well, I never. I became a member of the College Board. I was pleased to be involved and it offered various opportunities to be more involved in the wider community. I got to know other teaching and administrative staff, catering staff, Charlie who ran the bar set up if students, adult learners, were doing a residential.

I felt comfortable there. A woman in the Finance section invited me to accompany her to a friend's wedding because she was between partners and did not wish people to feel sorry for her. It turned out there was an intention on her part I should form one half of this 'between partners' sandwich! The wedding was fine, a nice meal, too much to drink, a passionate coupling at her flat afterwards, which was a mistake, followed by shamefaced shuffling along corridors for a couple of months afterwards.

I was in the fortunate position of having a room in the residential block, subject to it being available anytime I wanted. It was often the same room, a corner site with a sitting area and a larger bedroom and bathroom than the student rooms.

It was a priority for visiting speakers who stayed overnight, but I needed to give notice to be sure of booking it. I contemplated leaving the Council and moving there permanently. There was a place for me, so the Principal told me.

It was a less frantic place to work, and I admit I swanned around, but if I were a permanent member of staff, it would be different. A chat with the Vice Principal who looked stressed about budgets brought me a touch of reality, the same hassles everywhere.

I did not travel to Ireland for the next year. I claimed to Nuala my work was busy and I was travelling abroad when I could take a break. The real reason was O'Dade. Deep down, I was not convinced O'Dade was finished with me.

He was in danger of making himself a serious enemy in Leo, one who played for keeps. The upshot was I preferred staying safe across the water, out of sight, out of mind.

In Belfast, the nurse squeezed Jess's arm. "It will be soon she whispered.

Jess nodded. She was conscious of Ann, beside her, crying into herself. Billy felt tears coming to his eyes but was determined to stay strong for his Mum, Ann, and his Dad.

## Reflection Leo

McFaul was a volunteer from the 1970s. I met him once when he came out of the Maze. His name never came up, nobody knew him or had heard of him, but he was a friend of Pat Kane's. Pat was an influential guy and someone you should not cross, McFaul was made of the same stuff.

O'Dade was a headcase from a family of headcases. I could not fathom his grudge, a stupid fight when they were in the Maze. There were always arguments and fights there. By bringing a national newspaper into an internal dispute, O'Dade crossed a bridge. The beating was a warning. If he did something else, there would be more than a beating!

I do not know why but, in certain circumstances, I believe McFaul could be violent. There was an anger behind his eyes. I love that look in volunteers---

# Chapter 13

# SO, THE END IS THE END

I wish I had been a more confident person; I try to hide it through humour and the odd swagger. Wishes, now there's a thing. I should have wished I were a kinder person, but kindness is overrated. A lot of assholes exist. Should I be more sensitive to others? My parents, Ramie, Dolores, Lisa, all might claim my behaviour, my insensitivity, my decisions, or lack of them, hurt each one. I know I have changed, matured but also become more cynical.

I have regrets, not just about important issues but trifles. It's not helpful to dwell on the past, people do reflect on their lives as they get older. I needed to stop blaming everyone else when something went wrong, a difficult step in a late maturation process. Consequences, it is all about consequences! I accepted I was not fated to fall in love and marry a lifelong partner. I am 46, and either I let women down, or they let me down, or so I told myself. My two most important relationships ended because both Ramie and Jess left me. That is not fair to either, especially Ramie, given the circumstances, but I maintain he was to blame, if only —.

Dolores Kelly was a serious person, a 'die for your country,' individual, rather than live for it. Lisa was carefree, full of energy and a 'live for the moment,' girl.

Remember, I was low, more depressed than any time since Ramie's death 25 years ago. I needed to blame somebody, anybody but me.

This negativity transferred into work, life was full of budget cuts, lots of disciplinary hearings which Fiona insisted I play my part as a Senior Manager. Other Managers claimed I never wanted to find fault with staff, pointing out I hadn't managed direct service units. They contended I had insufficient experience in dealing with certain issues. If I worked in an operational, managerial career instead of somewhere safe like training and research, they suggested, I would back up a lower tier Manager even if they were an absolute 'haddy.' Fiona said she 'led' the department, other Managers 'managed' it and I 'chaired' it! I promised not to let logic and intelligence impede on any other disciplinary hearing. Fiona was not convinced I got the message.

She confronted me: "Joe, I like you and you have been a super addition to our Management Team. Training is of a high standard in Fife, as good, better than anywhere else in Scotland and the small Research Unit you created is a nugget. The Members consider you wonderful for that alone but, sometimes, I wish you visited planet Fife more often. You are away in the stars too often; in a world you think should exist, not one that does."

How others see you is often salutary! Was I the problem, not the solution I assumed I was? Once I accepted this, my mood brightened. I even got in a little parenting. Bella came to stay at Uncle Joe's for a long weekend. It started with sleepovers, and I loved those times messing about on beaches, exploring rock pools, watching scary TV shows.

Lynn would never let her watch. She always promised she would never tell her Mum and when I dropped her back, she would jump out of the car and shout, "Uncle Joe, let me see Indiana Jones and there were monsters—"

Lynn would give me a look and Gavin would turn away so she would not see him laughing.

"Lynn, how am I doing as a parent?" She gave me a look.

"Now I understand why you have never tried to pair me off with one of your single girlfriends?" Again, no response, but she stuck her tongue out. Gavin told the story so often, even Lynn laughed.

Life took an unexpected and unpleasant turn, as it has a habit of doing. Growing up as a kid, a young teenager in Belfast in the late 1960s/70s, I got used to the sounds of bombs and shootings. Even cities without civil wars have their own sounds. Rural Fife was different, something I loved. When I first moved into the cottage, I didn't sleep well. The silence was… loud.

I grew accustomed to the sounds of the country, which changed with the seasons, with what farmers were doing, what the bird life was doing. After a while, I accepted it.

One night after a couple of days of heavy rain, the roads around my cottage were flooded. I drove in the centre of the road, allowing other traffic to pass. Anyway, it wasn't first light, about 3.30 am, and I was wakened by a sound on the pebbles where my car was parked. I woke, listened, and all was quiet, and I fell asleep only to be wakened a second time. If I stayed in bed, I would drop off again. Was someone trying to steal my car? I looked out the window. A car was driving in the distance towards St Andrews. It must have been a mile away. I went back to bed after looking around.

The next morning, after breakfast, I was heading off to Edinburgh for a meeting. The rain stopped, and I went out with my briefcase. There were footsteps on the grass, not mine, and mud trailed towards the car. My visitor, or visitors used the grass to avoid the pebbles as much as possible. They didn't try to gain entry to the vehicle, there were no marks on the doors. An instinct stopped me from getting into the car and led me to peer underneath. The underside of a car is dark, but I noticed an off-white package about eight inches by six under the driver's seat. While I had only seen dummy ones, I guessed it was a Semtex car bomb.

I felt sick and went back inside. Then I phoned the office and asked a colleague to give apologies for my non-attendance at the Edinburgh meeting, claiming I was not well. For an hour I sat there trying to work out who, what, and why? It must be O'Dade. Despite Leo's warning, he was determined to kill me. I humiliated him in the Maze and at the roadblock. What passed between us was not serious enough to warrant this reaction. The kicking at the Roadblock should have evened out the incident in the Maze and that would have been that. Of course, he guessed I grassed on him. We never shared a proper conversation. Calling with my Mother, involving a newspaper, the funeral encounter, they were way over the top, an obsession. Scotland represented safety, coming here made me so angry, encroaching on Scotland was like defiling sacred ground. Whatever happened in Belfast should stay in Belfast. I was mad; I mean, seriously mad. The subsequent adrenaline kick focussed my mind.

I phoned the Police in St Andrews but could get no sense out of whoever I spoke to, He threatened me with arrest for 'Wasting police time,' so helpful! I was no longer frightened; I was in a rage and incomprehensible. I needed to calm down and decide on a plan. I phoned a Chief Inspector at the Fife Constabulary HQ in Glenrothes, I knew. He and I went on joint training and socialised at the College afterwards. We were not friends, but friendly. He knew I lived in Belfast during the Troubles but didn't know I was a member of a banned organisation or been in prison.

I told him about the time I saved the lorry load of bricks! He did courses with RUC guys who come over to Scotland and taken them to play golf. He wasn't available, but he returned my call an hour later. I was calmer and said to him, "There might be an explosive device was under my car."

"Joe, are you sure? Why do you think you were targeted?"

He was trying to figure out what to do next.

I suggested, "Look, there was bad feeling with a para-military group in Belfast way back."

"Right, I will send out some cops."

He also agreed to contact Bomb Disposal, who were based with Strathclyde Police in Glasgow.

The two cops were from Kirkaldy, one was a young guy who chatted with me, and we drank coffee. His companion was older. He looked under the car. He told me he was a soldier in Northern Ireland and, although not Bomb Disposal, he had enough training to recognise a car bomb. I almost said, 'me too,' He phoned the Chief Inspector who arranged for the Bomb Disposal unit to come to my cottage. They got a helicopter to Leuchars, and a Fife Police vehicle brought them and their equipment to the cottage. I was so remote no attention was generated, and they removed the bomb, took it to the firing range at Leuchars, and detonated it.

I wanted to put the next part of my plan into action. Then two detectives arrived, took a statement, and pushed me quite hard about who I thought planted it and why. They came back the next day. I was quite impressed at a couple of bog-standard Fife detectives grilling me with such focus and expertise. Turned out they were Special Branch from Glasgow! They told me I was not to discuss this with anyone. I guessed they contacted the new Police Service of Northern Ireland (PSNI) and accessed my records. The clue was they went from calling me Mr McFaul to 'Joe'.

I returned to work checking my car in the mornings. I phoned Leo on his mobile number.

"Leo, it's Joe...,"

He cut me off with a "I will phone you."

When the phone rang a few minutes later, it was a different number than the one I just used. I explained about the bomb; there was a sharp intake of breath. He grunted: "He should have got the message last time. It was enough to sort it."

Leo told me to come to Belfast but to tell no one. From Leo's tone, it was going to be sorted this time. I told him I would be in Belfast for the rest of the week. Took a week's leave, not saying I was going to Ireland and booked into a hotel in East Belfast. I did not contact Nuala.

On Friday Leo phoned. "We have him. I will pick you up at the usual spot."

Of course, it would be outside Dunville Park. We drove to a house in Ballymurphy. It looked derelict, as did the neighbouring houses. We went into the house, a re-run of the previous experience. O'Dade was gagged and tied to a chair. It looked rickety. He was unmarked, although one leg was encased in a support and was sitting at an unnatural angle. Leo spoke softly, with no sense of seeking a response. "We told you to stop. What is wrong with you?"

O'Dade glanced up, saw me and his face was transfixed with hate. He moved in the chair, which sounded as if bits were breaking. He could not speak, but the sight of me enraged him.

Leo beckoned me. "I don't know what his problem is, but it is destabilising. The newspaper business has a lot of folks still angry, and he stole Semtex. Christ, how did he even know where to find explosives?"

So, it was not about me. It was about O'Dade. He was out of control, like Driller Doyle, a serious liability. Leo took out a pistol. It was Beretta 92. I never fired one, but I heard about them. They were used by guys who came into the Maze before I was released who used them as personal protection weapons.

Leo handed me the gun; it was my call. Brilliant. The organisation did not want tarnished! I took the gun, shrugged. This bastard leant on me for too long. Inside I was raging but outwardly calm. I walked into the kitchen; the two boys stood with their hands clasped in front of them.

Were they the same two as the last time, what can you say of small, 20-year-old shaven headed Belfast guys? When he caught sight of me, O'Dade threshed again. The boys exchanged exited glances and left the room. They would not be witnesses to what followed.

I put my left arm around O'Dades neck. He struggled. The chair was almost gone, but I was holding him in his sitting position with two legs of the chair buckled and the others about to fold. I twisted his head to one side, brought the pistol up to just above his ear, and fired twice. The recoil hurt my wrist, O'Dades body jerked me forward. The chair and O'Dade collapsed on the ground, spewing blood and brain all over the floor. It was done.

Colum Delaney was right. I would shoot someone to protect myself, not because I was ordered to, it's all about Joe.

Leo appeared. "We'll take it from here."

The sleeve and the bottom part of my coat were covered in blood. Leo suggested he take the coat, but I refused. He took the gun. It would have my fingerprints on it. The coat would have plenty of O'Dades DNA, but I attempted to wash it in the kitchen sink as best I could, pointless.

How did I feel, traumatised, in denial, I guess? I was told never to think too much about a violent event. Leo drove me to the city centre. We did not exchange a word until I got out of the car.

He said, "It's done now."

And it was. Were Leo and I comrades bound by my awful deed, which he facilitated? O'Dade was never leaving that kitchen alive. The decision was already taken elsewhere. It was just a question of who would kill him. I never heard of O'Dade's body being found. They knew how to make people disappear.

How did I feel about shooting an unarmed man tied to a chair? Fine. It was always going to be me or him. When he ignored Leo's 'warning' and when he planted the car bomb, there could only be one outcome. I agonised over other events much more, ones which made me angry. They built up inside me, my parents' deaths, Ramie's death, also so violent. I stood for a moment outside the room in Ballymurphy with Leo. It came down to this. I never expected I would pull the trigger. I did not have time to think. It was O'Dade or me, and I chose him.

Within me, there was one discernible change which took a while to absorb. For the first time in thirty years, I wasn't angry. A deep-rooted anger simmered within me. I am not sure what caused it and I never discussed it with a soul, but it was always there. Many reasons caused it, expecting criticism, being abused for my religion, my employment, my time in the RA or my failure to be effective there. I was not haunted by the O'Dade killing.

Notice how I word it, not 'by my shooting O'Dade' or 'my murdering O'Dade.'

I defined any negative event in Northern Ireland as something from the past which intervened in my present. My response was to forget about it. One thing worried me, if either of the young guys was picked up, they might use the O'Dade slaying as material to barter. One of them was at both incidents. I was not worried about Leo being caught and identifying me. Then I realised the boys could not give me up without bringing Leo into it. They would not risk identifying him. I understood why Leo handed me the gun. It was not to give him a bargaining tool if he was arrested. As the shooter, it ensured I could offer nothing if I was lifted. The weak link was me, the one who would crack first and identify the others. Oh well, it all happened in Belfast, and I did not want to live there.

I returned to work peaceful in my own skin. At the beginning, I said Belfast was a different place in my life and it was a different time, too. Someone once described the 'Tet Offensive' in the Vietnam War as 'a time, not a place,' Belfast in the 1970s and 1980s, much the same.

I visited Nuala and Paul a few times a year and I drove to Liverpool, content with regular contact with my family.

Once when I was over, Paul said, "I hear your pal Delaney's funeral is tomorrow."

We now bantered each other about our different sides.

During Delaney's time as a Senior Minister in the Northern Ireland Executive, when he and other ex-paramilitaries came on the news, Paul would say. "I was involved in at least three of his arrests," or "better he spouts on finer points of the Education Bill as opposed to lying in a street in Ballymurphy shooting an Armalite at poor cops trying to keep the peace."

This was calculated to get a rise out of me, and I served it back in kind. I never mentioned Delaney beyond saying I met him twice and Paul then christened him, "Joe's friend Delaney."

To my immense satisfaction, Pat's name never arose, even when he appeared.

I went downtown the next day and, on a whim, went up to watch Colum Delaney's funeral. I was not grieving. I did not know him, but I was curious to see who was there.

Because of his recent Government involvement, politicians, civil servants, people from non-political organisations would have attended out of respect. The Republicans decided they wanted a Republican funeral, which put off people he worked with at the end of his life. It possessed all the usual paraphernalia without any volley of shots over the grave.

I stood at the side of the road near Milltown Cemetery and watched the cortege and the marchers, a lot of well-known faces. Pat was there and, in the row behind, Leo. I kept my head lowered. As the last of the marchers went past, I noticed the crowd on the other side of the road and O'Dade was staring straight at me. I felt faint, my knees buckle, and I wanted to be sick.

This girl standing beside me gave me a funny look and moved away. I staggered towards a lamppost and held on for support. I looked over at O'Dade. He stared back, ignoring me as he turned away with a couple of mates, and they wandered off down the road. Taking a deep breath, I got myself together and boarded a bus to the city centre and a taxi back to Nuala's. Later I asked Paul if knew the O'Dades, but he shook his head. I pursued it and he said he would ask ex-colleagues who spent most of their careers in West Belfast. When I phoned, he said no one got back to him. I did not let it go. On one occasion he was out, Nuala said.

"Paul wanted to tell you about this guy you asked him about." she couldn't remember what he was going to say. I tried not to sound too anxious. If, by a miracle, O'Dade survived, I needed to know. On the pretext of wishing him a happy birthday, I phoned Paul. It was two months later, 'Oh sorry, I got confused with Graham's.

"Yes, a pal of mine remembers the O'Dades. Petty criminals all their lives, four brothers all born about three years apart, unusual in Catholic families, but to coincide with their Dad's release from his periodic custodial sentences."

He added, of course, "They were all involved with your mob. My pal said you could always identify if one of the O'Dades was involved in something because they all possessed the same face!"

It explained why the O'Dade looked so like Padraig. It was one of his younger brothers, with the same face.

Paul said more; "The second brother, Padraig, disappeared a while back. The family say he went to Cork, they never made a missing person referral. One of them got away."

'He didn't get away,' I said to myself.

Over the next few years, I returned to my old haunt at the college. This Friday night I finished chairing a conference we were taking around Scotland to prepare for new legislation, and I led a planning meeting with the steering group to prepare for our next venture in Ayrshire. I stayed in my room at the college. They now charged me a nominal overnight stay because of financial issues. I stood in the bar chatting with Charlie, the barman.

The college encouraged local people to use the bar to generate income. They didn't advertise it, but staff, friends and neighbours would use the bar if they wanted a quiet drink.

It did not have a huge turnover but helped the facility break even.

There were 15 of us in the bar, a group of four older people, two separate couples, one of whom Charlie said neither spent nor drank much, but they were quiet folk. There was also a group of six women. They were noisy and consuming quantities of booze.

"Off the leash," in Charlie's opinion, and he was well qualified to judge.

Charlie was on about his favourite topic as Scotland was about to embark on another international tournament. It would, of course, lead to failure and national despair heightened by the Scottish football media's unrealistic appraisal of its team's capabilities. I told him again about my first attendance at Hampden Park in a World Cup, or was it a Euros match, between Scotland and Cyprus? I went with the Brennan's, Tommy, and Gabriel, who were hyper! Cyprus would bring the football weight of Arran or the Isle of Mull to the pitch, while the boys in dark blue would take five or six of them. The Cypriot team was a group of waiters, taxi drivers and bare foot lobby dancers while the stars of Celtic, Rangers, Liverpool etc. were the consummate seasoned professionals.

It didn't go according to plan. The waiters and dancers scored first in the fifteenth minute and Hampden Park fell silent, except me, who burst out laughing as much with the shock. I could have been lynched and Tommy and Gabriel would have led the charge!

Charlie listened ruefully; he knew the well-worn script. There was a burst of giggling from the women's table.

"I might need your help tonight, Joe. The group of Irish girls could create. They are not used to the drink."

Irish girls, not able to handle drink, unlikely. I turned my head, Irish yes, girls not so much. They all looked to be in their mid-forties. According to Charlie, they hired three rooms through their church for a few nights and were shopping and sightseeing in the East of Scotland. As I watched, one 'girl' with large curly permed hair, very eighties, got up to buy a round. We knew she was called Gloria because of a comment shouted at her.

"Gloria, just the drink. Leave the boys at the bar alone." She turned to the group and made a face and they all burst out laughing.

Charlie served her, and she gave him a bit of chat. Two of the drinks were soft drinks.

The girls drove to Dunfermline in a church minibus. I assumed the driver and co-driver were being sensible.

As Charlie took the money and wandered over to the till, Gloria turned to me and said, "How are you doing?"

"I'm fine. Are you enjoying your visit to Scotland?"

"Oh my God, you're from Norn Iron."

I laughed out loud. Earlier, I said to Charlie if he wanted to banter the 'girls,' he should say to them, 'Are you from NORN IRON? 'It is the closest a Fifer will get to a Belfast accent.

"Where abouts are you from?"

You may assume it was a loaded question, meaning what religion are you? Wrong. Away from Northern Ireland 'Norn Iron', folk are interested in the answer. It leads to 'do you know X,' 'or have you been to a night out at Y?' I have a set response; it goes like this:

"Ah, the last time I was in Belfast, I was in Carryduff. I have been in Scotland since 1982."

There are two answers here, but I make it sound like one, as if, 'I used to live in Carryduff, then moved to Scotland.' It was where our Nuala lived and was the last place in Belfast, I laid my head. I doubt if there were many people from Carryduff in the IRA, deflection was the intent. It should not have helped Gloria in her quest for the information though she was dying to share with her pals. As she returned to her table, she tossed back. "Oh, we are from further down the Saintfield Road," then her pals called her back with the drink.

Just my luck. My answer would heighten the curiosity, not dampen it. I was enjoying the chat with Charlie and was reluctant to head off to bed to avoid further inquisition from the Irish 'girls.' I ordered another pint.

About half an hour later, I saw from Charlie's reaction another one of the "girls" was coming with a drink order. I stood back and appraised my erstwhile country woman as she ordered. This time, half the drinks were non-alcoholic; Charlie might not have much of a problem when he closed the bar. This 'girl' was petite, with blondish highlights in short darker hair.

As I was looking at her, she turned and smiled at me. An unmistakable smile and one shocked me.

"Jess…. Jess Morton?" I gasped.

She appeared startled, stared at me wondering who this guy was and how did he know her name. She hesitated." Joe, Joe… McFaul."

I nodded. Before I could stop myself, I hugged her. This made her uncomfortable, and I stepped back, and we gazed at each other. Her rowdy table went quiet.

"Jess, my goodness, how lovely to meet you after all this time," I ventured in my politest tones.

I was Mister charming. Her smile was part of many dreams and fantasies over the years, during my imprisonment. The sparkle in the eyes was missing, the sparkle I pretended was reserved for me. After twenty years, she must have believed she changed.

"How did you recognise me?"

"Ah, Jess, you are unforgettable." (Joe you old charmer you.)

She flushed. "So how are you, Joe? What are you doing here?"

Charlie came over to add to a mate's street cred, he interjected, "Joe runs the College."

Whatever Jess understood about my background, College Principal was not the obvious career route. One of the other Irish women approached us. She eyed me with more than a hint of suspicion.

"Jess, what about our drinks? Are you coming?"

I moved quickly. "Which is your drink, Jess?"

I took the coke she showed off the bar, putting it to one side with a big smile motioning Jess and her pal to take the other five drinks to their table. Gloria lifted three. It was up to Jess now; she could deliver the two remaining drinks, come back, take hers and return to their table, or she could take the two drinks to her friends and return to talk to me.

She returned. As she walked back towards me, I looked past her at the table. Her five friends went into what University Challenge would recognise as "conferring mode." All five heads were bowed down together as they tried to make sense of what was happening. Jess did not stay to allay their fears or satisfy their curiosity.

I took our drinks to a table with more comfortable seats.

"This is more private. "I said. Motioning at the table.

She nodded. "Are you the head of the College?"

She recognised how that sounded, flushed again, "I mean --- I don't mean." I laughed.

"I am in Social Work these days; I teach a bit at the College; I am also on the Management Board as the Council's representative."

"You have done well."

Karim's and Paul's advice was,' get the hard bit out of the way.'

"I got into trouble back home and I was in Prison.

"I know," Jess interjected, "Robert told me."

Robert was bound to raise his head. Fair enough, all I wanted was to rekindle a friendship.

"The local news was on, mid-1970s. I was in the kitchen and Robert shouted, 'look it is Joe, isn't it?' and I saw you"

I forgot on the afternoon the Court sentenced me, a leading IRA figure got 20 years for being involved in killing a Catholic judge. There was heavy media presence outside the court. I was in a group of prisoners, handcuffed, and led out to the prison vehicle.

We came into Court through the tunnel between Crumlin Road Prison and the High Court, but we were going to Lisburn, to the Maze. After a few miles, we were diverted back to Crumlin Road. I found out years later the IRA planned to ambush the vehicle and free the high-profile prisoner. No doubt the rest of us, too.

I talked a little about various events, especially the death of Ramie, but I said to Jess, "Enough about me. What about you, your kids, and how is Robert?"

Jess's eyes met mine, her eyes filled with tears, and she whispered," Robert died two years ago. He got cancer —- I nursed him over his last eighteen months."

What could I say? There was a lot of pain there? I didn't notice, but Gloria arrived from the group to see how Jess was. Jess looked at her.

"Gloria, this is Joe, a friend from way back. He hadn't heard about Robert."

Gloria nodded, patted Jess's shoulder, and walked back after a brief smile in my direction.

We chatted about our last brief meeting on Royal Avenue when I first started at Brewster's. Then she said: "I shouldn't be surprised to see you. Ann mentioned she met you at a course in Scotland. It was during the tough times," and her voice fell.

I longed to ask if Ann told her grandfather, but I did not. It would spoil the moment! Jess sat with her hands clasped together, and I placed a hand on top of hers. She talked in a calm, reasoned manner, though telling someone for the first time is hard.

She went through a lot, a strong woman. Jess chatted about buying their first house. She and Robert then bought a bigger one on the Saintfield Road, about a mile from Carryduff. Their children were, Billy, he used to be William when he was a wee boy, and Ann. Billy took his Father's death badly and was still angry. He no longer went to church on the strength of it. Ann was her Mother's rock. Sounded similar to Jess. She was engaged, but still at home.

"I hadn't asked Ann where she met you. Robert was ill and I…," she tailed off. She gave no clue what reason she gave Ann about how we knew each other. Billy lived with his girlfriend in Ballymena and worked for her Father, who owned agricultural implements stores in Ballymena, Limavady and Coleraine.

We chatted away, her sister, her brother, and my siblings and parents. We touched on sad times. She was interested in my transition from prisoner to lorry driver to Social Worker. I told her I had obtained an OU degree and my Masters. Another emissary from the group arrived, and I was introduced to Grace. Jess and I were laughing remembering the football match in the Cregagh estate and poor Lorna.

Grace said, "We are going to our rooms. Have you got your key?"

Grace was sharing with Jess. Lucky Grace. Jess nodded and said, Don't worry, I'll be quiet."

After the women left, I looked over at Charlie and nodded. They were the last customers and if we left, he could close the bar. I suggested to Jess we go out for a walk, she agreed.

It was dark now, but still quite warm. Somewhere along the way, we held hands. We walked and talked. I told her about my cottage, and she asked if I was married. I told her about Dolores and Lisa. Jess was quite old-fashioned. Getting married and having a family was a priority for her. As we returned, it must have been close to 11.30 pm. I suggested we go up to my room. Jess hesitated.

"I don't mean, "I spluttered. (Although I did)

Jess laughed, and we sat in my room for another couple of hours chatting. We kissed and cuddled a little.

Exhausted by the lateness of the hour, we just crawled into my bed. I was wearing a tee shirt and boxers, Jess with her bra and pants. We lay there holding each other, nothing more than. We both fell asleep; it was reminiscent of an encounter in a sleeping bag in Sligo all those years ago. I awoke about 8.00 am. Jess was in the shower.

I was tempted to join her, but as that 'entertaining thought 'came into my mind, she came out wrapped in the bath towel.

"You will have to use the smaller towel. Now go have your shower so I can get dressed."

'Damit' I said almost to myself.

Jess said the "girls" were heading to Edinburgh for retail therapy and an evening meal. They would return to Dunfermline and travel to Cairnryan on Sunday, via Glasgow, and more shopping. In the shower, I came up with a plan. It was now or never, "Why don't you stay up in Fife with me? We could go to St Andrews, you can see my cottage and on Sunday, I will drive you to Cairnryan in time for the boat, I promise."

Jess hesitated: "OK."

She disappeared downstairs to her room. I dressed and waited by the window as the women got onto the bus. The angle did give a clear view, and I couldn't be sure how many climbed into the vehicle. How many five or six? I worried Jess might have been talked out of staying. As it drove away, there was a knock on my door. It was Jess with her overnight case.

"You must have had some explaining to do."

Jess nodded. "You wouldn't believe it. Grace said I planned it from the moment I said she wouldn't hear me come into our room."

Jess planned it. If anyone planned it; it was me!

We drove to my cottage. Jess used all the right words, enthused about the setting, the new kitchen I installed and the gardens. Thank you, Mr and Mrs Hepburn.

Now the interior of my cottage was strong on comfort and weaker in style. Jess looked around and made positive comments about the cottage, but I got the impression, if it was up to her, it would be gutted. Going into the spare bedroom, or as Jess put it, "my bedroom, tonight," "now there's a disappointment," I suggested. She sniffed but said nothing.

Eugene used it about four weeks ago and I had not been in it since he left. Jess went over and opened the window. I mumbled something about changing the bedding. She was amused at my crestfallen attitude to my failings in the domesticity stakes. For goodness' sake, there were cushions around even on my bed, a clear sign a woman has tried to influence the decor. I pointed out my sisters made minor alterations to improve the house. I made a late breakfast, eggs, bacon and toast and we sat out in the back garden. Ahead, the sky stretched until it merged with the sea, and you could not be certain where one ended and the other began. We talked and talked and after a while just sat and watched the land and the sky.

Later we drove up to the beautiful fishing village of Crail and walked along the shore and the golf course, then up to St Andrews, mooching around the shops. Jess found a classy shoe shop, and I insisted on buying her a pair of ankle length boots she liked.

"You are going home tomorrow, but when you put these boots on you will think of me."

I was uncertain what I wanted from Jess. Meeting her after all this time was unexpected. We did not have a proper closure all those years ago. We were so young. Many events happened in her life, for a time I was special. It might be I could settle for rekindling an old friendship--- I am not sure.

We enjoyed the meal, went back to the cottage, went out the back, chatted, sipped hot tea wrapped up in old woolly jumpers as the evening got cooler. We moved into the front garden and sat on the wooden bench watching the setting sun disappear. Jess laid her head on my arm and closed her eyes as if letting a deep worry recede. We were so relaxed with each other despite our tough experiences, and it was nice to share time without either seeking an agenda or creating any demands.

That night, Jess slept in my bed. It started the same as the previous night, gentle holding, kisses, a few caresses. I wanted more. I touched her intimately, expecting her to recoil, but she responded. We were kissing and as I caressed her breasts, she became more passionate, we consummated our relationship; Such a long wait, in my opinion we loved so long and with such passion, finally sleep took us.

I knew the minute she came out of the shower I wanted to make love to her. An instinct stayed my hand, told me it was not the time. The passion, more than I expected, allowed a release of emotions some older other more recent.

I was afraid the next morning Jess would be angry, believing I took advantage of her grief. Instead, she was chirpy and natural. We headed down to Edinburgh for breakfast. She visited it on holiday and as I was depriving her of the Glasgow visit, it was the least I could do. I did not want to be late for the boat, so we left Edinburgh just after noon to avoid being late. There was a nice roadhouse with a shop full of quality but expensive clothing. Only our Nuala could afford to shop in it, but it also sold crafts, nick knacks' and it did a nice mid-afternoon tea.

We made it to Cairnryan just ahead of the minibus, about 5.00 p.m. We talked about everything on the way, but I stayed clear of the future, afraid to ruin the moment. If we did not talk about it, I could dream. We walked over to join Jess' pals, and I was introduced to all of them. They appeared a pleasant, if bemused, bunch. Jess mentioned she left her overnight case in my boot. I am certain she did it so we could go back together and say goodbye away from prying eyes. She marched off, tossing over her shoulder, "Come on Joe, I need to get my case."

As I turned away from her friends, Grace murmured to me, "I have not seen Jess this happy in five years." I liked that.

We got the case, and a long lingering kiss. I went round and put the case in the minibus. Jess got in last and with a wave, they drove onto the ferry. Jess kept looking back, I hope… I wanted to believe.

The return to Fife was long, and I was tired. I already covered 150 miles and it would be the same going home. My mind was bouncing full of the last three days. I should have been sad at Jess leaving, yet I was also excited. Would I ever see her again? We agreed I was to phone on Wednesday night at seven. The next two days were busy at work and, although I fretted about Wednesday, I was tired after the emotional activity, and work and driving though I slept well.

On Wednesday, I was not myself, people commented on how subdued I behaved. I went home and watched the clock above Mrs Hepburn's fireplace. When I went back for a second viewing, she told me how she wanted to do up the fireplace and put one in to blend with the old-world character of the cottage. Mr H could not see the point. He wanted a warm house with money spent on central heating. It wasn't an either-or situation.

Never show a woman you are too keen, so I waited until 15 seconds after 7.00 pm and phoned Jess's number. It rang for a while. I panicked. She would know it was me and would not answer or she considered it too silly or regretted sleeping with me after all these years. She could have forgotten I was phoning and gone out. My mind raced and then… then a voice answered, "Hello."

"Jess, it's Joe," Ann might sound a bit like her, and a phone distorts accents.

Silence.

"I hope your journey back was OK, not too much inquisition from the girls."

Please speak Jess, I prayed to myself I will know a lot from your tone.

She laughed, a positive sign, "They were well behaved, and you have new fans in Grace, maybe Gloria too."

The old Joe came out, "Have you their phone numbers handy?" I asked. Silence again. I remembered the look of jealousy when Robert said I fancied Lorna at the football match all those years ago.

"Neither would be your type."

"Not like you." I pushed it and regretted it.

"It was a lovely weekend, I enjoyed it and wanted to thank so you so much, for everything including the lovely boots, Ann wants to borrow them."

In for a penny, in for a pound. "I am coming over to my sister Nuala's in two weeks. I hope we can see each other."

A brief silence "Oh, Joe," oh no hesitation "I would love to."

Our conversation became more relaxed, she asked about my work, I asked about Ann and Billy. She did not say what she told Ann. Anything would be too much too soon for Billy. I suspect it would always be much too soon for him. We agreed I would phone her on Saturday night at the same time. She offered to phone me, but I could not cope with waiting for her. At least if I phoned, I controlled the anxiety. Do Jess and I have a future. I do not know; I will just take it as it comes.

## Reflection Joe

I spent my whole life not knowing what I wanted and now I knew.

Lightning Source UK Ltd.
Milton Keynes UK
UKHW010356200422
401742UK00001B/49